Imperious

C. M. Sutter

AUTHOR'S NOTE

ABOUT THE AUTHOR

C. M. Sutter is a crime fiction writer who resides in Florida, although she is originally from California.

She is a member of numerous writers' organizations, including Fiction for All, Fiction Factor, and Writers etc.

In addition to writing, she enjoys spending time with her friends and family. She is an art enthusiast and loves to create gourd birdhouses, pebble art, and handmade soaps. Hiking, bicycling, fishing, and traveling are a few of her favorite pastimes.

C.M. Sutter

http://cmsutter.com/

Contact C. M. Sutter - http://cmsutter.com/contact/

Imperious: A Psychic Detective Kate Pierce Crime Thriller, Book 2

Two female students at a community college have died during finals week, and the college and the city of North Bend want answers. With no witnesses to the crime and no obvious signs of foul play, these disturbing occurrences may be nothing more than unusual coincidences. The sheriff's office and medical examiner have their hands full as they try to find logical explanations for the deaths.

Detective Kate Pierce begins to show signs of physical distress whenever she's near the bodies, and further research leads her to believe she could be experiencing psychic transference—she's feeling the same symptoms these students did when they took their last breaths.

Kate is determined to be heard, and when the shocking results of the toxicology reports are revealed, she and her colleagues know they're headed down the right path. There can be only one answer and only one person involved—they just have to prove it.

When another student goes missing and is soon found dead, the case breaks wide open, and the final showdown between Kate and the suspect puts her transference theory to the ultimate test.

See all of C. M. Sutter's books at:
http://cmsutter.com/available-books/

Find C. M. Sutter on Facebook at:
https://www.facebook.com/cmsutterauthor/

Don't want to miss C. M. Sutter's next release?
Sign up for the VIP e-mail list at:
http://cmsutter.com/newsletter/

Chapter 1

He flicked the cigarette butt out the window and munched three aspirin without water. As he kept an eye on Becca's door, he thought back to that fateful day two years ago. Today was Monday, and a new week of final exams was about to begin.

Becca's apartment was several hundred feet away, and from that distance, she wouldn't notice his vehicle. He was a patient man and would wait for her to drive away in that rust bucket of hers, turn left at the lights, and head toward the freeway. Becca wouldn't dare miss her exams, and she'd be gone most of the day. He would have plenty of opportunity to do what had to be done, yet he needed only a few minutes.

The memories of Isabelle's demise flooded his mind as he tapped his fingers on the steering wheel. He grimaced as he remembered the look on her face when she'd realized something was terribly wrong, yet five minutes before, things had been fine—or so she thought. She clenched her throat and gasped after she took that first swallow. With horror written across her face, she stared at the drink he handed her. He spewed something at her about payback being a bitch. He watched as

1

she frantically tried to breathe, but her airways were closing, and her fate was sealed. Blood spots filled the whites of her eyes, and her lips went from a healthy pink to a grayish blue. The cyanide worked, and her swollen tongue confirmed it. Her own body had suffocated her. It was too late for Isabelle; the deed was done, and she died a frightful and agonizing death.

Cyanide poisoning was extremely rare, and he couldn't risk having her body found. An autopsy would surely reveal the manner of death. He'd prepared a bath of special ingredients and carried Isabelle to the bathroom. With gloved hands, he lowered her into the lye-filled tub. Her body would be completely dissolved by the week's end. He knew it would take years before her life insurance policy paid out but it would be well worth it. She had a two-million-dollar policy, and until then, he'd do fine on his own.

That was then, and this was now. Since he was in a different city and using a different name, nobody knew his past or what he was capable of doing when wronged. He had nothing to lose.

Movement at Becca's door brought him back to the moment. She was leaving.

There you are, you little bitch.

He rubbed his hands together in excitement as he watched her exit the ground-floor apartment and climb into her car. Two years had gone by without that feeling of power. He needed it again and was ready to kill—it was time. Now with a valid reason to kill, he had several people in mind. They deserved death just as much as Isabelle had. He didn't take betrayal lightly.

He felt at ease in Becca's apartment, and as the owner, he had access to every unit in that eight-apartment building. He turned the key and walked inside. Memories of their few intimate times together filled his mind yet enraged him. He knew in his heart that she despised him, but he needed to stay focused on the task at hand. Becca was about to die since her threat of exposing their arrangement didn't sit well with him. He was calling the shots, not her, and she would find that out the hard way.

He opened the thermal bag he'd brought along and browsed through the sealed containers. He needed to use something that would kill her in less than twenty-four hours, but he had no idea what she'd eat or drink later when she was back from her exams. He grabbed a chair from the two-seat table in the corner of the galley kitchen, pulled open the refrigerator, and took a seat while examining everything inside. With the bag on his lap, he twisted the lids off several containers. He added clostridium botulinum to her milk, coffee creamer, and jug of filtered water, and castor beans to the three-bean salad that sat on the shelf. He knew her evening and morning routines. Melatonin with a glass of water helped her sleep at night. A bowl of cereal and coffee with cream were her staples in the morning, and dinnertime was anyone's guess, but the container of deli bean salad told him she might enjoy some of it that evening.

Satisfied that his job was done, and now all he had to do was wait, he locked the apartment door behind him and returned to North Bend. A sinister smile lit his face as he drove to the west side of town. No matter what, Becca would die a painful death within twenty-four hours.

She deserves the agony she'll go through before she dies, and I hope there's plenty of it.

He wondered what he could do to witness her demise.

Chapter 2

As she drove toward North Bend Tuesday morning, Becca hoped to massage away the stomachache that was increasing rapidly. She would have stayed in bed that day if it weren't for her exams, and now, the ten-mile drive to the university seemed like a hundred.

What the hell is wrong with me?

She thought about the carryout calzone that she'd had the previous night from Pizza Pie, a local restaurant only a block from the efficiency apartment she rented. It was delicious, but now she wondered if it had made her sick. She knew the salad was good since she'd had a small portion just the night before last, and the label said the expiration date wasn't until four more days.

But can I possibly have food poisoning?

The nausea overwhelmed her, and the ringing in her ears was getting louder. That bitter taste of bile climbed up her throat and made her gag. Becca held her breath and willed away the urge to vomit.

I've got to get to the hospital. This pain is unbearable. I can't take it anymore.

She pressed the gas pedal deeper against the floor, and the car sped down Highway 45, passing dozens of morning commuters.

She frantically grabbed the cell phone from her purse and tried to read the names on her contact list, but each one blurred into the next. Becca pressed every name in a wild attempt to reach someone, but the stabbing pain stiffened her body, and her vision faded into blackness. Her muscles began to seize. The car swerved right and then left and sent her across the median into oncoming traffic.

Tires squealed, and drivers took to the gravel shoulder to avoid colliding with her. One car hit the ditch and flipped before landing upside down on its roof. Another hit the rear end of the car ahead of it, then a semi, trying to avoid the cars, jackknifed and took out two vehicles in a violent explosion. The early morning normal was interrupted by crunching metal, cars in flames, a semi on its side, and a car smashed into a tree and on the wrong side of the highway. As smoke poured out from under the hood of her crumpled car, Becca sat motionless, her face pressed into the airbag.

Chapter 3

Concerned citizens raced from their cars to render aid to the injured while others snapped pictures and bystanders called 911.

The emergency lines were flooded with incoming calls. Patrol deputies and ambulances were dispatched to the scene of what was described as a horrific multicar pileup on Highway 45 in the northbound lanes. Silver and Donnelly were the first of the patrol units on the scene, and three ambulances and a fire truck arrived seconds later. The emergency vehicles pulled to the shoulder, and the EMTs rushed to the cars that looked to be in the worst condition while firemen with extinguishers ran to the cars engulfed in flames.

Silver leapt from his car and pointed toward the ditch. "Holy shit. That car smashed against the tree is facing oncoming traffic. It had to be what caused this mess." He shielded his eyes and looked out across the median. "Yep, see those deep ruts? They're heading in this direction. We need Forensics out here to photograph the scene."

Donnelly let out a whistle as he walked the shoulder and

scanned left to right, assessing the devastation. "I'm counting seven demolished vehicles, including the semi that's blocking two lanes. If we don't get the debris and disabled cars off the road, there's going to be even more crashes." Screeching brakes sounded behind them. He pointed at the bottleneck starting on the road to their rear. "We need to block off the two outside lanes and fast. Give the county road crew a call and tell them they're needed out here ASAP. The traffic needs to be diverted to the inside lanes a good mile back. Tell them to set up barricades to funnel drivers into the far-left lanes. We need more units out here too to slow down the traffic." Donnelly looked to see if every smashed car had an EMT attending the injured. He tipped his head toward the people standing alongside their vehicles—there were five in total. "I'll get started on the witness statements." He headed toward a man on the opposite side of the road, standing next to a white Ford Explorer. "I'll take him."

The man, leaning against his driver's-side front fender, smoked a cigarette and stared at the EMTs across the road as they worked on freeing Becca from her car.

Donnelly pulled out his notepad as he ran toward the SUV. "Sir, did you witness the accident?"

The man took a deep drag and nodded.

"I'll need to see your ID if you don't mind."

The man complied and pulled his driver's license from his wallet and handed it to Tim.

Donnelly jotted down the information and gave the card back to him. "Can you walk me through what happened?"

The witness let out a sigh and dropped the cigarette to the

gravel in front of him, then he ground the butt back and forth with the toe of his shoe. "Never saw anything like it in my life. I was sure more cars on that side of the road were going to get tangled up in the crash, but most of them parted on both sides of that oncoming car. It reminded me of that movie where Moses parted the Red Sea."

Donnelly scratched his head. "*The Ten Commandments?* You some kind of biblical scholar?"

The man ignored the comment. "Obviously, I was going the same direction as the person who caused the accident, but I was lucky. Being several car lengths behind them, I saw everything unfold. I hit the brakes so hard my vehicle began to skid. Even from this side of the road, I could tell that everyone was locking up their brakes. I don't think anyone could believe their eyes."

"Understood. So, what did you actually witness?"

The man tipped his head toward Becca's car. "Is that person dead?"

Tim looked over his left shoulder and saw the rescue team using the extraction tool on the driver's-side door. "I don't have any information yet, sir. Can you give me the actual details of what took place?"

"Just a normal morning when out of nowhere, I saw that car swerve violently left and right. Suddenly it veered left, plowed through the median, and headed right for the northbound lanes. Horns blared, brakes squealed, and cars went every which way. A good six or seven of them smashed into each other, a couple exploded, and there's that upside-down one too. But when that semi jackknifed—well, that was just like in the movies." He shielded his eyes and peered across the median. "Those people have to be pretty messed up."

"The EMTs are assisting the injured, sir."

The man shook his head. "It was over with in a few seconds. The red car that caused the mess went straight for that big oak tree." He pointed. "And there it sits with smoke pouring out of it."

Silver interrupted the conversation. "The county crew should be here in a couple of minutes. They'll close the two right lanes and keep the two inside lanes open." He noticed a woman pacing alongside her vehicle on the shoulder of the northbound lane. "I'll get her statement."

Donnelly turned back to the man. "Did you notice brake lights when the car veered across the median?"

"Humph… can't say that I did."

"Okay, thanks. I guess that's all the questions I have. If you think of anything else, please contact the Washburn County Sheriff's Office and reference this accident."

"Sure thing."

Donnelly crossed the median then turned back and watched the man drive away. He cupped his mouth and called out to Derrick Gray, the head EMT. "What have we got on that red car?"

Derrick watched as his colleagues lifted Becca onto the gurney and wheeled her to the back of the first ambulance. He shook his head. "She's gone. We called it at eight thirteen." He rubbed his chin as if something weighed heavily on his mind.

"Derrick, is there a problem?"

"Not quite sure. She was wearing her seat belt, and the airbag did its job. It seems off."

"Off how?"

"Like she shouldn't be dead. She didn't collide with any other cars, only the tree. Direct impact with properly working airbags—which they were—would usually result in a collapsed lung, possible head injury, and maybe a few broken ribs, but dead at the scene, especially a young person? That doesn't feel right." He reached in his pocket and pulled out a cell phone then handed it to Donnelly. "This was under her body. Texting while driving could have caused the accident, but that still doesn't explain her being deceased by the time we arrived."

Donnelly huffed. "Damn cell phones and kids. They can't seem to understand how dangerous it is to drive and text, let alone that it's illegal in Wisconsin. Did you get an ID?"

Derrick reached into the mangled vehicle and pulled a purse from the passenger side footwell. "Here you go, Tim. Unfortunately, her family is about to have a bad day."

Donnelly nodded. "That vehicle has to go to our impound lot. We'll need tow trucks for the rest. What about other injuries?"

"Not good. Two more dead, another with severe burns, and the man from the rolled-over car sustained broken bones. He's in the second ambulance, and they're getting ready to head out. The rear-end collision didn't cause any injuries, so that'll be an accident report and insurance claim."

"What a mess, and the morning has just begun." Donnelly rubbed his forehead. "I'll send another deputy over there to take care of that."

11

Chapter 4

Jack exited his office with his coffee in hand and took a seat in Adam's guest chair. He blew out a breath and raked his fingers through his hair. "Multicar pileup out on 45 this morning. What's with young people these days?"

"Are you talking to me specifically?" Billings asked.

"Yeah, I guess so. You're the only person here who has a college-aged kid."

Adam frowned. "Do you take issue with college-aged kids?"

"Nah, high school kids would probably fit the bill too. It's a sad situation, though."

I shook my head at Amber and rolled my eyes. "Jack, can you stop talking in riddles and just tell us what's on your mind?"

"Sorry, guess I went off topic. Silver called earlier from the scene, where there were multiple fatalities, an overturned semi, and burned-up cars. The accident happened halfway between Kewaskum and North Bend. I guess somebody driving in the southbound lane caused it. Silver needed me to call the county crews and get them out there to block two lanes on the northbound side."

I frowned. "Didn't you just say the accident was in the southbound lane?"

"I should clarify that. The car was driving south but veered across the median into the northbound lanes and slammed into a tree. Of course that caused a chain reaction of collisions. A half dozen cars and that semi got tangled up in the mess. Some of the witnesses Silver spoke with said it happened so suddenly they thought the car that caused the accident may have had a tire blow out."

"Did it?" Amber asked.

Jack took a sip and continued. "Not according to Silver. He said all the tires were fully inflated. As far as I know, two other people sustained serious injuries, and EMTs are transporting them to the hospital now. Three in total were dead at the scene."

"Wow, that's horrible. Did the person who caused the accident survive?" Clayton asked.

"Nope. That person was a young female, and she was pronounced at the scene along with the two who burned in the collision with the semi. The EMTs found a cell phone beneath her body when they lifted her out of the car. She may have been texting while driving." Jack checked the time. "Donnelly is heading back with her phone and purse. According to her driver's license, she was only nineteen years old."

Amber groaned. "That is more than sad and such a waste of a life."

"But if she was texting, she caused other people to lose their lives too," Clayton said.

Adam agreed. "Texting while driving is a dangerous thing all right. Thank God Mia doesn't have a car."

I snapped my head in his direction. "And that matters why?"

Adam glared at me, and Amber rolled her eyes as she watched us begin our usual morning debate.

"Mia could be a passenger in somebody's car while the driver is texting. The danger factor is still the same." I turned to Jack before Adam had a chance to respond. "How would anyone know that texting caused the accident, anyway?"

Jack shrugged. "Donnelly said the time stamp on her phone showed texts sent to a handful of people seconds before the crash, but they were just a bunch of scrambled letters that made no sense. Anyway, our county, our problem. I'll have to locate her next of kin from her phone contacts."

Seconds later, the security door opened, and Donnelly walked in. "What a tragedy," he said as he plopped down in Clayton's guest chair. "Deceased individual that caused the accident was a Becca Morbeck."

I sighed. "Of course she'd have a sweet name."

Donnelly continued. "According to her driver's license, she's from Tomah. Not quite sure how her being in this area plays out."

"I'll follow up on everything as soon as I read the witness statements. Has her body been transported downstairs yet?" Jack asked.

"Yeah, the EMTs were checking her in with Lena just as I got back. Here are the important items from her car, sir." Donnelly handed the purse and phone to Jack. "The deceased burn victims are en route right now."

"Appreciate it. Is Silver still at the scene?"

"He is until our flatbed loads Becca's car and leaves. Ebert and Lawrence will stick around until the scene is cleared, the other vehicles are towed, and the county crew opens up the far-right lanes."

"Do you have Silver's witness statements?"

"Right here, Boss." Donnelly handed them to Jack. "I've already entered the accident reports into my car's computer."

Jack nodded and rose. "Thanks, Donnelly. Okay, back to work, people, and I want to know when Becca Morbeck's vehicle arrives."

Clayton spoke up. "I'll let the garage know to call me when they check it in."

"Thanks." Jack crossed the bull pen to his office and closed the door behind him. He sipped on his second cup of coffee, now cold, as he read the witness statements.

This doesn't make any sense. The car veered left and right, flew over the median, and hit a tree. Nobody Silver and Donnelly spoke to from the southbound lanes said they noticed brake lights as the car crossed into oncoming traffic.

Jack rubbed his forehead as he continued reading.

No signs of a blowout either. What the hell caused the car to swerve, cross the median, and crash?

He picked up the receiver and dialed Lena, hit the speakerphone button, and set the receiver back on the base. "Lena, it's Jack. Donnelly said the first victim from this morning's Highway 45 crash is in your possession?"

"That's correct. Has her next of kin been notified?"

"No, I'm still reviewing the witness statements. According to what the people interviewed from the southbound lanes said, there was no attempt to brake before the car crossed into oncoming traffic. Wouldn't that be a natural instinct if the driver was coherent at the time?"

"Absolutely. Are you thinking she was under the influence?"

"Possibly. Her driver's license shows she's from Tomah. She's a long way from home at seven thirty-five in the morning. I need to contact her family, but I wanted answers to some of their questions before they ask them."

"Should I put her in cold storage until you learn more?"

"Yeah, that's a good idea. Her car is being towed in, and I want the garage to go over it to rule out foul play. It could have been brake failure." Jack's mind went back to Jade Monroe's near-death car accident after criminal Warren Ricks tampered with her brakes. She was lucky to be alive. "Hold off until I know the car wasn't the problem. If it wasn't, then it means Becca Morbeck either had a medical or psychological issue or she was under the influence of something. I'll let you know how to proceed once I reach her family." Jack ended the call and looked up to see Clayton approaching his door. He waved him in.

"Boss, the Morbeck car was just dropped off downstairs."

"Okay, thanks." Jack pushed back his chair and left his office. The lower level housed the technical department, the forensics lab, the coroner's office, and the impound lot and garage. He took the stairs down two flights and spoke to George Abrams, the head mechanic. "George, I need that car up on the lift right away."

"Yes, sir, and what are we looking for?"

"Faulty brake lines, signs of tampering, or anything that would cause a car to barrel across a highway and crash into a tree with no signs of trying to stop."

"That sounds more like a stuck accelerator."

Jack nodded. "Call me as soon as you know something."

"Will do."

Back at his office, Jack scrolled through Becca's contact list. He stopped on the name Mom. It was time to make that unpleasant call. Letting out a long sigh, he dialed the number, pressed Speakerphone, and engaged his recorder. He waited until someone picked up on the other end.

"Hi, honey. Aren't you supposed to be taking exams right now?"

"Mrs. Morbeck?" Jack heard her startled reaction through the phone lines.

"Yes. Who is this, and why are you talking on my daughter's phone?"

"Ma'am, this is Lieutenant Jack Steele with the Washburn County Sheriff's Office. Your daughter is Becca Morbeck?"

"Of course. Is Becca okay?"

Jack hesitated for a second, knowing full well that as soon as the words came out of his mouth, the family's life would change in an instant.

"Ma'am, I'm sorry to inform you that Becca was involved in a fatal car accident this morning."

"No, no, no!"

Gut-wrenching sobs sounded on the other end of the phone. Jack waited until the woman was able to speak.

"Why, how, where? I have to see her. Where is she?"

"Ma'am, Becca is at our coroner's office at the sheriff's department. Where are you located?"

"We live in Tomah, Lieutenant. I need to be with Becca now." She continued to wail into the phone. "I have to call my husband. We'll leave as soon as he gets home."

"Thank you, ma'am. We have questions that I'm sure only you and your husband can answer. Please, drive to our sheriff's office and ask for me directly when you get here. Again, I'm Lieutenant Jack Steele."

She coughed into the phone. "Thank you, Lieutenant Steele. We'll be there by lunchtime."

Jack hung up and walked out of his office. "Kate, run downstairs and tell Lena that Becca's family is on their way from Tomah. She can go ahead with the pictures and prepare the consent paperwork if the parents agree to an autopsy."

"You got it, Boss."

Jack turned to Amber. "You went to UWWC, didn't you?"

"Yeah, and Jade did too."

"And Highway 45 would have been the most logical route since Becca was driving south."

"As far as going to school?"

Jack took a seat on Amber's guest chair. "The mom asked why she wasn't taking her exams."

"It is finals week, but there's also Moraine Park Technical College. She could have taken Highway 45 south to either school, depending on where she was coming from."

"And I don't have that information, but I guess the school

is irrelevant. My concern is the cause of the crash. Maybe the parents can shed some light during the interview." Jack stood and headed for the door. "Come on, Kate, I'll walk down with you. I need to see if George discovered anything suspicious with the car."

Chapter 5

He shook several aspirin into his hand and popped them in his mouth. That excruciating pain had become a constant in his life. Checking his surroundings first, he slipped out of his SUV and into her empty apartment. That time of day, most people were at work, anyway, and with her apartment being an end unit, he easily entered unseen through her side door. He could take his time—he knew full well she wouldn't be back. He'd witnessed her death firsthand, yet he had to be certain there wasn't any evidence or mention of his name inside her apartment. He intended to check every square inch of the space to make sure.

See what happens when you resist me, and then you threatened to expose our agreement. Tsk, tsk, Becca. Totally not your smartest move.

He crossed the tiny living room into her bedroom. Memories of their last night together filled his mind as he ran his hand across her pillow.

You could have had everything handed to you on a silver platter if you had played by my rules, but no—your morality took the place of common sense. Now your career plans and ambitions are dead in the water, and you—you're just dead.

He knew every dream and aspiration Becca had and recalled when he met her last fall at orientation day. She seemed hopeful and innocent and matched all the qualities on his bullet-point list of the type of woman to pursue—an easy target. An image of Isabelle took over his thoughts for a split second, but he quickly erased her from his mind.

You were nothing but a two-timing whore.

He lifted the pillow, held it against his face, and drew in a deep breath. The scent of Becca's shampoo lingered on the pillowcase.

Stupid bitch had to ruin everything.

He lingered at her underwear drawer and studied the lace that accented her bras and panties. She'd fulfilled every fantasy in his mind, but deep inside, he knew she was never truly on board.

"Why couldn't you just go along with it? You didn't need to die."

He went back to work and looked through every drawer, cabinet, and closet. If she had a journal, he'd find it. A half hour passed before he finally found the book squeezed between her mattress and box springs.

"There it is. Now let's see what you wrote, Ms. Morbeck."

He pulled out the leather-bound journal and took a seat on the bed. Page by page, he read how she'd despised him and how he made her skin crawl. He had power over her and held her future career in his hands. He swore he'd ruin her life if she mentioned their relationship to anyone. She feared him but hated him even more, and it was finally time to expose him for the sick control he had over her. She'd find a way to get through the mess he would create and the lies he would tell—she had to.

Rage filled him as he read each entry.

Why didn't you want to be with me?

He stood and stared at his reflection in the dresser's mirror.

I'm not ugly or ignorant. I'm an educated man, for God's sake, and have a lot going for me. You should have felt honored that I gave you my attention.

He threw the journal across the room and continued searching for something else that might have mentioned his name. He snickered his resentment. "You certainly aren't the only woman on my list, Becca. There's plenty more where you came from."

Once satisfied that he had cleared the apartment, he opened the refrigerator and pulled out the containers he needed. The milk, creamer, and water went down the drain. The empty jugs, the salad, and the journal were dropped into a plastic grocery bag and slung over his left arm. He pushed back his sleeve and tipped his wrist—10:57. He had to be at work by eleven thirty. With a final scan of each room, he walked out and locked the door behind him.

Chapter 6

I cut left, and Jack turned right. Lena's office was just down the hall. I called out her name as I entered.

"I'm in the back." Lena was in the refrigerated room, where a dozen individual compartments were situated side by side within the wall.

"Hi, Kate. Just putting Becca Morbeck in her own space for now until I get further instructions. The burn victims will be arriving any minute." She looked at the young woman's sheet-covered body as it lay on the compartment's retractable surface.

"May I?"

Lena nodded, and I stared at Becca's scuffed face. "Airbag injury?"

"Yep. They can cause bruising and scuffs. Her body sustained injuries from the impact, but there shouldn't have been anything forceful enough to cause her death. She isn't cut up, and there wasn't noticeable bleeding."

"How about internal injuries?" I brushed Becca's blond hair out of her face.

Lena sighed. "Maybe. I'll know more if her folks consent to an autopsy."

"What a pretty girl and just starting life as an adult. Such a waste, especially if the accident was really caused by texting while driving."

"Is that what you guys are thinking?"

I shrugged and dropped my hand to my waistline. "It's a theory."

Lena saw me rub my stomach and noticed the sour expression on my face. "You okay, Kate?"

I tried to make light of it, even though the pain was intense and came on suddenly. "I think so. Whoever prepared the coffee this morning probably made it too strong. Acid buildup, I guess, and a bile taste in my mouth." I sucked in a slow breath and continued. "Anyway, Jack said her folks are en route." I tipped my head toward the door. "He walked over to the garage to see if George found anything wrong with the car and wanted me to tell you to go ahead with the photos and paperwork for Becca." I grabbed my left side and bent forward. I squeezed my eyes closed and held my breath, hoping the stabbing pain would pass. "Oh my God, that hurts."

Lena led me by the arm. "Sit down on this chair and don't move. Your pain seems far worse than something caused by a cup of acidic coffee. I'm getting Jack."

"No, wait, it'll pass." I clenched the chair's arm and pushed through the pain. "It's going away."

"Are you sure?"

I nodded. In that moment, it hurt too much to speak. I inhaled through my nose and exhaled through my mouth. Slow, easy breaths were beginning to help. "I just need to get to the bull pen. I have antacids in my desk drawer."

"I'll help you upstairs."

"Just give me a minute." I stood and assessed how I felt. "It's getting better."

Lena stared at me as if she was trying to read my face. "Are you lying to me?"

"No, I'm okay, really."

"All right and tell Jack I'll have everything ready when Becca's parents arrive." The buzzer rang at the back. "They're here with the other bodies."

I left the coroner's office and rushed to the stairs, where I hunched over and grabbed the handrail. "What the hell is wrong with me?" I wiped the perspiration off my forehead with the back of my hand and sucked in deep breaths.

This has to subside before I go upstairs.

I looked right toward the double-glass doors at the end of the hall, and Jack was still talking with George in the garage bay.

I need to get back to the bull pen before he sees me like this. I'll be fine once I'm at my desk and munch a handful of antacids.

I climbed the two flights and entered the bull pen, faking the best normal expression I could muster. Nobody realized anything was wrong.

Minutes later, Amber caught a glimpse of me popping something into my mouth. "Hey, no hiding food. Whatcha eating?"

"Just peanuts." I lied.

She held out her hand. "Give me some."

"Sorry, I just polished them off."

"Thanks a lot, you oinker." She gave me a scowl and continued sorting her paperwork.

Chapter 7

Thankfully, the antacids helped since my stomach pain had gone away. Nobody was the wiser, but I'd sworn off that toxic-tasting coffee for the rest of the day.

Jack's phone rang just before lunchtime. Since he had his door open, I heard his side of the conversation and knew Jan was on the line. I assumed Becca's mom and dad had arrived. I saw Jack take in a deep breath, likely to steel himself for the tough conversation he was about to have. Talking to distraught parents who had just lost their child was never an easy task, and in those situations, I didn't envy his job at all. With the handset back on the receiver, he stood and walked out of his office.

"Kate, you're going with me."

My head snapped in his direction. "What?"

"Don't worry, I'm not going to introduce you as a psychic detective. Becca could have been the sole cause of that accident, but the fact that she didn't apply the brakes makes me think something else is going on. George didn't find anything wrong with the car, which is even more suspect, but something caused her to careen into oncoming traffic, and the press is going to want answers. I need your read on the parents to see if they're withholding anything. Becca could have had a serious medical or psychological problem. She could have been suicidal or had substance abuse issues too. We won't know anything, though, until we talk to her folks." He cocked his head toward the door. "Let's go."

I grabbed my notepad and pen from the desk drawer and walked out with Jack through our security door, which led to the dispatch station and reception counter. I saw Becca's parents sitting in the waiting area adjacent to the building's entrance. Their slumped shoulders and folded hands told me they were already grieving—that day was likely the worst they'd ever had. My heart ached for them as we reached out to give our condolences.

Jack introduced us. "Mr. and Mrs. Morbeck, I'm Lieutenant Steele, and this is Detective Kate Pierce. We're very sorry for your loss."

Mr. Morbeck's expression changed dramatically. "Detective? Why is a detective involved? Was Becca involved in a crime that led to her death?"

"Sir, we don't know anything other than what was described at the scene. We're hoping you two can fill in the gaps." Jack motioned toward the hallway. "Let's talk in our conference room where it's more comfortable, shall we?"

Jack led the way with Mr. Morbeck at his side, and I walked with Mrs. Morbeck behind them. We entered the conference room, and Jack closed the door behind the couple.

"Please, have a seat. May we get you coffee or water?"

They agreed on water, and Jack gave me a head tip. I stepped out, got four bottles of water and a box of tissues, and was back within minutes. With the water handed out, I settled in with my notepad and pen ready, then gave Jack a nod and he began.

He opened the folder in front of him, which contained the five witness statements. The people who were transported to the hospital hadn't given statements yet, but Jack would make sure that was done when and if they were able. Each statement in the folder was given a quick once-over, then Jack removed his own notes compiled from all of them. He closed the folder and cleared his throat.

"The 911 calls flooded in this morning between seven thirty-five and seven forty-two about a car in the southbound lanes of Highway 45 that crossed the center line. It caused multiple accidents—two that were fatal—in the northbound lanes, and then slammed into a tree just off the highway. Witnesses state they saw Becca's vehicle swerve back and forth before it headed for the median, yet nobody noticed brake lights."

Mrs. Morbeck crumbled into a round of tear-jerking sobs. Jack slid the tissue box closer to her and waited.

"I'll give you a minute, ma'am."

She waved him on.

"Are you sure?"

She nodded as her husband consoled her.

Jack continued. "One man was hospitalized with multiple injuries, another with severe burns, two victims died when their cars caught on fire, and several other people were banged up but cleared at the scene and didn't need emergency treatment." Jack glanced at his notes. "Becca was pronounced dead at eight thirteen this morning. I have several concerns about that. Her body wasn't seriously injured because the airbag and seat belt worked properly. She was young, and according to the lead EMT and our medical examiner, that should have been a survivable accident, especially for somebody her age." He looked from one parent to the next. "Is there anything you'd like to share as far as any medical problems or substance abuse Becca had? We need to understand why this accident occurred since there's a good chance of multiple lawsuits. We need full disclosure here, nothing held back. The car was checked out, and there weren't faulty brake lines or a stuck accelerator to blame." Jack went silent and waited.

I held my pen over my notepad, ready to write.

Mrs. Morbeck coughed into her hand then began speaking. "Becca lived in Kewaskum in an efficiency apartment while she was going to school at UWWC. She had nearly a ten-mile drive to school every day, but she chose to be frugal. Her apartment was tiny but affordable and in a decent neighborhood. Everything available near the university was twice as expensive. Becca saves"—she looked at her husband and dabbed her eyes—"or saved all her summer earnings to pay her own way. She paid for her own car too, even though it was a clunker. She was so proud to be making her own way in the world, Lieutenant, and no, she didn't do drugs."

I jotted down *no drugs.*

Mr. Morbeck took over for his wife. "Becca was a healthy nineteen-year-old and participated in sports. She ran track and was on the women's soccer team. She followed the straight and narrow and had real goals—she didn't hang around with that kind of crowd."

I thought back to that morning, when I saw Becca lying on the table in the refrigerated compartment. She did appear very fit, a perfect example of an athletic young lady.

"What was she studying in school?" Jack asked.

Mrs. Morbeck gave Jack a thoughtful smile. "She wanted to be involved in biochemistry after grad school, she just hadn't narrowed down the exact field she wanted to work in yet. She had a long way to go and was just beginning her dream. The semester had just ended, and it was finals week, so she wouldn't have missed any exams. Becca was very responsible."

"Did she ever mention feeling overwhelmed? Did she seem down or depressed?"

The mother shook her head. "Everybody does at one point or another. Like I said, it was finals week, and all kids have anxiety over that, but in her normal life, she seemed happy."

I wrote that down and made a note to talk to some of her professors.

"Does Becca have siblings that she would have confided in?"

"A younger brother, Brent, but he's only eleven. She'd have no reason to confide in him."

I added that to my notes.

Jack scratched his cheek. "When did you see Becca last?"

"She came home over Memorial Day weekend. We had a wonderful time, and she caught up with her high school classmates. We even hosted a barbecue at our house, and several of Becca's friends showed up."

Jack nodded. "Sounds like a normal lifestyle. So you wouldn't say she had suicidal tendencies?"

"Oh, God no! Becca would never consider doing something like that. She had her religious faith too, Lieutenant, and suicide goes against our beliefs. She'd never put us through that kind of agony." Mrs. Morbeck squeezed her husband's hand. "When can we see her? I need to hold my daughter in my arms."

"Ma'am, it doesn't work that way, especially since we may be looking at a criminal investigation here. Once Becca's body is released to you, you can spend as much time as you like with her, but right now, it's by photo identification only. I'm truly sorry."

Becca's father buried his face in his hands. "So you're thinking Becca was involved in some criminal activity?"

"Not necessarily, sir, but we do have to get to the bottom of things. The accident happened for a reason. The car wasn't defective, so that puts the accident back on Becca. You said she didn't have medical issues, she didn't do drugs, and she wasn't depressed. Is there anything we didn't cover?"

Mr. Morbeck stared at the table. "Nothing I can think of."

"How about her driving habits?"

"Meaning?"

"Her cell phone showed text messages sent out to several contacts just seconds before the accident, but they were only jumbled letters that made no sense. Was she prone to texting while driving? That is illegal, you know."

Mrs. Morbeck shook her head. "I don't think she did that, but I couldn't say for sure. I'm not around her all the time."

"Has she ever been ticketed for inattentive or reckless driving?"

"No, only failure to come to a complete stop at a stop sign."

I made a note to dig deep into her driving record. Many times, attorneys in court had the charges changed to faulty taillights or failure to come to a complete stop when the real violation might have been something far worse. It was a practice commonly used to reduce fines and point violations.

Jack continued. "Okay, then the next step is an autopsy, and the medical examiner will need your permission to conduct one. It's the only way to rule out, or include, a physical problem. We'd like to be able to fill in the box that states a cause of death other than *unknown*. I'm assuming you'd want to know why your daughter passed away this morning. Am I correct?"

"Yes, of course. We need to know why Becca died."

"Thank you, and I'm sure the autopsy will answer the questions we're all looking for. I'll have the coroner join us and go over everything with you. She has the consent paperwork you'll need to sign and the photograph of Becca for an ID." Jack pushed back his chair and nodded at me. "Excuse us for a minute."

I walked into the hallway with Jack. "Do you need me for anything else, Boss?"

"Yeah, run downstairs and get Lena and tell her to bring the photo and autopsy consent form to the conference room. I have to call the county and find out when all the highway lanes will be reopened. Tell her I'll meet her in the hallway in five minutes."

"Sure thing." I took the stairs to our lower level and turned left toward the coroner's office. As soon as I stepped through the doorway, I felt that sharp pain in my stomach again. I backed out of the room and called out to the coroner. "Lena, Jack needs you in the conference room with Becca's photo and the autopsy consent form."

She craned her neck around the office door. "Why on earth are you standing in the hallway?"

"I'm not sure. Call it being cautious until I know more."

Lena shook her head as she pushed back her chair and walked my way. "Are you okay?"

"Yeah, but something weird is going on. I'll figure it out sooner or later. Anyway, did you hear what I said?"

"Yes, hon. How are the parents holding up?"

"Not well. They swear Becca wasn't on any drugs or medication. They said her mindset was fine and she was the picture of health."

"Humph… and they agreed to the autopsy?"

"They did."

"Well, what I do know from previous experience is that people hide the truth, and autopsies expose the truth. We'll have our answers soon enough."

Chapter 8

When he saw Daphne Cole walk into the library, he slammed the laptop closed. His online research confirmed what he would use next, and Daphne was about to get it in spades. He was furious with her inattention and lack of concern for him.

Daphne was a blond beauty—tall, willowy, and model like. He thought about the night to come and how he'd tangle his fingers in her hair and make love to her one last time before killing her. It was the least she could do to please him—but in that moment, he was outraged. He checked the time and glared at her as she approached the table.

He defiantly folded his arms across his chest. "More important things going on this morning, Daphne? Do you want to pass your exams or not?"

"Of course I do. My future career depends on it."

"Then you'd think finals week would prompt you to give a shit about showing up on time."

She pulled out the chair opposite him and sat then looked around—the library was full of students. She leaned across the table and whispered. "Sorry, but my boyfriend was late picking me up."

"I don't want to hear your lame excuses, and I don't take kindly to conversations about your boyfriend. I've already told you to get rid of him. I'm the one you should concentrate on since I can make or break you."

She snarled her response. "He's my boyfriend, and I like being with him."

"As opposed to me?" He leaned across the table. "I said to get rid of him."

She pulled back. "You can't be serious!"

"I'm as serious as a heart attack. What's more important to you, your career or a boyfriend who will probably be history by the end of summer break?"

She buried her face in her hands and remained silent.

"That's what I thought. Now get out your textbook and notes. Your hour-long tutoring session has just been reduced to forty minutes. Let me remind you, you'll be sorry if you're late tonight. I have plans that you aren't about to screw up."

"But—"

"But what?" He cocked his head and locked eyes with her.

She reached into the backpack and pulled out her textbook, pen, and spiral notebook. "Nothing. I'll be there on time."

Chapter 9

When Jack finally cut through the bull pen at two o'clock, I looked up. He appeared distraught as he headed toward his office. I wanted to know what was going on since we'd learned that the cause of that morning's accident could be harder to determine than we'd thought. The only person who knew the truth was dead.

"Did the Morbecks leave?"

Jack stopped, took a seat in Amber's guest chair, and let out a long sigh. "They did about an hour ago. The autopsy is underway, but they'll be back as soon as Lena has the final results. That was a tough one, especially since I don't have answers to their questions."

"You don't have to. The autopsy will tell us everything. Facts are facts, and they can't dispute the truth."

Jack raised a brow and let out a puff of air. "True enough, Kate. Right now, we're in a holding pattern until the preliminary results are in. Learning more will take time, and that's when the real investigation begins."

"Sounds like foul play is on your mind," Clayton said.

"Just thinking out loud." Jack glanced at the wall clock

then at Amber and me. "Are you two busy?"

Amber spoke up. "Nothing that can't be pushed back. Why?"

"I want you to head over to St. Joe's and interview Mr. Charles. I was told he's out of surgery. Go find out if he noticed something that nobody else did."

I was happy to leave the building since it looked like a beautiful afternoon. "Sounds good to me. Let's go, Monroe."

The drive was a short ten minutes from door to door. Amber and I had been in that hospital enough times that we were on a first-name basis with most of the administrative staff. We approached the check-in and information counter and gave a head tip to Anna, the receptionist at the moment.

She gave us a wide grin. "No blood or broken bones, and you're walking in under your own power. That's always a good sign. So, what can I do for you ladies?"

I leaned forward and spoke quietly. "We need to know what room Bill Charles is in. We have to interview him about the car accident he was involved in this morning."

Anna cupped her hand around her mouth. "I heard three people died at the scene, one being a college-aged girl."

Amber nodded. "Unfortunately, that's true. Such a sad day for all three families."

"I can't even imagine. Give me just a sec." Anna tapped her computer keys. "Here we go. He's on the third floor in room fourteen." She raised a concerned brow. "His surgery was only three hours ago. You sure you want to interview him already?"

"Boss's orders," Amber said. "We'll see how he responds. Thanks, Anna."

"You bet."

The elevators were thirty feet to our left, just beyond the gift shop. Amber and I rode up with an orderly attending to someone in a wheelchair. I gave them a smile and kept silent. When the doors parted, we stepped out into the third-floor hallway.

"Who's conducting the interview?"

Amber gave me a nod. "You are. You can read between the lines better than I can because of your voodoo abilities."

I chuckled. "Knock it off. Do you really think so?" We headed to room fourteen.

"Uh-huh. Nah, just kidding. Go ahead and start asking questions. I'll butt in whenever necessary, and I'll do the note taking."

"Got it."

Amber knocked on the partially open door. Beyond it, a privacy curtain was pulled closed, and a TV played quietly in the background.

A raspy voice from inside the room said to come in, and the TV went off. Amber popped her head around the curtain.

"Mr. Charles?"

"That's me," he said, "but you don't look like a nurse."

We entered the room, and Amber smiled. "And for good reason. We aren't nurses. I'm Detective Amber Monroe, and this is my partner, Detective Kate Pierce. We're from the sheriff's office."

He nodded. "You're here about the accident, right?"

"That's correct, sir. The deputies at the scene didn't get a witness statement from you for obvious reasons—you needed immediate medical attention. How are you doing?"

He shrugged. "Guess I'll be here for a few days and then on medical leave for six weeks. Broken ankle and cracked kneecap on my right leg, broken arm on the left, and multiple cuts and contusions. Overall, it isn't my best day."

"I bet it isn't. Do you mind if we sit and ask you a few questions?"

"Do I need my attorney present since I intend to sue for injuries?"

I took my turn. "No, we'd need a witness statement regardless of whether you sued or not, and the insurance companies would insist on a copy of it too. What we want is your true recollection of the accident, but first we need to know that you're coherent and can answer our questions with a clear mind. Are you fully awake? No residual grogginess from your surgery?"

"I think I'm okay. I'm due for some pain meds, but I'll wait until after the interview."

I gave him a nod. "If you don't remember anything, that's understandable considering the circumstances."

"Oh, I remember everything, and to be honest, it was pretty frightening." He tipped his chin at me. "Go ahead and ask away."

Amber pulled out her notepad, and I began.

"Okay, where were you going this morning when the accident occurred?"

"To work. I live here in North Bend, but I work at F. P. Lyons Construction in Campbellsport. My medical compensation is only three quarters of my actual weekly pay, and that doesn't figure in the amount of overtime we work. Summer is our busy months, you know."

"Yep and noted. So, you were driving north on Highway 45, and then what happened?"

"Then I saw a car behaving erratically in the southbound lanes. The cars around it swerved to get out of its way, and then they backed off. I thought the driver had fallen asleep and then overcorrected when they felt the rumble strips, but it swerved again. That time, it jumped the median and came directly at me, toward the center lane. A semi was skidding behind me, and other cars were to my left and right—I had nowhere to go. It was like bumper-car madness with everyone trying to avoid getting hit. I was within twenty feet of a head-on collision when there was enough space to swerve left. My car crossed two lanes and hit the ditch. That's when it flipped on its roof."

"That had to be horrifying," Amber said.

Mr. Charles wiped his eyes with the back of his right hand. "I thought I was going to die, and before it was all over, I wanted a good look at the face that caused my death."

My eyes widened with disbelief. "And what did you see?"

"Not a damn thing. The driver's side visor was down."

I thought about when the accident occurred. The sun would have been overhead in the east to southeast skies, and the highway did have a few slight curves. Becca might have lowered her visor because of the glaring sun, and I wondered if that could have been a factor that led to the accident.

We ended the interview when Bill's wife showed up, and with a thank-you and wishes for a speedy recovery, Amber and I left the hospital.

I climbed into the passenger seat, and we headed to the sheriff's office. "We need to mention the sun's position in the sky to Jack. Maybe it blinded Becca enough to cause her to swerve, especially if somebody ahead of her braked for a second. The witnesses may need to be interviewed again."

"I agree, and let's get his take on it. I'd be happy to conduct some interviews while Billings and Clayton sit at their desks and file paperwork all day. It's too beautiful outside to be cooped up indoors, anyway."

We entered the building and headed for the bull pen. Jack saw us walk through the security door and motioned us toward his office. Inside, we took seats on his guest chairs, and Amber pulled out her notes.

"Let's hear it. Did you have an aha moment after speaking to Mr. Charles?"

"Possibly," I said. I knew Jack was half kidding with that remark, but his surprised expression told me he was all ears. "We asked Mr. Charles to walk us through what he remembered from this morning. His account was pretty much on target with what the rest of the witnesses said as far as Becca's car swerving left and right before speeding across the median. Mr. Charles thought she was about to hit him head-on and said he wanted to see the face of the person who was about to kill him."

"That sounds ominous."

I nodded. "No kidding, right? I asked him what he saw, and he said he saw nothing. The driver's visor was pulled down."

Jack's shoulders slumped. "That was your aha moment?"

"No, it was the fact that her visor was down. It got me thinking about the sun's position at that time of morning. Maybe the east to southeast sun glaring through her windshield blinded her enough to cause the accident."

Jack rubbed his chin. "Okay, that could make sense."

"I hear a *but* coming," Amber said.

"Yes, you do. *But* why wouldn't she brake or just pull to the shoulder to compose herself? It was like she was in a runaway car."

Now it was *my* shoulders that slumped. "So, there's no point in asking the people in the southbound lanes who left witness statements if they remember the sun glaring so much this morning that it made it difficult to see clearly."

Jack opened the witness statement folder that was lying on his desk. "Hang on. I believe there were only two people from the southbound lanes who stayed behind to give statements." He licked his thumb and index finger and paged through the notes. "Here we go, one woman and one man, each in separate cars."

He handed the witness statements to me with their names and contact numbers, and I passed one to Amber.

"I believe simple phone calls would be all it takes to get the answers you need." Jack tapped the desk with his fingertips. "Okay, go ahead and make those calls, and I'll pull Becca's driving records and get a warrant for her phone calls. They'll show me if she was prone to texting while driving or not."

Chapter 10

I noticed the grin on Clayton's face as we left Jack's office. "Hoping to go for another drive, weren't you?"

"Eavesdropper. Don't you have paperwork to file?"

"Not that much anymore since I'm going to share it with you."

"Whatever." I fired off a frown at Clayton as I passed his desk and took a seat at my own. Once I was situated, I called the phone number on the witness statement, and Amber did the same with hers. We were hoping to hear answers that would explain everything, but it wasn't meant to be. Both parties said the sun didn't seem to factor in at all on their morning drive south. That discounted my theory of Becca's accident being caused by temporary sun blindness.

I felt discouraged as I thanked the gentleman for his time and placed the handset back on the base. I had hoped I was onto something, but I wasn't. "I guess we're back to square one. We'll have to wait for the autopsy report to know anything definitive." I reached for the stack of files Chad had placed on my desk and dug in.

Moments later, Lena walked in and headed for Jack's

office door with a folder in her hand. I was sure it was the early results of Becca's exam. I cleared my throat loudly, causing Jack to look out into the bull pen. He saw Lena coming his way and exited his office. He met her next to Amber's desk. My plan had worked, and I hoped Jack would allow her to share the information with all of us.

"Whatcha got, Lena?" Jack pointed at Amber's guest chair as he rolled his shoulders and neck. He took a seat in the chair next to my desk.

"Just some early information about Becca's autopsy, primarily the basics. The detailed results will come back with the blood work and urinalysis." She opened the folder and began with Jack's go-ahead. "By all appearances, Becca Morbeck was a healthy nineteen-year-old female. Her weight and height were proportionate at five feet six inches and one hundred twenty-six pounds. Her muscle tone was excellent, and her body fat was a low fifteen percent."

I added my take. "She did look very fit."

Lena nodded. "And she was. She had shoulder-length blond hair and green eyes. Her teeth were well cared for with only three fillings in her entire mouth. No tattoos or piercings. Her heart looked normal, and there weren't any signs of internal bleeding." Lena gave me a subtle smile. "Her lungs appeared healthy, so I'd say she wasn't a smoker. Under the microscope, her stomach contents looked like breakfast cereal, so she obviously ate before leaving home this morning. The only thing that looked off to me was her esophagus and stomach lining itself."

Jack's forehead creased. "Off how?"

"Red and inflamed, which unfortunately could be caused from a handful of problems from chronic acid indigestion and GERD to esophageal and stomach cancer. I'm not sure what I should test for since it's unlikely that any medical issues like those would send somebody flying off the freeway into oncoming traffic. Before any type of medical problem became severe enough to disable her while driving—other than a massive heart attack—she would have felt the symptoms of the disease and would have been under a doctor's care. Having her parents pull her medical records is a good place to start."

"Assuming she passed out behind the wheel, what would cause that to happen other than being sleep deprived? Because of finals, many students stay awake all night cramming for exams. I know I did."

Lena turned to Amber. "Do you know she passed out? If she was up all night, she probably drank caffeinated beverages, which would make her wired, not sleepy."

Amber shrugged. "Just throwing out ideas that obviously don't make sense. A person who doesn't instinctively slam on their brakes in a situation like that seems abnormal to me."

"Same here," Jack said. "I'm leaning toward her being under the influence of something, passed out, or already dead."

Lena glanced at her notes one more time then turned to Jack. "Ask her folks if Becca ever had heart problems, even as a youth, and then ask them to pull her medical records. I'll send out her blood work for drug testing, but the appearance of her stomach and esophagus still sticks in my craw. I'll test for cancer too even though that wouldn't have led to her accident."

"Is there a cancer drug that could have rendered her sleepy or unconscious?" Jack asked.

"Not sure, but I'll check into that. You'd think her parents would be aware of something as serious as cancer, though. I'll see if I can get the lab to put a rush on the blood and urinalysis tests. I should have more answers by tomorrow, at least about being under the influence of drugs or alcohol."

Jack let out a hard breath and thanked Lena for what she had so far. "Okay, guys, call it a wrap. There's nothing to follow up on now until Lena gets us more answers."

"How about talking to some of her friends and professors? They, if anyone, would know if she was under stress or not getting enough sleep because of exams," Amber said.

"Yeah, but let's save that for tomorrow. I'll have Tech pull her social media accounts too. They're usually full of helpful information."

Chapter 11

"Something on your mind?" Amber glanced at me as she waited at the stoplight.

"Sort of." I stared out the window as I thought of Lena's startling comment about Becca's stomach and esophagus.

"Do you want to expand on that or keep it to yourself?" Amber pressed the gas pedal and continued through the intersection.

I swatted the air. "You don't want to hear my nonsense."

"Sure I do, and sometimes you actually make sense."

I gave her the middle finger. "You sure?"

"Uh-huh, go ahead."

"Okay, if you insist. Twice today, I had to go to Lena's office, and the first time, bile came up my throat and stabbing pains shot through my stomach while I was standing next to Becca's body. The second time, I barely entered Lena's office and it began again. I backed out, and it went away."

"That's ridiculous. Do you think her office holds some bad juju?"

"No, not at all. Actually, I blamed it on the coffee until it happened the second time. I think it's related to Becca.

Remember what Lena said in her description of Becca's organs?"

"Yeah, sort of."

"Let me refresh your memory. She said Becca's stomach and esophagus were red and inflamed."

"Right. And your stomach hurt and bile came up your throat. Are you thinking it's transference? Becca's medical problems are now yours? Is that even possible?"

I shook my head. "Hell if I know. Look at the husbands who claim to have morning sickness alongside their pregnant wives."

Amber snickered. "You're talking about attention hogs. They're just men who feel left out."

"Whatever. But on a serious note, nothing like that—if it's related to my psychic abilities—has ever happened to me before."

Amber pulled into the driveway and tapped the garage door remote. "I know what you should do while I'm making dinner."

"Research transference?"

"Absolutely."

Inside, we found Jade talking on the phone. She gave us a hello nod, continued for several minutes, then hung up. She pulled three beers from the refrigerator, handed them out, and took a seat next to me at the breakfast bar. She peered over my arm, clearly wondering what I was conducting a search on.

"Transference? Why are you looking into that?"

I pulled back. "What's with all the nosy people today?

Clayton was eavesdropping earlier, and now you're eyedropping."

"That was funny." Amber stuck her head into the lower cabinet and pulled out a saucepan.

"Is this about the big accident on 45 this morning?"

"Yeah, you heard about it?"

"No, but that was Jack who just called. He wanted to know how it felt and what I did once I realized my brakes were gone, thanks to Warren Ricks."

I set down my phone. "Sorry for snapping at you."

"That's okay. It was a cute comment and pretty clever. Anyway, I told him I was petrified and kept hitting the brakes even though it didn't help. He gave me the short version of the accident and said the witnesses never saw brake lights."

Amber lit the burner and set the pot of leftover homemade chicken dumpling soup to a low setting. It would simmer for a half hour, and we'd have grilled cheese sandwiches to go along with it. She joined us and took a seat on the barstool. "Kate thinks she felt the symptoms of something Lena mentioned about the condition of Becca's stomach and esophagus."

Jade furrowed her brows. "Really? Is that even possible?"

"No clue. Transference is usually the feelings and emotions of one person to another, primarily stemming from childhood issues. It isn't normally a physical thing, *but* there is that twin phenomenon when one gets sick then the other falls sick too."

Amber craned her neck around Jade. "And don't forget the pregnant-husband syndrome."

"Yeah, and that."

Jade chuckled. "Sounds like you guys already did the research."

After dinner and a few TV shows, I pulled a limp cat off my lap and announced I was going to bed. Spaz bristled at me for disturbing his sleep. "I'm beat. I'll see you guys in the morning." Jade and Amber wished me sweet dreams as I headed for my basement bedroom. I hoped for a restful night, and sweet dreams would be a plus.

Chapter 12

She covered her mouth and yawned. "I really should go. Tomorrow is another day of exams." Daphne tried to be discreet as she glanced up at the wall clock.

"Do you think I was born yesterday? All you want to do is get out of here so you can meet up with your piece of shit boyfriend. That lowlife has nothing going for him, but look at me, I went out of my way for you with a perfect four-course dinner. We made love, and I could tell you enjoyed it. Your enthusiasm was obvious." He stared at her. "So what's your hurry, Daphne?"

She appeared nervous as she picked at her cuticles. "Nothing, I'm just tired. I want to be wide awake for tomorrow's tests."

"One more glass of wine won't kill you. It's only ten o'clock."

She reluctantly agreed. She had seen his intimidating side and didn't want to go there again.

"Stay put. I'll fill our glasses." He rose from the couch and took the wineglasses into the kitchen. Earlier, when she was showering, he'd scooped up her car keys and dropped them into his pants pocket. There was no chance of her sneaking away while his back was turned. At the counter, he tipped the shaker of fentanyl over her wineglass then returned it to the cabinet on his left. With a plastic spoon—so she wouldn't hear the stirring—he made sure the powder was dissolved before walking back to the living room with a glass in each hand.

"Here you go. I promise this will be the last glass of wine for you tonight." He handed the left glass to Daphne and took a seat at her side. "Let's make a toast."

She forced a smile. "To what?"

"To a night to remember."

Daphne frowned. "I don't understand."

"We had a wonderful dinner and then some. Yes?"

She looked at her lap and nodded.

"Then it's a night worth remembering. At least I'll always remember it." He tapped his wineglass against hers. "Cheers." He took a deep sip and watched her do the same. He was sure she'd guzzle it as fast as possible in hopes of leaving soon.

Sweet Daphne, you aren't going anywhere since you'll be dead in a matter of minutes.

He watched as her expression changed to confusion then panic. She held her hand to her throat and coughed as if something had blocked her airway.

"Did the wine go down wrong?" He feigned concern and watched her every move.

Watching you die fills my heart with pleasure.

"I… I… can't breathe." She sucked in gulps of air, but

they weren't filling her lungs. Her passageway was closing. Her raspy voice cried out as she clawed for his help. "Please, my heart … I think I'm having—"

He backed away to avoid being scratched. "What? I can't understand you, Daphne. Speak up. What seems to be the problem?" He watched her thrash and convulse for several minutes before she went still. He pressed the back of his fingers against her throat and felt for a pulse, but there wasn't one. Her mouth gaped open, and her blue eyes bulged. He stared into those eyes and saw emptiness.

"That'll teach you to screw around with me. You wanted a passing grade, but you weren't willing to pay the price to get it. Everyone wants a handout these days. See what happens when you don't take my warnings seriously."

He crossed to the kitchen, chewed a handful of aspirin, then grabbed the dish towel. He returned to her side, and with the towel covering his hands, he closed her eyes and mouth so rigor wouldn't freeze them open. Satisfied, he slugged down the rest of his wine and dabbed his lips. "Finals week is a real killer, isn't it?" He thought of his options.

I can't risk taking you to your apartment since the boyfriend might be there, but I can leave you at the university. You'll surely be found first thing in the morning.

He knew where every camera was located at the campus, and there weren't any facing the faculty parking lot. That would be the best place to leave Daphne and her car. He could slip into the shadows unseen, walk to town, then order a driver through his phone app. He'd be home before midnight.

He gathered her things, turned off her phone and his own, and slipped on a pair of gloves. After wiping down her phone and keys to remove possible fingerprints, he carried Daphne to her car and placed her in the passenger seat. The click of the seat belt secured her in an upright position, then he climbed in behind the wheel and headed down the driveway. Because he lived on the outskirts of town, off country roads, she had no doubt gone unnoticed as she drove to his house earlier that night. He'd slip out just as quietly as Daphne had slipped in. Memories of Isabelle filled his mind as he drove the short four miles.

Women can't be trusted. Isn't that right, Isabelle? You cheated on me dozens of times, but you were too wrapped up with those college boys to realize I knew what you were doing all along. Paid the price too, didn't you, bitch?

He killed the headlights and turned in to the empty faculty parking lot then checked the time—it was closing in on eleven o'clock. Hugging the outside edge of the lot, he used the tree canopy as cover and inched forward until he settled on a spot a good distance from the pole lights illuminating the area. In the morning, the parking lot would fill up quickly, and the unfortunate person who parked next to Daphne would definitely notice something was wrong.

A quick scan of the lot told him he was still alone. He stepped out of the car, reached in, unfastened her belt, and pulled her across the console. It was a struggle to situate her in the proper position, but it had to be perfect. He placed her feet at the pedals, her hands in her lap, and the driver's side seat belt over her chest and right hip, then he clicked it closed. Another look at his surroundings confirmed the coast was clear. He rounded the vehicle to the passenger side, pulled the phone from Daphne's purse, turned it on, and set it in the cup holder. He placed her purse on the passenger seat and made a final check of the interior.

Keys in the ignition, purse on seat, phone turned on and visible, and Daphne correctly positioned behind the wheel. I'm good to go.

He headed for the tree line, where the shadows swallowed up his movements as he walked east toward town.

Chapter 13

I ran for my life, but he closed in rapidly, like a wild animal chasing its prey. The claws were out, and the deadly strike was only seconds away. I looked over my shoulder and saw him mere inches behind me.

He's after me again. Why won't Robert Lynch die?

The cornstalks slapped my face as I raced through the field, doing what I could to hide from my attacker, but I tripped over the furrowed rows again and again. He was gaining speed and getting too close—I couldn't outrun him. Dirt clods flew up behind me as he neared, and I felt his hot breath on the back of my neck. Any second now, I'd feel him reach out and grab me, then he'd have me and pull me to the ground. He'd gut me with his Bowie knife that glinted in the moonlight, and I'd be dead.

My feet came out from beneath me. He jerked me backward by the hair, and I fell hard. It was over, and I closed my eyes and accepted my fate as he straddled my body. The first searing strike hit me in the left side under my ribs. He raised the knife again and buried it to the handle, then he gave it an extra twist for good measure. Strike after strike, I felt the burn of the blade puncturing my flesh and organs. I prayed to God for a speedy death.

I was shaken into the moment by Amber, who was sitting on the edge of my bed.

"Kate, Kate, wake up! You're having a nightmare." She clicked on the table lamp and brushed my hair out of my face.

I held my stomach and cried out in pain. I looked down, expecting to see my disemboweled intestines, then I stared at my hands and wondered why they weren't covered in blood.

"Kate, it was a dream."

I looked into Amber's eyes, still confused. "He... I'm... the knife—"

"There's nothing wrong with you. You're safe in your own bed."

I looked at the doorway, and Jade was walking toward me with a wet cloth in her hand.

"Here, hon, hold this against your forehead. You're drenched in sweat."

"What happened? My pain is real." I winced as another attack seared through my midsection.

As Amber headed for the door, Jade took her place. "I'll get you a cup of peppermint tea and the heating pad. They'll help your stomachache."

With my shaking hand, I wiped my tears. "It was Robert, Jade. He was in that cornfield again, and this time he caught me. He stabbed me repeatedly with his Bowie knife, and I think I died."

"But you're alive, and the dream probably came on

because of your stomachache. Take some deep breaths and lie back. Amber will be here with the tea and heating pad soon. They'll help. I'm sure of it."

I heard Amber's footsteps as she descended the stairs.

She set the cup and saucer on the nightstand, plumped the pillows behind my back, and placed the heating pad at my side. She handed the cup to me. "Here you go."

"Thank you." I took a sip. "It's good. You know I never get stomachaches, right?"

Amber nodded. "I've never known you to have them until today."

"Robert was stabbing me in my dream, and Jade thinks that's why I felt the pain."

"Then why the stomachache in Lena's office?"

"Good question, but I truly believe it has something to do with Becca. The description Lena gave of her stomach and esophagus and the timing of my sudden stomachaches are too coincidental. I believe whatever caused Becca's organs to look that way is what killed her."

"And you may be onto something, Kate." Amber reached for the cup. "How is the pain now?"

"It's starting to go away, and I appreciate your help, both of you. I know my dreams interrupt your sleep, and I'm so sorry."

Amber swatted the air. "They solve cases too, so don't give it another thought."

"I need to talk to Lena tomorrow about Becca. I'm positive the toxicology results will solve that case."

Chapter 14

Jack noticed my lack of attention during our morning update. "Is there somewhere else you'd rather be, Detective Pierce?"

"What? Sorry, Boss, I guess my mind is on Lena."

Jack frowned. "Why Lena?"

"I need to talk to her about Becca Morbeck's case. I—"

Amber interrupted. "Kate had a nightmare last night, and she thinks it's related to Becca."

I rolled my eyes and glared at her. "Can I tell my own stories?"

Clayton chuckled. "Here we go."

Jack held up his hand. "Will everyone please stop?" Jack turned to me as he took a seat on the edge of my desk. "Lena is in meetings with the families of the burn victims. She might be a while. Want to share your dream?"

I huffed. "Thanks, Amber. I wanted to get Lena's opinion before I voiced my ideas to the rest of you, but"—I tipped my head toward her—"apparently she knows best."

Amber began her rebuttal, but Jack gave her a zip-it gesture. "Go ahead, Kate. Your instincts are usually right."

"The dream isn't completely related, but I've had several instances of severe stomach pains and bile in my throat after Becca was brought into the coroner's office. Then when Lena described Becca's red, inflamed stomach and throat, it made me think the two were related."

Jack raised a curious brow. "As if her condition transferred to you?"

"I guess that's the only way to say it, but yeah. I'm thinking she's using me as the conduit to tell us what killed her."

"That's an interesting theory, and there may be some merit to it. I'll text Lena and ask her to let us know when she's finished with her meetings. I'd like to sit in on the conversation too if that's okay."

I nodded. "Thanks for having an open mind."

Jack pointed at Clayton. "Okay, let's begin. What's on your agenda today?"

"Whatever you need me to do."

Billings spoke up. "Same here."

"Then I want the two of you to head to the university and find out what courses Becca had finals in this week. Interview those professors and ask if anything seemed off with her. Talk to her advisors and find out who her friends were. Get a list from Admissions of the classes she took over the semester and talk to everyone she knew." He turned to Amber and me. "You ladies can start working on a press release. Of course, we don't know the cause of the accident yet, but you can organize what we do know according to the scene and witness statements. I'll look it over before we hand it off to the press."

I gathered my laptop and legal pad then jerked my chin at Amber. "Come on, bigmouth. Let's work in the conference room."

Jack's office phone rang just as the four of us were about to leave the bull pen. "Hang on a minute, guys," I said. "This could be Lena with some additional information."

We dropped back into our chairs and waited. When I heard cursing coming from Jack's end of the call, my head snapped toward his office.

I cupped my hand and whispered. "Whatever that's about can't be good."

Seconds later, Jack stormed out and motioned to all of us. "Let's go. A call just came in that a student was found dead in her car in UWWC's faculty parking lot. Clayton, tell Forensics to head out, and let Lena know she'll have to wrap up her meetings."

Billings clipped his badge to his belt. "Holy shit. I have a feeling it's going to be one of those weeks."

We checked out two cruisers and headed west. Silver and Ebert were already at the scene and had the parking lot blocked off with crime scene tape. Thankfully, the campus wasn't as populated during finals week as it normally was, but there was no way to keep the death of another student under wraps—the yellow tape was a dead giveaway. Social media accounts would blow up and wild rumors of UWWC students dying would hit the airwaves within hours. The news would go viral in no time.

We parked at the taped barricade ten minutes later. Once we exited our vehicles and dipped under the tape, Jack shouted out orders to the deputies. "Ebert, keep those students back at least a hundred yards, and Silver, block that car with your own until Lena gets here with a portable barrier. I don't want to see any cell phone pictures on the news or social media."

"Right away, Lieutenant."

Ebert lowered the tape so Silver could block the view of the victim's car with his own.

Jack approached Ebert. "What have we got? Walk me through this."

"Car is registered to a Daphne Cole, aged twenty, and lives with a roommate on Fifth Street in an upper duplex. DMV shows a previous address in Manitowoc."

"Her parents' house, maybe?"

"Probably."

"Who discovered the body and at what time?"

Ebert pointed at a woman standing with a good twenty other people near the faculty entrance. "The woman wearing the orange sweater called it in. Her car is the black one pointing at the nose of the vehicle with the deceased student in it."

"So she parked and noticed someone sitting in the other car and thought to take a closer look? Why?"

Ebert shrugged. "No idea. The interview halted when you guys arrived."

"Sure." Jack shielded his eyes, looked around, then jerked his chin straight ahead. "Take her over to that bench. I'll be there in just a minute, and I want the rest of these gawkers gone. Tell those professors or whoever they are to go inside the building. I want this lot, the sidewalks surrounding it, and the building entrances cleared. The only people out here should be law enforcement and county personnel. Got it?"

"You bet, Lieutenant." Ebert headed toward the woman in the sweater.

Amber and I joined Jack as he gloved up and approached the vehicle. We stood at the driver's-side window and peered through. He tried the door, but it was locked.

Jack groaned. "Jesus. What the hell is going on with young kids these days?"

"If we only knew." I stared at the blonde, whose chin was against her chest. Her hair—tumbled forward—hid the sides of her face, and the clasped seat belt suspended her inches from the steering wheel.

Amber rounded the vehicle to the passenger side and looked in. "Her purse is clearly visible on the seat, and there's no sign of an attack, plus her cell phone is sitting in the cup holder. It's apparent she wasn't trying to call for help."

We followed Jack to the driver's-side door of the black car and faced the victim's vehicle. That vantage point didn't show us without a shadow of a doubt that we were looking at a dead person sitting behind the wheel.

Jack pointed at the victim. "If you glanced at her while getting out of this car, would you automatically think she was dead, or would you think she was looking down at a cell phone in her hand?"

Amber responded. "I wouldn't think anything of it, and I'm a cop."

"Exactly. Kate?"

"To be honest, I'd say she was looking down."

"Then why would anyone walk over to investigate? Most people park their vehicles, grab their stuff, and go about their business." When car doors closed at our backs, Jack looked over his shoulder. Forensics and Lena had arrived. "I'm beginning to think finals week is cursed. Too much stress on the students. They're either killing themselves or each other." Jack's frustration was showing. "Okay, I'll update these guys quick, and then I have to talk to that witness."

"What do you want us to do?"

Jack looked at me. "Damage control. Chase those students off the sidewalk and into the building. Make sure nobody is lurking around and taking pictures from the tree line either. Clayton and Billings, go inside and talk to other faculty members. Find out if anybody saw something or someone that seemed out of place when they pulled into the parking lot this morning."

Clayton elbowed Billings and tipped his head toward the building. "On it, Boss."

Amber and I headed for the sidewalk. "How's the stomach?"

"It's behaving. I'm not looking forward to the autopsy on the latest victim, though. Who knows what might have caused her death."

Chapter 15

"Okay, people, the show is over. Go on inside. I'm sure all of you have exams to take."

Groans sounded throughout the crowd, and questions were flying at Amber and me.

A man stepped out of the crowd and addressed us. "Who's in that car? Are they dead?"

Amber pointed at the coroner's van. "You do see what it says on the side of that vehicle, right?"

I nudged Amber and gave her a frown then took the lead. "Sir, unless you're a family member, we can't disclose information to you or anyone else. Are you?"

"No, but—"

"Sorry, then you'll have to go inside with the rest of the group. This is a sheriff's office matter. You'll know what's going on once we release information to the press. We'll have questions for certain people later after we learn more about the victim." I turned back to Amber. "What was that about?"

"Nothing, I just don't do well with people who fake ignorance."

"Maybe he wasn't faking." I noticed a young woman

among the crowd who was wiping her eyes, and I called out to her. "Do you know the person in that vehicle?"

"Yes, I recognize the car. It belongs to Daphne Cole, my best friend and roommate."

Whispers and gasps sounded among the growing crowd.

I wiggled my finger at the female who made the comment. "You're coming with us. Everyone else, keep moving." I whistled to get Ebert's attention. "Come take over for us. We have questions for this young lady."

Ebert headed toward the sidewalk, and Amber and I led the student to our cruiser.

I opened the back door. "Have a seat and tell us what you know about Daphne."

The young woman stared at Daphne's car in the distance. "What happened to her?"

Amber pulled a notepad and pen from the console. "We don't know yet. What's your name?"

"Jennifer Tenley."

"And you and Daphne were best friends?"

Her voice cracked as she responded. "The very best." She covered her face with her hands and broke into sobs.

Amber handed Jennifer a travel-sized pack of tissues from the glove box. "Here you go."

"Thanks."

"Can you think of any reason that Daphne would park in the faculty lot?"

She shook her head and dabbed her eyes. "Not a clue. She's never done that before, plus she doesn't drive to school that often."

I cocked my head. "You take turns?"

"No, Vince takes her to school when she has late classes."

Amber jotted that down. "Vince who, and what was his relationship to Daphne?"

"Vince Meroni, her boyfriend."

"Is Vince a student here?"

Jennifer nodded. "Sometimes. He shows up just enough to avoid getting expelled."

"Is he here now?"

"I don't know. I haven't seen him, but I know Daphne had exams today. I assumed she spent the night with him since she didn't come home last night. But now that I see her car—"

I glanced at Amber. "When did you talk to Daphne last?"

"Yesterday. She had two exams, then she mentioned spending the rest of the day with Vince."

"Where does he live?"

"At the Trace, in apartment three. He's so disgusting, but Daphne likes bad boys." She blew into a tissue. "I mean liked."

I tipped my head at Amber, and we excused ourselves for a minute. "I need to update Jack on this Vince character. He needs to be interviewed right away."

"Go ahead. I'll keep Jennifer talking."

"Good enough." I crossed the lot and joined Jack, Lena, and the forensic team at Daphne's car. "What's the word, Boss?" I rubbed my chest and coughed into my hand. The air suddenly felt thick, and breathing was difficult.

Jack glanced my way. "You okay?"

I nodded. "Must be the humidity."

Lena popped her head out of the car and asked Jason to get the gurney. She shook her head as she backed away from the vehicle.

Jack stared at her. "Well?"

"Her large muscles are completely stiff. I'd say she's been dead for at least eight hours and getting her out of the car isn't going to be pretty or easy."

Jack grimaced. "Can we push the seat back as far as it goes and then recline it?"

"Yeah, that's our only option, and I hope it works. Kyle, get a few more shots of the way she's sitting and the seat position before we pull her out."

"Any obvious signs of a struggle?"

"Nothing. Give me a minute, Jack." Lena helped Jason position the gurney alongside the vehicle.

"Sure thing." Jack turned to me. "What did you get from that witness?"

"Her boyfriend's name and that he's probably the last person who saw Daphne alive."

Jack whistled and waved to get Clayton's attention then looked back at me. "Got this boyfriend's address?"

"Sure do. His name is Vince Meroni, and he lives at the Trace in apartment three."

"Good."

Clayton jogged over. "What do you need, sir?"

"Is he a student here or not?"

I nodded. "The witness said he is once in a while."

Jack frowned. "Okay. Chad, the deceased had a boyfriend

named Vince Meroni. See if he's here, and if he isn't, call the PD and have someone meet you and Adam at apartment three at the Trace. You need to shake Vince's tree and see what he knows. If you can't find him, have the locals pull his DMV file. He'll likely be wherever his vehicle is. They can put out a BOLO for it."

"On it."

Jack raked his fingers through his hair. "Got your notepad handy?"

"Yeah, one second." I pulled the notepad and pen from my pocket and flipped to an empty page. "Go ahead."

"Write down the boyfriend's name, the young lady that Amber is with, and Jeanette Fry, the woman who made the 911 call. At this point, unless Lena rules Daphne's death a suicide, they are people we'll be touching base with again."

I looked toward the faculty entrance and the area was empty. "Did Jeanette explain why she walked over to Daphne's car?"

"Yeah, something about assigned parking. She was going to ask why Daphne was parked in a designated spot. Guess the faculty members have parking stickers on their windshields. Sounded innocent enough."

"What about Becca Morbeck, Boss? This new development kind of overshadows the reason Clayton and Billings were coming here to begin with."

Jack let out a puff of air. "I know, and now Lena has her hands full with another victim. Speaking of that, what's the story on Daphne's family?"

I shrugged. "We weren't working on that."

Jack scratched his cheek. "That's right, it was Ebert who

69

said her previous address was in Manitowoc. Go inside and track down somebody in Admissions. Find out Daphne's emergency contact person and get their phone number and address."

"Wouldn't a family member's name be on her phone?"

"Forensics already bagged it to check for prints. We need to get a handle on these deaths and fast. Speaking of that—"

I followed Jack's eyes to the curb in front of the campus. "Shit, the press is here, and they're heading our way."

Chapter 16

"How many times do you think the city boys have arrested people here?" Adam looked from apartment to apartment and shook his head. People sat on their porches, smoking cigarettes and drinking beer from tall boys. They watched life go by with no apparent ambition to do anything other than what they were doing.

"Probably more than I care to count. This place is known as Trouble Central due to fistfights, disorderly conduct, drugs, and domestic abuse. In my opinion, the Trace should be bulldozed into the ground."

Adam laughed. "And then what, put in another soccer field? How many are in the county now, seven?"

"Or more." Clayton jerked his head. "A patrol car is pulling in. Let's see who they sent."

They climbed out of the cruiser just as the patrol car rolled to a stop at their side.

Clayton nodded. "Billy Bachaus, good to see you."

The officer killed the engine, got out, and shook hands with Clayton and Billings. "Vince Meroni again?"

"You know him?"

"As well as I know my next-door neighbor. He's been nothing but trouble since age nine."

Adam frowned. "Yet he's a college student? How does that work?"

Billy swiped the air. "No different than athletes who have zero interest in academics, yet they get a free ride to college in hopes of getting picked up by a professional team. Grandpa foots Vince's rent and expenses as long as he's enrolled in college. The thing is, the kid never goes to classes, and honestly, I'm surprised he hasn't been expelled. So what has he done now?"

Clayton shrugged. "We don't know that he's done anything, we just need to talk to him about his girlfriend's death. We were told he may have been the last person to see her alive."

"Jeez, who's his girlfriend?"

"The student who was found dead in her car at UWWC this morning."

"No shit? Then let's go bang on his door and see what he has to say." Billy led the way to the front of the building. "It's right here." He balled his hand into a fist and rapped hard against the dirty tan door. "Did you notice an old black Altima in the parking lot?"

"Can't say that I did or didn't."

"So you didn't look for it?" Billy banged again.

"It's your jurisdiction, dude." Clayton took the sidewalk to the parking lot and looked out over the fifty or more cars parked there. He jogged back to the door where Adam and Billings still stood.

Billy looked at Chad. "Well?"

Clayton glanced at his notepad. "Tags are TXK-640?"

"That's the one." Billy banged again, harder that time. "Police. Open the door, Vince. I know you're in there." He cocked his head. "I hear footsteps."

The door cracked open, and a pissed-off Vince Meroni stood there in his boxer shorts. "What the hell, dude, I'm trying to sleep."

Billy pushed past him. "Aren't you supposed to be taking finals?" He looked around the disheveled apartment.

Vince laughed. "Yeah, I'll get right on that as soon as I remember what courses I'm enrolled in. What do you want, and where's your warrant? In my book, this is the definition of harassment." He began to close the door.

"Leave it open. It stinks like shit in here." Billy glanced at the overflowing garbage can. "Have you been home all day?"

"Does it look like I'm dressed to go out?"

Clayton spoke up. "Did you see Daphne Cole this morning?"

"What did I just say, dude?"

"The name is Detective Clayton."

"Whatever. No, I haven't seen Daphne, and I haven't left my apartment. She said she felt sick last night and went home around six o'clock. I haven't seen her since. I called her phone last night to check on her, but it went straight to voicemail. I figured she was sleeping. Why?"

"The sheriff's office received a 911 call from the university this morning about a dead student in the parking lot. It was Daphne."

Vince grabbed his head and squeezed. "No, that's impossible. She was alive last night. I mean, I just saw her."

"You said she felt sick?" Billings asked.

"That's what she said. Is this some kind of a joke? I know you cops hate my guts."

"It isn't a joke, Vince," Billy said. "Now get dressed. You're coming to the station to give your statement."

"I just did for crissakes!"

"It wasn't on record. Just so you know, you're the last person who saw her alive."

"No, I told you she went home. Talk to Jen, her roommate. She'll verify it."

Clayton responded. "We did, and she didn't. Jennifer said Daphne spent the night with you. Now get your pants on and go with Officer Bachaus. He has an interview room with your name on it."

Chapter 17

I had to look away when Jason wheeled the gurney past me. I couldn't catch my breath, and my chest felt tight. I turned my head and coughed into my shoulder.

Amber wrinkled her nose. "Are you getting sick? Maybe that's what your stomach pain was about yesterday. It could be something as innocent as the flu."

I cleared my throat. "I hope not. I've had the flu, and it doesn't feel very innocent."

Jack watched Jason as he loaded the gurney into the van, then he turned back to us. "Did you get information on the parents?"

"Yeah, the address in Manitowoc is theirs, and I thought you'd want to make the call."

Jack lifted his sunglasses and rubbed his eyes. "The hardest part is telling two families their daughters are dead and we have no idea why."

Clayton and Billings returned minutes later and joined us as Daphne's car was loaded onto the flatbed.

Kyle addressed Jack as he and Dan watched from the sidelines. "We'll give the car a thorough going through, sir, as if it were a criminal investigation."

"As far as we know, it could be. Do the same with Becca Morbeck's car. We've only checked it for tampering. I want the cars gone over with a fine-toothed comb. Check both vehicles for blood, DNA, and fingerprints, especially on the door handles and steering wheel. Pull out every slip of paper you find—do the works. Somebody, or something, is killing female students from UWWC." Jack turned to Billings. "What'd you get from the boyfriend?"

"Nothing. He swears he hasn't seen Daphne since early yesterday evening. The kid just crawled out of bed, and that was only because we were banging on the door. His story and Jennifer's contradict each other. He said Daphne went home because she felt sick, and Jennifer said Daphne didn't come home at all, so she assumed Daphne was with Vince."

With his brows furrowed, Jack pressed on his forehead. "Damn headache coming on. Daphne was somewhere last night, and whoever she was with knows why she's dead. Where's Vince now?"

Clayton spoke up. "Downtown giving a formal statement to Billy Bachaus."

"Good. Kate, go get Jennifer Tenley. I want to have a word with her myself."

"You bet, sir."

Jack lowered his sunglasses as the clouds parted. "Clayton, you and Billings go inside and work the Becca Morbeck case. It's why you were coming here to begin with. Find out who her friends were at school and talk to every professor she had who's here now. We'll interview other people later."

I went inside the building and had Jennifer paged. Moments later, I saw her walking my way. "My boss needs a word with you."

"I told you everything I know."

I shrugged. "Not my call. Let's go." We dipped under the police tape and walked toward Jack. "Jennifer, Vince said Daphne went home last night because she was sick, and you said she wasn't there. Somebody is lying."

Panic took over Jennifer's face. "I swear I told you the truth. Vince is a piece of shit, and he'd lie about anything to keep from going to jail again. That place is his second home."

I sat on the curb with Jennifer while Jack spoke on the phone. He held up five fingers as if to say five more minutes.

"That was tough," he said when he finally clicked off the call.

"Daphne's folks?"

"Yeah." Jack looked at Jennifer. "Seems we have contradicting stories between you and Vince Meroni."

"I didn't lie to anyone. Daphne never came home."

Jack pulled me aside. "I'll talk to her in a minute. Right now, I want you and Amber to go back to the sheriff's office and see if Lena has anything new on Becca. I'll be a few hours behind you. I need to interview her"—he tipped his head toward Jennifer—"then follow up with Clayton and Billings and talk to the advisors myself. Maybe Becca and Daphne had some courses in common."

Chapter 18

Alone in that room, he had a bird's-eye view of the faculty parking lot from the second-story window. Three hours after Daphne was discovered, detectives, deputies, and the man who was calling out orders still milled around two stories below.

He had heard Jennifer Tenley's name being paged earlier and wondered why. He retraced his steps from the night before as he watched the coroner and her assistant struggle to get Daphne out of her car.

I wiped down the keys and phone. The keys were left in the ignition, and her phone was off until I got here. I didn't change the seat position, and I was gloved the entire time I was in her car. I think I'm good.

With back-and-forth motions and a lot of tugging, they finally freed Daphne's body and placed her on the gurney. "Rigor is a real bitch." He spun at the sound behind him. Meredith Carlson stood in the doorway, staring at him. "Meredith, you startled me."

"Sorry, I thought I'd be alone up here. Were you just talking to yourself?"

"Yeah, guess I'm busted." He tried to make light of it, hoping she hadn't actually heard what he'd said. "It's a bad habit, especially when I have no idea somebody is eavesdropping on me."

Her face went bright red. "But I—"

He grinned. "No worries. I'm just pulling your chain."

"Oh, okay. We have a botany exam in fifteen minutes, right?"

"That's why I came in early." He tipped his head toward the window. "I've been watching the commotion in the parking lot. It looks like they're finally wrapping things up and just hauled away the car and the body."

Seconds later, he saw Jennifer cross the parking lot with one of the two female detectives he'd noticed earlier when they told the students to go inside. She escorted Jennifer to the man who looked to be in charge.

"Isn't that Jennifer Tenley?"

Meredith crossed the room and looked out the window. "I think so, but I can't be sure from this distance." She sighed. "Yesterday Becca Morbeck died in that accident, and now this? I didn't know either of them well, but nobody their age deserves to die."

He inhaled deeply and caught a fresh lavender scent coming from her hair. "So you only deserve to die if you're older?"

She blushed again. "I guess that came out wrong."

The room began to fill with students. He gave Meredith a subtle smile. "I guess we better take our seats. It's exam time."

Chapter 19

We walked into the sheriff's office and took one flight down to the lower level. I stopped in the hallway and grimaced.

Amber looked over her shoulder at me. "What are you doing?"

"Debating."

She looked up and down the hallway. "With whom?"

"With myself. Go ahead and talk to Lena. I'll wait out here."

"No way. If you really think there's some transference going on, the only way to be sure is to go with me. You haven't had a stomachache today, have you?"

"No, just a tight feeling in my chest and a cough."

"Oak pollen. Now let's go."

I reluctantly crossed over the threshold with Amber and looked around the corner. Lena's office was empty. I felt relief and turned back toward the door.

"What the hell, Kate?"

"She isn't here. Let's go upstairs."

"Just hold your horses." Amber called out Lena's name.

"I'm examining Daphne in the autopsy room."

Amber grabbed my arm and whispered. "You'll never know if you don't face your fears."

"I understand, but this has never happened to me, and I don't know what to expect."

"Expect to learn something new about yourself if this really is a psychic phenomenon." She smiled. "It's a good thing, you're honing your skills."

"Says the person who has nothing to lose."

We entered the autopsy room and saw Daphne lying, still somewhat contorted, on the stainless-steel table. A sheet, draped over her body, covered her to the collarbone, and her neck was supported with the headrest.

"I'm beginning the initial exam, and honestly, I haven't seen anything yet that looks suspicious."

Amber stepped closer and studied Daphne's body. "No signs of a struggle, strangulation, or suffocation?"

"Homicidal suffocation is hard to detect unless we had a crime scene such as a bed and a pillow. If she had been strangled, there would have been evidence around her neck and petechiae in the whites of her eyes, which she doesn't have."

I leaned against the wall of cabinets and began coughing. Amber and Lena glanced up at me then continued talking. My chest began to tighten just as before, and my left shoulder down to my elbow ached. It was becoming harder and harder to breathe.

"I need to leave." I quickly exited the autopsy room and ran for the outer door that opened to the hallway. I caught my breath as I held the handrail and panted.

Amber followed me out. "What the hell? Are you okay?"

"No, I felt like I was having a heart attack. It's going away now." I rested my head against the wall and sucked in mouthfuls of air. "You need to ask Lena if it's possible that Daphne died of a heart attack."

"You can't be serious."

"I am—dead serious." I took in long, slow breaths to relax my body as I rubbed the numbness out of my shoulder. "I have to go upstairs and do some research. Find out if Lena has Becca's blood work results yet. We need to know what was wrong with her stomach and throat."

"Okay, okay, I'll ask."

"Then ask her to come upstairs as soon as she has time so I can go over possible causes of death with her." I glanced down the hallway. "I can't go back in there."

"I will." Amber squeezed my hand. "Can you get upstairs on your own?"

"Yeah, I should be okay as long as I stay away from the victims."

Upstairs, I was glad to be at my desk and alone. I didn't want eye-rolls or ridicule. I was certain Amber and Lena thought I was crazy as it was. I needed to find documented cases of transference in order to be taken seriously. First, I had to record my own physical symptoms, starting with Becca. When I stood alongside her body, I had developed severe stomach pain, nausea, and the taste of bile. It came out of the blue with no earlier indications of feeling ill, and then it happened again later when I attempted to enter Lena's office. It went away when I backed out. I wrote that down, then thought about earlier, as I stood in the parking lot near Daphne's car. My chest tightened, I had trouble breathing, and I found myself coughing for no apparent reason. Once again, it happened downstairs in the autopsy room when I was in the same vicinity as Daphne.

There has to be a connection. Are they trying to tell me how they died? What else could it be?

I found stories of empathetic transference and psychic energy moving from person to person yet proving that someone could literally feel the same symptoms that caused the death of another human being was hard for even me to accept. Some psychics swore they were conduits between the dead and the living, but not many people took psychics seriously. I felt I was on my own and would have to convince Lena to check for possible ways Becca and Daphne might have died.

Chapter 20

I checked the time as I completed my online research. It was nearing one o'clock. Amber busied herself at her desk and glanced over when I rolled my neck.

"Did you find what you were looking for?"

"I found what was documented, but of course that information comes from the psychics themselves, not an impartial outside source. When is Lena coming up?"

Amber shrugged. "She said she would when she had something to tell us."

I shook my head with frustration.

Amber set down her pen and closed the report she had been working on. "We're taking your claims seriously, Kate, she's just really busy now that there's two dead students downstairs and families that want answers."

"Right, and I could help narrow down the causes of death if she'd give me a minute of her time."

"She needs to do her job, and she didn't have the blood work report yet, anyway." Amber pushed back her chair and got up. She filled two cups at the coffee station at the far end of the room then handed one to me and sat back down.

"Thanks."

She nodded. "Can I be candid with you?"

"I suppose so even though I have a feeling I'm not going to like what you're about to say."

Amber sighed. "Put yourself in the place of Becca and Daphne's families. They want to know why their healthy daughters died. Whose report do you think they'll take seriously, a medical examiner's or a psychic's?"

I stared. "Wow, that was really harsh."

"No, it was honest. Law enforcement knows your history of solving crimes, but the public—especially grieving parents—doesn't want to hear that. They want facts."

I was about to start my rebuttal when the beep from the security door sounded. I looked over my shoulder to see Clayton, Billings, and Jack walk in.

Jack jerked his chin toward the hallway. "Kate and Amber, gather your notes. We're headed to the conference room."

Moments later, with paperwork scattered across the table, the five of us sat in the conference room and began brainstorming.

Chad and Adam had interviewed dozens of students and professors. They all said Becca and Daphne seemed like well-adjusted young ladies with plans for the future. Becca didn't have a boyfriend, but her love of sports kept her busy. According to her professors, she did okay academically although chemistry was her weak spot. Jennifer described Daphne as someone who was focused on her career goals, but because she was so wrapped up in Vince, her studies suffered.

Both girls had a bad case of nerves over finals week, and both were being privately tutored.

"Did they have any classes in common?" Amber asked.

I fidgeted and waited for my opportunity to speak. I needed to explain my theory again and that I had new symptoms similar to a heart attack when I was near Daphne's body. There had to be a reason it was happening now since being around deceased victims had never made me physically ill before.

Clayton checked his notes. "They both had chemistry lab. Daphne was fifteen months older than Becca and ready to graduate with her associate degree, so they weren't actually in the same class, so to speak. They may not have even known each other or had friends in common. We haven't checked that out yet."

Jack scratched his forehead. "And what was it Becca wanted to be after completing college?"

Billings spoke up. "Something in biochemistry, her folks said. No idea what career fields that involves, but it sounds like master's degree stuff."

"That's right, and Daphne's parents haven't been interviewed yet." Jack glanced at the clock. "As a matter of fact, they should be arriving any minute. We'll have to pick up where we left off after I speak to them."

"But, Boss—"

The conference room phone rang as I was about to plead my case. Jack answered, said a few words, and hung up. "Yep, we'll continue this later. Mr. and Mrs. Cole are here. You guys keep at it. Find a connection between both girls, someone or something they had in common." He stood, rounded the table, and walked out.

"Damn it."

Clayton and Billings gave me a side-eyed glance.

"What?" Clayton asked.

"Can somebody give me a second to speak?"

"The floor is yours," Billings said.

I let out a relieved breath. "Finally, and I need you guys to be open-minded."

Billings rolled his eyes then grinned. "Just giving you shit. Go ahead."

"Okay, what if I really *do* have physical transference and the reason it's come to light now is because neither girl shows an obvious cause of death. The blood work results may be in for Becca. I don't know. I haven't talked to Lena yet, but testing for something specific that may have killed one or both of them could take forever if we don't know what their symptoms were. Maybe I'm getting the symptoms, as a clue in a way, so Lena knows what to test for."

"It sounds logical if you're a psychic, but is physical transference an actual condition one might get?" Clayton asked.

My shoulders dropped. "That's the problem, Chad. I don't know. What I do know is that Becca's autopsy showed damage to her stomach and throat. I had physical pain in my stomach and nasty bile coming up my throat when I was near Becca. Today, I felt like I was having a heart attack when I was near Daphne."

"No shit? Why didn't you tell us that earlier?" Billings asked.

I shrugged. "It scared me, but we were also knee-deep in an investigation."

Amber nodded. "I did witness Kate's symptoms firsthand, and they were real."

"Sure, then besides stomach and esophageal cancer, GERD, and chronic acid indigestion, what else could Becca's inflammation be from?"

I stared at Billings. "It had to be something painful enough to make her pass out or die and send her flying off the road. That has to be why she didn't hit the brakes."

Chad nodded. "Let's start a list of possible conditions and have Lena double-check those organs. How about appendicitis?"

I wrote that down, along with colitis, gallstone and gall bladder issues, ulcers, pancreatitis, a ruptured aortic aneurysm, obstructions to the small intestine or colon, and the list went on.

"Lena would have noticed those conditions, though, right?" Billings asked.

Amber poured water for everyone. "One would think, if she took every organ out of Becca's body and examined it, but she only mentioned the heart, lungs, and stomach. I think she's waiting for the blood work results to come back tomorrow before looking for other problems."

"Okay, let's move on to Daphne. Tightening of the chest, trouble breathing, and pain and numbness in my left shoulder to the elbow. Those are the classic symptoms of a heart attack, aren't they?"

The group nodded.

"Can you think of anything else that causes those symptoms?"

Amber took a sip of water and added her opinion. "Only when people go to the hospital because they think they've had a heart attack only to find out it's indigestion. I think they end up with a bad case of embarrassment."

"That's true, but I don't know of anyone who has actually died of indigestion."

Clayton looked at the faces around the table. "I concur with Kate. I truly believe she's experiencing the symptoms of the causes of those deaths. Becca and Daphne are reaching out to you, Kate, and it's up to us to follow through."

I patted Chad's hand. "Thanks. Now we just have to get Lena on board."

Chapter 21

We returned to the bull pen at three o'clock with our notes and theories organized and ready to present to Lena. Through the wall of glass, I saw Jack was still talking to Daphne's visibly distraught parents.

Clayton set his coffee cup down and answered the ringing phone. "Clayton here." He nodded. "Go ahead and put her through." He placed his hand over the receiver. "I'm getting Jack's calls while he's with Daphne's folks. It's Lena calling with the blood work results." He raised his brows at me. "Should I ask her to come up?"

"Absolutely." I glanced toward Jack's office. "He shouldn't be much longer."

"Lena, yes, Jack is still with Daphne's family, but he asked us to keep working the cases while he's with them. How about coming to the bull pen? We can start going over everything together, and I'm sure the parents have to sign consent forms, anyway, if they agree to an autopsy. Why don't you bring those with you?" He looked my way and gave me a thumbs-up. "Yep, ten minutes is fine." Clayton returned the handset to the base. "Are we ready to present our case to her?"

I rolled my eyes. "I've been ready for hours." I steeled myself for the theory I was about to present to her. Lena knew some—but not much—about my psychic abilities since our skills didn't often overlap. I was sure she'd think I was off my rocker, but my gut told me I was on the right track. The clock ticked away as I stared at Jack's office door. He would be the perfect person to act as a go-between with Lena and me. She trusted his opinion completely, and he trusted my instincts.

Mrs. Cole picked up her purse, then she and her husband pushed back their chairs and stood. They shook Jack's hand, and the three of them walked out. I lowered my eyes and pretended to be busy.

Seconds later, Lena entered the bull pen through the back hallway, and Jack made the introductions between the Coles and her. "We were headed down to your office next. What can I do for you, Lena?"

"I was coming up, anyway. First off, Mr. and Mrs. Cole, you have my deepest sympathy for the loss of your daughter. If your intentions were to go forward with an autopsy, I have the consent form right here in my folder."

Mrs. Cole spoke up. "We do, and that's why we were coming to see you. We need to know why Daphne died. Most twenty-year-old women don't die unexpectedly."

"I agree, and I promise to do my best to find out why she passed away." Lena turned to Jack. "Can we use your office for a few minutes?"

"Sure thing." Jack opened the door and allowed them in. "Take your time." He looked toward us as he closed the door and took a seat on Amber's guest chair. "So, what's the word?"

"The word is I need to explain my theory to Lena. That's why she came up here."

Jack looked over his shoulder. "I'm sure she won't be long, and I'd rather you ran it past me first, anyway."

Clayton nodded. "That's really the best way to go, Kate."

I explained to Jack how my symptoms came on only when I was in the proximity of the bodies. "Boss, I really don't think it's a coincidence, and I've never had this type of premonition, if you will, before in my life. It's a new realm in my personal psychic world, and I can't explain it other than how I did. I'm confident that the pain I feel in the presence of Becca and Daphne is them telling me the symptoms they had when they died. It really isn't much different than me seeing villains and crimes being committed in my dreams except I'm physically experiencing the pain instead of dreaming about it."

"Although, you dreamt *and* felt it the other night," Amber added.

"You're right, I did."

Jack raked his hair. "I understand, but you *do* realize how strange that sounds, right?"

"Yes, and I'd prefer to keep it close to the vest, anyway, but we need Lena to check for those diseases. If you seriously think foul play is involved, then ruling out natural causes is the only way to know for sure." I handed the sheet of potential causes to Jack. "Becca may have had such severe stomach pain that it rendered her unconscious or killed her as she drove. That's ruling out a sudden heart attack, of course."

"Uh-huh. So if Lena excludes all of these diseases, it could be something else that masked a serious ailment?"

Amber piped in. "Exactly, and it's the perfect way to murder someone and get away with it. The same goes for Daphne. For all intents and purposes, it appeared as if she had a heart attack."

Jack took his turn. "And I asked her parents if she had heart issues, and they said no."

"Daphne's case may be a little easier to figure out since a thorough examination of her heart should tell Lena if there was an underlying problem or not," I said.

Jack tipped his head toward his office. "Looks like they're finishing up. We'll meet in the conference room as soon as the Coles leave. If Becca and Daphne's deaths turn out to be foul play, then we have our work cut out for us. Not only will we have to interview the people in their personal lives, but UWWC has well over nine hundred students and faculty members combined who may have to be interviewed."

Chapter 22

When I heard Lena's heels tap against the tile floor, I let out a nervous breath. She was coming down the hallway. I didn't understand my fear but knew Lena was all about business, and she didn't appear to be the type who gave too much credence to the world of the unexplained. *Every abnormality has a logical explanation behind it*, I'd heard her say. I was ready to debate that comment.

She entered the conference room with two folders in hand and took a seat near Jack then tipped her head as she glanced at the rest of us.

"The Coles have agreed to an autopsy, so I'll get started on that as soon as we wrap this up." She looked at Jack. "They mentioned talking to you about heart problems?"

"They said Daphne didn't have any."

Lena sighed. "They told me that as well, but seconds later, Mr. Cole said he'd had a quadruple bypass only three years ago and that his own mother passed away at age fifty of a sudden heart attack. That just made Daphne's odds of having heart problems rise significantly."

I couldn't help myself and blurted out a statement I

wished I could have taken back. "But you'll examine her heart closely, won't you?"

Lena frowned. "Of course I will, Kate. It's my job."

"Sorry."

Lena continued on. "Becca's blood work came back as negative for cancer, and I checked her stomach for tumors and polyps. I didn't see unusual cells under the microscope either. I'm assuming her irritation came from a serious case of GERD and nothing more."

I slid the list across the table to her.

"What's this?" Lena lifted her reading glasses from the lanyard and perched them on her nose. "A list of possible stomach and intestinal issues?"

"Not only issues but something so painful it sent her flying off the road." I sighed. "Lena, we're trying to narrow down things that could have killed Becca or rendered her unconscious. That means the pain came on suddenly or worsened as she drove. She didn't have a heart attack, did she?"

"Her heart looked very healthy. Jack, did you get her medical records from the parents?"

"They gave me her primary doctor's name, and I made the call myself. He said Becca never came to him for anything unusual as far as internal pain. She had colds, the flu, and a few sprains over her lifetime but usually no reason to see him other than sports physicals."

Lena closed the folder. "Maybe you guys are overthinking this. It is possible that texting while driving actually *was* what caused the accident."

Jack spoke up again. "The injured people and the families of the two who died when their cars caught fire are going to want answers. I'm sure there will be lawsuits, and the attorneys and insurance companies are going to need thorough autopsy reports."

"And they'll get them. I know how to do my job, Jack. Now are we done?"

I knew it was time to say what I was thinking, and I hoped my colleagues had my back. "Not yet, Lena. I have to say what's really on my mind."

Over the next forty-five minutes, I explained to Lena how my dreams and premonitions had helped solve cases. Jack, Amber, and the guys substantiated everything I'd said. At first, she dismissed my claims, but as I gave her case numbers as proof, she seemed to listen with more curiosity.

"So what do you want me to do, Kate? Pull every organ from Becca's body, test it, send it out to another lab, or what?"

"Close examinations of those organs would tell us if they were healthy or diseased, wouldn't they?"

"A visual exam along with microscope work should do it since her blood and urinalysis reports came back normal. So if everything is okay, what then? What caused those severe stomach pains you had the other day, a coincidence?"

"Normally I'd have said yes until I had symptoms of a heart attack when I was near Daphne. If her heart is normal and looks healthy…" I paused, almost afraid to utter the words nobody had yet heard me mention.

Jack raised his right brow. "Then what?"

"Then I'd have to say both women were likely poisoned."

Chapter 23

He drove home after exams and thought about that week. Women couldn't be trusted, no matter what their age. Isabelle, the wife he'd loved dearly, was in her thirties, yet she cheated with college students fifteen years her junior.

You did love your job, didn't you, Isabelle?

Becca and Daphne had only one thing in mind when it came to him—getting through finals week. He was a means to an end, and once they'd passed their exams, he'd be tossed to the curb like yesterday's trash. He wouldn't be needed anymore, and rejection enraged him.

Tutoring didn't help—the girls lacked focus and wanted the easy A. The only alternative was giving them passing grades for intimacy, and both women grew tired of his constant demands. They turned the tables on him and threatened to expose the secret arrangement to the campus counselors. Becca and Daphne were young and full of life, with other people and activities on their minds. He was of no significance to them, and he knew it.

They had to pay, just like Isabelle did. I won't be dismissed by the youth of today. I'm a man of substance and intelligence, and they should have felt privileged that I gave them my time.

His eyes lit up as he recalled the way he'd killed each woman. Isabelle succumbed to a pulverized cyanide pill mixed in with her iced tea. Becca died from either botulism or the deadly castor bean, he wasn't sure which, and Daphne drank a lethal dose of fentanyl mixed with her wine. He considered himself lucky and thankful to have access to those poisons and many more.

I'm resourceful and a hell of a lot smarter than everyone in this town, and I know the cops will never figure it out.

Chapter 24

We were back in the bull pen by four thirty, and Lena had returned to her office to research my suggestion. I hoped she'd forgive my forwardness, but I was a cop and a damn good one. It was my job, as well as the job of my colleagues, to find out why these women had mysteriously died. It was Lena's job to prove or disprove my theory, and I prayed I was right.

Jack grabbed a pen from the cup on Clayton's desk, a souvenir from his vacation to the Bahamas years back. He jerked his chin toward Chad's desk drawer. "Hand me a legal pad." He took a seat on the guest chair and scratched his cheek. "Okay, where are we so far?"

"Billy Bachaus took Vince downtown and got his formal statement. Vince swears he doesn't know anything and he's sticking to his story, but the city boys are keeping an eye on him and getting a warrant to search his apartment."

Jack jotted that down. "And I interviewed Jennifer the second time myself. There's got to be a reason her statement and Vince's don't match up."

Amber piped in. "Yeah, one of them is lying—and I'd

venture to say it's Vince. Or Daphne made up the story about feeling sick and went somewhere else that neither of them knew about."

"So she may have had secrets," I said, "and there could be some merit to that. Maybe she was seeing somebody else. From what Jennifer said, Vince is a real creep."

Billings chuckled. "That's an understatement."

"But if Jennifer was Daphne's best friend, why wouldn't she know about another guy in Daphne's life?"

Jack nodded at me and wrote that down. "Go interview her again. I want every friend of Becca's and Daphne's interviewed one more time. Relatives too. We have to ask the right questions, people. Was there a secret man in their lives? Were there skeletons in their closets? Was somebody blackmailing them, or vice versa, that sort of thing."

"They seemed too young to be involved in something that sinister."

Jack cocked his head. "Yet you're the one who suggested poison."

I smiled. "Touché."

"What else?"

Adam flipped through the pages in his notepad. "Normal medical results for Becca, and Daphne hasn't undergone her autopsy yet. Dan and Kyle printed both cars but didn't get any hits that were in the system. They didn't find blood evidence anywhere either."

"Okay, I'll call Becca's parents and update them on her autopsy results. No matter what, we can't release her body until we know definitively what the cause of the accident was." Jack looked at Amber and me. "Did you ever get that press release written?"

I smirked. "We started it, but now we have to add something about Daphne."

"Only give the press what we know—two deceased girls, unknown causes, ongoing investigation, yada, yada, yada. I'll look it over before it goes out. What about the burn victim? Has anyone checked on his condition?"

Clayton answered. "He's in an induced coma—no interview for the foreseeable future."

"Damn, that doesn't sound good." Jack wrote that down and stood. "Okay, let's talk to the witnesses at Becca's accident again, and then we'll wait to see what Lena comes up with." He pointed at me. "Finish the press release"—he checked the time—"and then contact the witnesses from Becca's accident. Tell them you'll be interviewing them again tomorrow and set up a time for each one. That way you won't be wasting your time chasing down people who aren't available. Clayton, call Becca's folks and press them about anybody that has been a nuisance to Becca or a new name she's mentioned. Find out who her best friends in Tomah are too."

"Sure thing, sir."

Jack opened the top button of his shirt. "Damn, it's hot in here. Billings, do the same with Daphne's folks. Push them for information. After that, go home. I'll update Horbeck and Jamison and task them with something that they can work on during the overnight hours." He rapped his knuckles on Clayton's desk. "Let's finish out this day with something positive. We should know more from Lena when we get in tomorrow."

I sat at my desk with Amber at my side. "Which do you want to do, call the witnesses or finish the press release?"

"I'll do the press release."

I opened my desk drawer, pulled out what we had started, and handed it to her. "Jack?"

He turned back. "Yep?"

"I need the witness statements with the names and phone numbers."

He tipped his head toward his office. "Come on in. They're in my desk."

I followed Jack, and surprisingly, he closed the door behind me. I was sure my coworkers were already whispering.

"What's going on?"

"Have a seat." Jack exhaled and sat in his own chair. "Take it easy on Lena. She's a little overwhelmed right now."

"And so are we, Boss. I'm actually trying to make her job easier by narrowing down the CODs."

"Why poison?"

"Not to make light of the situation, but I do watch a lot of crime shows on TV. Many sudden deaths are attributed to unknown sicknesses, but once the correct tests are run, primarily for poisons, the real cause of death is exposed. Testing for poison isn't part of the normal autopsy procedure, as you know, especially if the death itself doesn't appear to be murder. The problem is, Lena can do the visual exams, but getting the results back from forensic toxicology testing can take a while."

Jack nodded. "That's why I asked about poisons in particular. Toxicology tests can drag out, and meanwhile, we're in a holding pattern without answers for the parents or the press. The university isn't happy either. They're getting slammed. The problem is, what if you're wrong?"

I stared at my lap. "I'll accept the responsibility publicly. In the meantime, we can try to root out anyone who may have had a grudge against the girls. It's somewhere to start. We need to dig into that while we wait for answers."

Jack tapped his fingers against his desk calendar. "Okay, go for it and do it aggressively. Nobody gets a pass—not friends, family, classmates, or the university staff. Everyone is on our radar until we've cleared them. If those girls were murdered, then we're likely looking at the same person. Find the connection, and you'll find the killer."

Chapter 25

Jack's words resonated through me during dinner that night. *Find the connection, and you'll find the killer.*

"And then with a swift kick to the face, I knocked Bigfoot senseless and saved Kate's life. Right, Kate?"

"Yep, that's right."

Jade and Amber broke into a round of laughter. I stared at them with a blank expression. "What's wrong with you two?"

"What's wrong with you? You haven't listened to or joined in on a single conversation we've had since we sat down."

"Sorry, my mind is too full right now to add anything else."

Jade stood and cleared the table. "Apparently. You didn't even hear Amber's comment about Bigfoot."

"Bigfoot?"

Jade swiped the air. "Never mind. You're a lost cause."

"So what is it that's taking up all the available space in your brain?" Amber dished up hot apple pie and passed around the plates.

"Just what Jack said when I walked into his office to get the witness statements."

"You mean when he closed the door behind you and you had a secret conversation?"

"Yeah, then. I mean, no—it wasn't a secret."

"Then spill." Amber winked at Jade as she took a bite of the pie. "Damn, this is good."

"He questioned me about being hard on Lena."

Jade coughed into her fist. "What did you do?"

Amber cut in. "She accused Lena of not doing her job right."

I threw a piece of piecrust at Amber. Spaz scurried across the floor and munched it down. "Liar. I simply asked her to look at Becca's organs closely and then check for poisoning."

"Poisoning?" Jade looked from me to Amber and then back to me. "Why?"

"Because there's no obvious reason either of the girls should be dead. It always turns out to be poison when nobody can figure out why somebody died."

Jade huffed. "Yeah, on TV. This is real life, Kate."

"And I had real symptoms that I believe to be clues. Most likely acute stomach pain in Becca's case and symptoms of a heart attack in Daphne's. So far, the autopsy results on Becca showed her to have normal organs except for redness and inflammation in her stomach and esophagus. Lena just thinks she had GERD."

"Maybe she did."

"My gut says otherwise—literally. You witnessed the pain I had during that nightmare. I don't think GERD is that excruciating, and I know my heart is in tiptop condition except when I've been near Daphne's body."

Jade gave me a somber look. "That's really creepy."

"Yeah, I know. Try being on my end of it. We'll find out more about Daphne in the morning, then Amber and I are going to start interviewing witnesses from the crash scene again. They have to give us more."

Amber scraped every crumb off her plate then licked her fork. "Clayton and Billings are going hard after every friend and family member. There may be somebody that we don't know about yet who pissed off those girls." She took our dessert plates into the kitchen and put them in the dishwasher. "Hey, you never told us what Jack said that's taking up your brain space."

"He said if we find the connection between Becca and Daphne, we'll find the killer. I'm thinking he's absolutely right."

Later that night as I sat on the couch, I racked my brain to come up with connections between the girls. With Amber and Jade's help, I wrote down everything I could think of. The girls went to the same university, and they might have had friends in common—that still needed to be checked out. They both took chemistry, meaning they possibly had the same professor. We needed to see if they were in any of the same extracurricular activities too. Did Vince have friends who knew Becca? The list went on and on. By the time I went to bed, we had compiled a list of fifteen additional things to work on tomorrow.

I woke the next morning relieved that I'd had an

undisturbed night's sleep. I was sure Jade and Amber were relieved too. Amber and I needed to be alert in order to tackle the amount of work that faced us that day. I couldn't wait to hear Lena's report on Daphne's autopsy. If her heart was healthy with no signs of abnormality, we'd be one step closer to ruling out a heart attack from natural causes and looking into something that mimicked heart failure.

At eight o'clock, we gathered in the conference room with a thermal carafe of coffee centered on the table. Everyone had their pens and paper ready for note taking. Jack filled the cups as we waited for Lena to join us.

The familiar sound of her shoes told me she was approaching, except this time I was excited to hear her verdict.

"Good morning, everyone."

We responded in kind, and I poured her a cup of coffee as she took a seat.

She gave me a quick smile, which I hoped meant we were back on good terms. "Thank you, Kate." She took a sip and began. "I have to admit, I'm stumped by the results of both women. Neither seemed to have any medical issues whatsoever, other than Becca's GERD."

I still had my doubts about that, but I kept quiet.

"After a thorough examination of Daphne's heart, I didn't find anything wrong with it. It wasn't enlarged, scarred, or damaged." Lena looked directly at me. "I reviewed poisons that could bring on or mimic a heart attack, and there are several—fentanyl, succinylcholine, potassium chloride—and of course there's the nearly untraceable air embolism. Luckily, the lab technicians in forensic toxicology know the usual poisons to check for. It just takes time to get the results back. I sent all the body fluids from both women to toxicology yesterday, but they didn't know to check for poisons at that time. When I spoke to them this morning, I told them it was imperative to complete the tests as quickly as possible. They'll do the best they can."

"And that's all we can ask," Jack said. "Will you update Daphne's parents?"

"I will. I'll also explain that until we have the toxicology report back, we can't release her body."

"Appreciate it." Jack jotted down the information and closed his folder. "Okay, guys, we have a busy day ahead of us. Let's get at it."

We rose from the table and filed out the door. I tapped Lena's shoulder before she parted ways with us. "We're good, right?"

She gave me a wink. "We're good."

Chapter 26

Jack had approved Amber's press release late yesterday, and we gave the information to the media.

I sipped my second cup of coffee as I looked over the list of appointments I had set up with the crash scene witnesses. We needed as much detail as possible and had found in the past that immediately after accidents, witness statements tended to be exaggerated. Emotions and adrenaline came into play and caused witness accounts to be skewed. Once they had time to calm down and process what they actually remembered seeing, the real scene unfolded.

"We have three interviews today." I hit Print then reached behind me and pulled the copy of the names and phone numbers of each witness out of the printer tray.

"Weren't there five witnesses?" Amber asked.

"Yeah, but two of them can't meet with us until tomorrow. We have a Mrs. Lynn Purdy at eleven"—I glanced at the time—"a Mr. Morton at eleven thirty, and Albert Ling at one o'clock."

"Are we going to their homes?"

"Nah, that's too much running around since it looks like

Albert comes from Fond du Lac. I asked each of them to meet us at the Coffee Bean in Kewaskum. We can have lunch there too between the meeting with Mr. Morton and Albert Ling." I exhaled a long puff of air.

"What?"

"Just wondering how interviewing these people again will give us a connection between Daphne and Becca. They're just random people who unfortunately shared the road with somebody who caused a fatal accident. It isn't like any of them knew Becca."

Amber leaned toward me and whispered. "Jack wants us to see if anyone has more information to share."

"Yeah, I know, so I guess we have to take advantage of it and ask as many questions as we can think of."

We pulled out of the sheriff's office parking lot at ten thirty and headed west, and we'd connect with Highway 45 five minutes later. From there, we'd turn north and drive the very route where the fatal accident took place. Prior to leaving, I called Lynn Purdy to make sure she wasn't going to be a no-show. In a roundabout way, I explained that this interview wasn't optional and a second statement was necessary. She promised to be there, and before hanging up, Lynn described herself as a five-foot-nine-inch redhead. That was all I needed to know, and I was sure she wouldn't be hard to spot once she walked through the door.

The drive to Kewaskum would take fifteen minutes, and I wanted to review Lynn's original statement before she arrived. Reading what she had said before, compared to now, would reveal how much, if any, her account of the accident might have changed.

I had heard good reviews of the Coffee Bean's breakfast and lunch menu, and it was a central location to meet, anyway. The restaurant was said to have a Pacific Northwest vibe—hippie mixed with a Seattle industrial flair. As we walked through the doors, I noticed that the décor was spot-on. Amber and I opted for a table near the rear of the restaurant. With lunchtime fast approaching and the restaurant filling up, we wanted to have a discreet conversation with the witnesses without broadcasting to the public why we were there.

We took our seats, and a shredded-jeans-wearing twenty-something pink-haired waitress with a pad and pen approached our table. Her name tag read Kylie.

"Hi. What can I start you off with?"

Amber took the lead and wiggled her finger for the young lady to come closer. "We're detectives from the sheriff's office and will be doing a few interviews over the next several hours. Right now coffee is fine, but we'll be having lunch a bit later."

"Way cool. Okay, would you like regular or decaf?"

We both spoke up. "Regular sounds great."

"Okeydokey, I'll bring a carafe right over."

I waited until she was out of earshot before discussing Lynn Purdy's original statement with Amber. "Scoot closer so you can read this alongside me. That way her first statement is fresh in both of our minds."

We silently read the three-paragraph account.

Amber's eyes bulged. "Wow, she was parallel with Becca's car when it began to swerve. That had to be scary. Lynn says she nearly hit the ditch to avoid being clipped by Becca.

According to this statement, she said the female driver was looking down." Amber stared at me. "Could Becca really have been texting?"

"Not if she was swerving back and forth. I don't think texting would be that important once she started losing control of her car." I put my index finger to my lip—the waitress was returning.

Kylie grinned as she placed the carafe on the table. "Here you go, Detectives, a freshly brewed pot. I'll admit, I've never talked to a real detective before. It's sick." She tipped her head toward the container on the table. "The cream and sugar are right there."

We thanked her, and she walked away and picked up an order. I shook my head. "Sick? Does that mean cool?"

Amber chuckled as she gave a side-eyed glance toward the front door. "I think so, and I believe our first witness is here." A tall redhead stood in the doorway and scanned the restaurant. Amber caught her attention with a wave, and Lynn headed our way.

I pulled out a clean sheet of paper and placed it on top of the witness statement folder. "It'll be interesting to hear if her story is still the same as before."

When Lynn reached our table, we stood and introduced ourselves. The only explanation we gave her for the second interview was that since several lawsuits were in the works, we needed very detailed and precise accounts of how the accident went down. Insurance companies and attorneys wanted answers for their clients.

Lynn settled in after pouring coffee into an empty cup for

herself. "So what can I do to help?"

"We need your best recollection of the accident because of possible lawsuits. Many times people recall things they forgot to mention at the time." I took a sip of coffee and continued. "Go back to that morning in your mind and just say what you see as if you were there right now."

"That's a scary thought."

"Sorry, but it's necessary." Amber and I waited in silence.

Lynn closed her eyes. "I had just left work and was heading home. I do overnight in-home health care three nights a week. I remember it being a sunny morning and even had my window lowered. Everyone was just doing their own thing when the car directly ahead and to my right swerved violently left. It almost took off my front bumper. I didn't want to slam on my brakes for fear of getting rear-ended."

Amber gave me a sharply arched eyebrow. "Go on."

"I swerved right to get as far away from it as possible and ended up on the shoulder, where I stayed. I remember my heart pounding in my chest."

I wrote down her comments. "I bet it was awful. Then what?"

"Then the car swerved right again. People slammed on their brakes and darted every which way. The car finally veered left through the median and into oncoming traffic. The rest was a nightmare."

"And did you see the car brake at any time? Or the person inside?"

"Neither, but I heard it was a college-aged girl." She paused as if she had a thought.

"Something else come to mind?"

"Um, yeah, just a flash of another car that was to the left of me. I remember glancing over to see who was driving because the music was so loud. It was a woman, and she wasn't even watching where she was going. She was looking down at her phone. People like that cause accidents."

I smiled. "But not in this case, right?"

"Oh no." She wrung her hands. "I'm so sorry. I was a wreck at the time, and I think I got my statement wrong. I didn't see the driver of the swerving car at all."

We stood, gave her our contact cards, thanked her for her time, then watched as she walked out.

Amber rubbed her forehead and sat back down. "So she mistook the car next to her for Becca's car when she gave her original witness statement. She never saw Becca at all."

"Apparently not, but that doesn't mean Becca wasn't texting. Remember what her phone showed?" I warmed up our coffees.

"True, but the texts were just garbled nonsense, so that's telling me she was already in distress."

With a quick glance at my cell phone, I saw we had only seven minutes before Mike Morton was due to arrive. I pulled out his witness statement and read it. "According to Donnelly, Mr. Morton seemed calm and strangely detached at the accident scene but was curious enough to ask if the person who caused the accident was dead. Odd that he wondered that after seeing a semi lay on its side after crashing into two cars that burst into flames, another car on its roof, and multiple fender benders."

"I'd say that's odd. What was his account?" Amber took a look at the front door. Nobody had come in yet.

"He said cars braked and skidded, including his own, after Becca's car started swerving wildly from one lane to the next. Humph."

"What?"

"Mr. Morton must be an odd duck in general. His next comment was that the way cars parted in the northbound lanes reminded him of how Moses parted the Red Sea." I frowned. "What a strange thing to say when you're staring at carnage unfolding right in front of you."

"It takes all kinds." Amber checked the door again just as a man stepped over the threshold. "Speaking of—"

"Yep, that's him. He said he'd be wearing a red shirt." I stood and waved.

He tipped his head and walked over with an outstretched hand. "I'm Mike Morton, and who are you little ladies?"

His demeanor instantly rubbed me the wrong way. I had already spoken to him on the phone yesterday and told him he'd be meeting Amber and myself.

"We're Detectives Kate Pierce and Amber Monroe from the Washburn County Sheriff's Office."

"That's right. Detectives, eh? Very interesting."

"What is?" I stared at the man, who appeared to be in his mid-forties. His medium-brown hair had turned gray at the temples, and a goatee wrapped his mouth. His hazel eyes seemed to be twinkling as if he enjoyed the limelight.

"That women are detectives these days, and here I gave my original statement to a mere male patrol officer."

"This is the twenty-first century, Mr. Morton, and that patrol officer would be Deputy Tim Donnelly." I nodded at the empty chair between Amber and me. "Why don't you take a seat? We have a few questions for you."

"Sure, why not." He turned and waved to get Kylie's attention since we were fresh out of clean cups on the table.

I rolled my eyes at Amber then squeezed them closed momentarily. I felt a headache coming on.

Mr. Morton turned his attention back to us. "Now, what can I do for you ladies?"

Chapter 27

"So what is it you do for a living, Mr. Morton?" I asked.

"I own quite a few rental properties and consider myself very lucky. I'm not at a nine-to-five grind where I'm stuck in the workplace and can't play my part of a concerned citizen to help out you officers."

Amber corrected him. "Detectives."

"Right. Anyway"—he glanced at his watch—"what do you need to know?"

"We need your statement again, if you don't mind," I said.

"Because?"

I smiled through gritted teeth. My headache didn't help the irritation I felt toward him, and he stank of cigarettes. I poured myself a fresh cup of coffee and remembered that at some point in life, I'd read that caffeine helped with headaches. "Because of insurance claims and lawsuits, that sort of thing. Lawyers want exact accounts since people get called into court on occasion to state what they saw if it goes that far. So whenever you're ready."

"Yeah, okay. I saw the car swerve left, then right, then left and across the median. The driver ended up in the northbound lanes, and cars scattered everywhere, but some were caught up in the crashes. It was a case of real-life bumper cars." He rubbed his brow and shook his head as a smile crossed his face. "I've never seen anything like it."

Amber pulled back, obviously irritated. "And why is that something to smile about?"

He shrugged. "I don't know. Call it an adrenaline rush if you like. You don't want to see it, yet you can't take your eyes off it."

I wrote down his comments, no matter how weird they were. "Where were you going that morning?"

He wrinkled his nose. "Nowhere in particular, just out for a morning drive. It was sunny that day and warm, as I recall. I had no idea I'd be witnessing something that intense. I mean, three people died in front of my eyes. They were alive one minute and dead the next. Damn crazy shit."

His stare unnerved me. It was as if he enjoyed every second he reminisced about the accident.

"Do you remember seeing brake lights flash?"

He swatted the air. "That girl never even tapped the brakes. She was passed out or dead before she hit the tree."

I leaned across the table, mere inches from his face. "And what leads you to that conclusion?"

"I'm an intelligent man, Detective, and it's pure physics. Fear of dying would have forced her to hit the brakes. It's a natural instinct. The autopsy must have confirmed something by now."

"We aren't at liberty to discuss that with you, Mr.

Morton. Is there anything else you remember that wasn't mentioned in the first interview?" Amber asked.

"Nope, I'm a thorough guy and never leave anything unsaid or undone. What you have in the first statement is what I stand by."

I pushed back my chair and stood. "Great, then I guess we're finished." A wave of dizziness washed over me, and I grabbed the table's edge. Luckily, Amber didn't appear to notice.

She stood and handed him a card. "If you think of anything else—"

He cut off her comment as he dropped a dollar bill on the table. "Yeah, make sure to call. Have a nice day, ladies." He turned and walked out.

I sat and steadied myself in the chair. I took in a slow breath and felt better. "That man was this far"—I gestured a space of an inch with my fingers—"from getting on my last nerve. I need more coffee and a handful of ibuprofen." I caught Kylie's attention and asked for a glass of water and two lunch menus.

Chapter 28

Suspicion filled his mind as he waited to turn left at the stoplight. He checked the time once more—botany exams were scheduled to begin in forty-five minutes.

What the hell did those bitches really want, and why did they choose me to talk to? It couldn't have been a coincidence.

His mind went to that dark place where paranoia and self-doubt crept in.

Women are deceitful—they cheat and lie. We know that from experience, don't we, Isabelle? Daphne and Becca, you got what you deserved too.

He thought about Naomi Hahn. She was the last one who still had exams, had also pleaded for a passing grade, and admitted she'd do nearly anything to get one. She made a deal with the devil, yet she always found a reason not to show up for their prearranged rendezvous. Mike would teach her a lesson in more ways than one, and he'd make certain she'd fail the botany exam that day.

He thought about those nosy female detectives again as he stepped on the gas.

Keep your distance, ladies, or you might get a failing grade too.

Chapter 29

It was one forty-five, and we were driving back to North Bend. I let out a hard breath as I looked over notes from the three interviews.

Amber gave me an eyebrow raise. "That sounded discouraging."

"It is. Nobody's recollection of the accident was different than before except Lynn's, and even then, it doesn't explain why Becca crashed and died."

I noticed Amber glance out the window as we passed the man-made ski hill to our right. A quick smile lit her face.

"Memories?"

"Definitely. I remember Jade and my dad trying to teach me to ski there when I was only five. I never did catch on."

"But it was the experience that counted, right?"

"It was priceless." She let out a heartfelt sigh. "Anyway, we won't have the answers I want until the toxicology reports come back."

"And until then? Do we just resume our usual activities of filing and closing out old cases?"

Amber shrugged. "Probably, but first let's hear what the

guys found out from digging deeper with the parents. The girls may have mentioned people from the university who slipped under our radar. Don't forget, we still have interviews to do with their hometown friends too. Two girls from the same university dying in the same week seems too coincidental to me, and the more people we talk to, the more chances there are of finding that one person they had in common. That might be all it takes to link their deaths."

We were back at the sheriff's office a few minutes after two. Amber pressed the code and pushed the bull pen door open, and we entered to see Clayton and Billings sitting in Jack's office with him.

Jack waved us in. "Anything worth mentioning?"

I rolled my eyes. "Yeah, the pounding headache I had is finally going away after a handful of ibuprofen and three cups of coffee. Witness number two got on my nerves the minute I met him."

"I'll second that," Amber said.

"Sorry to hear it. Anything else?"

"Not really, and certainly nothing that gave us reason to think Becca's accident happened any other way than how the witnesses originally said."

"Okay, go downstairs and get the cell phones from Forensics. I want both of you to work on the contact lists for the rest of the day. Interview everyone who answers their phones. Find out if either girl talked about new aches and pains to their hometown friends and get names of anyone they may have mentioned from school that they possibly had issues with."

"Good enough." I handed the witness interview statements to Jack along with what we'd gathered from our meetings that day. Amber said she'd retrieve the cell phones and headed for the door. Back at my desk, I placed my purse in the drawer and pulled out a legal pad, ready for note taking. I glanced at Chad when he and Billings returned to their desks. "Did the parents provide anything helpful?"

"Becca's mom said as close as they were, Becca didn't discuss people from school with her. I'm assuming it's probably because the mom didn't know them, anyway."

"Did she give you the names of Becca's closest friends in Tomah? We can cross-reference them with the names on her cell phone list."

"Yep, here you go, but there's only two names." Chad opened the folder lying on his desk and pulled out the top sheet of paper. "According to the mom, Becca had plenty of acquaintances in high school, especially on the track-and-field team, but only two friends she hung out with on a regular basis."

I looked at the names—Jodi Prentice and Marie McFarlane. "I guess only having two best friends isn't that unusual. I hope there are more than that on her contact list, though. How about you, Billings?"

He held out his sheet of names. "Daphne had a lot of hometown friends. Maybe you guys can split up the list."

I thanked him and counted the names he had gathered from Daphne's parents. There were fourteen in total but no phone numbers. We'd retrieve them from her phone's contact list. "She probably had more friends because

Manitowoc is larger than Tomah—more students to know."

Billings nodded. "Maybe."

Minutes later, Amber was back with both cell phones. "Forensics doesn't need them anymore—none of the prints were in the system. Once we're done with the names, the parents can have them." She handed Becca's phone to me. "Jack did get warrants for the phone records, didn't he?"

Clayton said that he had.

An idea popped into my mind when I thought about the social media angle Jack had talked about several days ago. The parents didn't know the social media log-ins, so our tech department was trying to gain access. "Cell phones are a wealth of information, you know. There's the contact list we'll work off of, but there's also pictures in the gallery that might be separated into folders."

Amber filled a water glass and took her seat. "Not a bad idea. Let's make the calls and then start looking through the pictures."

"Good, tear your sheet in half. Daphne knew more people than Becca did." I tapped Becca's gallery to take a look before I started on the calls. She had four folders and dozens of recent photos that hadn't been placed in the folders yet. "Here's a good example," I said. "Becca had a few folders— home, school, sports, and miscellaneous, and I bet some of those pics will come in handy."

Amber and I dug in with phone calls, each taking eight, while the guys went over the interviews from yesterday to tighten down comments from peers along with names of classmates and classes they had in common. I got through to four of the eight names I called and left messages for the rest. Of Becca and Daphne's personal friends, no one reported that either girl talked about unusual medical issues they were experiencing. One new name popped up, and that was from Becca's friend Jodi Prentice. She said Becca had mentioned a Mike and how he had a thing for her. She couldn't wait until summer break so she wouldn't have to see him again until the fall semester began—if he was still there. I jotted down that information and went back to Becca's picture gallery while Amber finished her calls.

I'll start at the beginning and work my way through the folders.

I opened the folder that said "Home" and began browsing the photographs. I felt as if I were spying and looking at a private part of her life, but it was necessary, and I swiped left as I went through her very personal images. The photos from home were just that, pictures of Becca with her parents and little brother, Brent. Swimming in the family pool, on camping trips, working in the yard, and at barbecues. It appeared to be a happy home life. I tapped the "School" folder and began paging through the contents. Dozens of outdoor and indoor pictures of the campus popped up along with a picture of Becca and Brent standing on the soccer field. I swiped again and saw a picture of Becca's parents, each with an arm around her shoulder—they looked proud.

That must have been orientation day.

I continued through the school photographs when one in particular caught my eye. I backed up, tapped the picture, and spread it with my fingers to enlarge it.

What the heck?

Amber had just ended her last call, and I motioned her over. "Hey, take a look at this."

Chapter 30

He glanced in Naomi's direction every so often and watched as she seemed to struggle with the two-hour botany final. He'd find an excuse to talk to her after the exam and arrange something for later that night. Her grade was hanging in the balance, and she wouldn't dare stand him up.

At his desk, he paged through the hardcover book that contained every species of plant life found in North America. A specific plant came to mind, and in his fenced backyard, he had many varieties to choose from. He ran his finger down the table of contents and turned to page eighty-seven.

Here we go, deadliest plants of North America.

He had harvested and preserved many plants over time. Nicotine extract from the leaves of one plant could be added to a beverage. Fresh salads might include the berries from the doll's eye plant, castor beans, or deadly nightshade, and dried and ground roots from the water hemlock could be added to any meal he decided to prepare. As a chemist, he had even more opportunities to be inventive. He'd have no problem coming up with the perfect chemical cocktail as he had in the past. Naomi's last chance to make the right decision would come that night.

Nah, she has to die, anyway. Can't have any loose lips.

Chapter 31

"What have you got?" Amber rolled her chair over to my desk.

"I was checking Becca's photo gallery from school and look who's in the background of this picture." I passed Becca's phone to Amber. "Go ahead and enlarge it."

She did. "Isn't that—"

"Mmm-hmm. Mr. Morton in the flesh. Why do you think somebody who owns apartment buildings is at what looks to be orientation day at UWWC?"

Amber shrugged. "We didn't ask if he was married or had kids. He could have a daughter or son who started college last fall. His age seems right."

My shoulders dropped. "I guess so. It's probably because we just met him and his demeanor irritated me. I think he actually gave me that headache."

"Maybe. So did you get anything from the phone calls?"

I had almost forgotten about Jodi's comment. "That's right. Nobody had anything to say about new health issues, but Jodi told me that Becca mentioned a Mike and how he had a thing for her. It didn't sound like the feelings were reciprocated."

"I'm assuming the Mike was somebody from UWWC?"

"That's what she said." I turned to Clayton. "Did you guys interview any students named Mike the other day?"

Billings paged through his notepad. "I didn't."

Clayton took a look too. "I had a Michael Taylor, an acquaintance of Daphne's from her botany class. I called him Mike, and he corrected me, saying he goes by Michael, not Mike. Does he need a second interview?"

"Maybe. Run it past Jack and see what he thinks. If he knew Becca too, we could be onto something, I'm just not sure what."

I heard footsteps coming from the hallway. I looked over my shoulder to see Lena entering the bull pen. Something was up. She never came upstairs unless she had something to share with all of us.

I checked the time. There was no way she could have any results from toxicology yet. It was way too soon.

Jack saw Lena from his half-opened office door and came out. "Lena, do you have something?"

She glanced at me then pointed at my guest chair. "May I?"

"Of course. Sit down, please."

"I have the initial tox results for Daphne. The standard tests were run before I asked the lab to check for poisons, and it appears that she had fentanyl in her system." Lena frowned at Jack. "Did her parents mention she was a drug user?"

Jack rubbed his forehead. "To be honest, I think I only asked about heart problems, and they told me she didn't have any."

"Fentanyl is fifty times stronger than heroin, Jack. There's a reason it was in her body. My question is, was she taking opioids for pain, or was she a drug abuser? The tox lab can't distinguish between pharmaceutical fentanyl and the black-market versions of the drug. Either way, I'd venture to say we just found out what killed Daphne."

Jack pushed off the doorframe. "Anything on Becca yet as far as the standard screening?"

"Nothing that they've found as far as drugs or alcohol. They've moved on to the poison screening for both girls."

Jack groaned. "Okay, thanks, Lena. I need to call the Coles and find out if Daphne was taking recreational drugs or had prescriptions for opioids, and if so, why. Maybe foul play wasn't a factor in either death. Becca could have been texting while driving like we originally thought, and Daphne could have overdosed—accidentally or deliberately. I'm sure those kids feel like they're under a lot of pressure during finals week."

"The tox lab is working hard to finish the screening. Here you go." Lena handed a copy of the report to Jack. "I'll let you know when I know more."

"Appreciate it." Jack jerked his head at us. "Keep doing what you were doing while I get to the bottom of this."

"Boss?"

Jack loosened his tie as he turned toward Clayton. "Yep?"

"There's a kid named Michael Taylor that Daphne knew, and I'd like to question him again. Maybe he knew Becca too."

"Question anybody who raises a red flag with you, once,

twice, or a dozen times. While you're at it, find out if Mr. Taylor peddles drugs at the campus." Jack raked his hair. "Better yet, find out who the offenders are at UWWC and where they're getting the drugs. Pull the jackets from anybody in the county who has been arrested for dealing, especially narcotics, and have a chat with them. I have more questions for the Cole family." He walked into his office and closed the door behind him.

I slapped my desk. "Come on, guys. We need a lead, and this Michael could be a good place to start."

Clayton rose from his desk and tipped his chin at Billings. "We have today and tomorrow before finals week is over and the students are done for the summer. Let's find Michael Taylor and have a sit-down with him again."

I fired up my laptop. "I'll see what the known drug dealers in the county have been up to lately. Amber and I may have to pay them a visit. If the fentanyl wasn't a prescription, Daphne got it from somebody."

Amber reached for her desk phone. "I'll call upstairs and see who we have in lockup."

Chapter 32

He recognized the cops as the same ones who had been sniffing around on the day Daphne was discovered. Along with other professors and students, he had been questioned about Becca and Daphne as standard procedure. He walked to the window, separated the slats, and peered out. Below was the faculty parking lot, filled with cars as if nothing eventful had happened there. He remembered watching the coroner load Daphne's contorted body onto the gurney.

"Shit happens when you don't comply." He heard a knock on the doorframe.

"Excuse us."

Mike Morton turned to see those very cops standing at the door's threshold.

I need to stop thinking out loud, damn it.

"Can I help you?"

Clayton cocked his head. "Did we already meet?"

"Possibly, and you are?"

"We're Detectives Clayton and Billings. We interviewed a number of professors and students the other day in reference to the deaths of Becca Morbeck and Daphne Cole."

"Of course, I remember now. Such a tragedy."

Billings raised a brow. "Aren't you a chemistry professor?"

"I am. Sometimes botany and chemistry cross over. What can I help you with, Detectives? I have exams in"—he checked the time on the wall clock—"twenty minutes."

Clayton took over the conversation. "We're looking for Michael Taylor. We were told he and Daphne were in the same class. Has he already taken his finals?"

Professor Morton nodded. "He finished up yesterday. I don't know if he has more finals this week or if he's done for the summer."

"Sure thing. Do you know if Michael and Daphne were close, as in a tight friendship?" Billings asked.

The professor took a seat at his desk.

I have to divert this conversation and quick.

"They seemed to know each other well. I have a lot of students, Detectives, so I couldn't possibly tell you what any of them do once they leave my classes."

Clayton and Billings turned toward the door. "One more thing, sir," Clayton said. "Do you know if Michael Taylor knew Becca Morbeck or if he's local to the area?"

He shrugged. "I have no idea on both questions. Check with the admissions office."

"You bet. Thanks for your time."

He watched as the detectives walked out.

I have to make sure I don't leave any loose ends. Naomi is the only girl left who can point a finger at me, and she'll meet her fate tonight.

Chapter 33

Jack tapped his pen against the notepad as the phone rang at the Cole residence in Manitowoc. He assumed the family took time off work to grieve even though they couldn't make funeral arrangements until the cause of Daphne's death was known and her body was released from the morgue.

Mrs. Cole picked up on the third ring. "Hello."

Jack pressed Speakerphone and placed the handset back on the base. He tried to roll the kinks out of his tensed shoulders. "Mrs. Cole, it's Lieutenant Steele calling."

"Have you found out anything new, Lieutenant?"

Jack heard the hope in her voice, yet the only news he had to tell her was bad and would likely raise more questions. "Ma'am, the initial toxicology report for Daphne came in. Those results tell us if alcohol or drugs were found in her system."

"Yes, and?"

Jack sighed. "Fentanyl was discovered."

"Fentanyl? I don't even know what that is, Lieutenant."

"Fentanyl is a very dangerous opioid if used recreationally. It's far stronger than morphine and heroin and causes many fatalities every year. Was Daphne taking any prescription pain medications?" Jack heard Mr. Cole tell his wife to click over to Speakerphone so he could add to the conversation.

"Lieutenant?"

"Yes, Mr. Cole. I need to know if Daphne has been on or had a reason to take prescription pain medication recently."

"No, not at all. Her medical bills would come to our home even if she went to a doctor in North Bend. There hasn't been anything. What are you saying?"

Jack had to ask the difficult question. "So if she wasn't taking pain meds out of necessity, do you have any knowledge of her abusing narcotics?"

"Of course not! Daphne was a good daughter who focused on her studies."

Jack thought about Vince and his questionable background. "Has Daphne ever mentioned a young man named Vince Meroni?" Jack heard the couple discuss it with each other.

Mr. Cole answered for both of them. "We aren't familiar with that name, Lieutenant."

"According to Jennifer Tenley, Daphne's roommate, Vince was Daphne's boyfriend. He's not the most upstanding citizen according to North Bend PD." Jack jotted down a note to himself to talk to Billy Bachaus about Vince and his arrest record. "Long story short, Mr. and Mrs. Cole, Daphne may have died from fentanyl poisoning. The lab is still working to see if the amount in her bloodstream was a lethal dose. I'll keep you updated as information comes in."

Jack hung up and cracked his neck. He picked up the phone again and dialed the North Bend PD. "Hey, Emily, it's Jack Steele. Can you connect me to Billy Bachaus? I have some questions for him about Vince Meroni."

Chapter 34

Clayton and Billings walked out of the admissions office with the most current address for Michael Taylor. He rented a one-room efficiency apartment at the back of a storefront in Allenton.

Ten minutes later, Clayton parked the cruiser in the gravel parking lot, and they walked to the rear of the building.

"Here it is," Billings said as he double-checked the slip of paper in his hand. He balled his fist and banged on the door.

The door opened seconds later, and Michael stood on the other side. A look of recognition and surprise covered his face. "Detective Clayton, what are you doing here?"

"Hey, Michael. Sorry to barge in unannounced, but we have a few questions for you. This is my partner, Detective Billings."

Michael tipped his head toward the door. "I was about to leave for work."

His khaki pants and navy-blue polo shirt with the store logo embroidered on the chest told the detectives he likely worked at the big-box electronics store in North Bend.

Clayton pointed toward the living room. "We only need five minutes of your time."

"Okay, I guess." Michael scratched the top of his head and took a seat on the couch. The detectives remained standing. "So, what is this about?"

"Daphne Cole and Becca Morbeck. You and Daphne had chemistry lab together?"

"Yeah."

"Were you close?"

He shrugged. "We were classmates and knew each other, but close? Not really."

"Have you ever been arrested, Michael?"

"Hell no. I'm a responsible guy who's just trying to work my way through college and land a decent job."

Clayton wrote that down. "Good for you, but you know we'll check, right?"

Michael nodded.

"Did you know Becca Morbeck?"

"Not personally, but I heard about her death like everyone else did."

"Have you heard of anyone at school selling fentanyl?"

"No, but I think Cory Norman sells OxyContin. Please don't mention my name. I have another year to go at UWWC."

"Does Cory live in North Bend?"

"Yeah, at the Trace."

Clayton raised a brow at Billings and glanced at his notes. "I think that should do it for now." He handed Michael his card, and they thanked him for his time.

Billings climbed into the passenger seat and fastened the belt over his expanding belly. "Do you think there could be a connection between Vince and Cory Norman?"

Clayton huffed. "There has to be. Everyone at the Trace knows each other. Maybe Vince found out Daphne was seeing somebody on the side and got Cory involved. If he already sells OxyContin, it isn't that much of a stretch to find somebody who will land him some fentanyl."

Billings did a search for the surname Norman in North Bend on the cruiser's computer. "Here we go. Jane Norman is listed at 107 East Decorah Road, North Bend. That's likely Cory's mother. I'll try that number." Billings dialed the number and hit Speakerphone. A female voice answered on the second ring.

"Hello."

"Is Cory home?"

"Yeah, hang on."

Billings heard her yell for Cory to come to the phone. He hung up and dialed the city PD. "This is Detective Billings from the sheriff's office calling. I need an officer to meet me at 107 East Decorah Road. Yes, at the Trace. Word came in that the tenant living there may be dealing drugs at UWWC, and my partner and I need to question him. Right, we'll be waiting in the parking lot."

Clayton lifted his right hip and fished his cell phone out of his pocket. He pressed Jack's name in his contact list. "I'll let Jack know what's going on. It could boil down to Vince being the culprit after all."

Jack answered immediately and listened as Clayton

140

explained the situation. "I just got off the phone with the North Bend PD myself. Vince has a lengthy criminal sheet but mostly for petty things like store theft and starting fights in high school. There's been a few vandalism charges against him too but nothing as far as dealing drugs. Looks like he's been up to no good since he was a kid, though."

"That's what Billy said. Maybe he's leaving the drug-dealing business to Cory. No need to compete with somebody who lives in the same apartment complex in the same town."

"Agreed. I'm heading out now, and I'll meet you there in ten minutes."

Chapter 35

I browsed through the records in the county's database and came up empty for anyone who had been busted for selling fentanyl locally.

I massaged my forehead as I tried to think of another angle. "I'm not getting anywhere with fentanyl arrests."

Amber leaned back in her chair. "Fentanyl is usually added to another drug, to make the high higher, isn't it?"

I slapped my desk in an aha moment. "That's what I'm missing. I'm looking for arrests for dealing fentanyl instead of heroin."

"But Daphne didn't have heroin in her body."

"True, but it still could have come from the same person. Maybe they lace the heroin with fentanyl on higher-priced deals." I went to the database and began jotting down every heroin arrest made in the last year. I'd go back further if I had to.

"I'll see if anyone is in lockup for drug possession with intent to sell." Amber pulled up the county jail log. "Sure as shit. Gunnar Tobias, our longtime drug-dealing punk, is right upstairs, awaiting his sentencing. This time he's going away for at least a nickel term." Amber jerked her head toward the door and grabbed a notepad from her desk drawer. "Let's go pay him a visit and see if he feels like chatting."

"Hang on. I'll call upstairs first and have Josh pull Gunnar from the cell and toss him in box number one." I made the quick call and arranged it. Josh said it would take ten minutes. "Let's write down our questions first so we don't overlook anything."

With that finished and an update call made to Jack, we walked to the third floor of our building.

"Hey, Josh, is El Chapo ready for his interview?"

Josh chuckled. "Not willingly, but yeah, he's in box one."

I gave Josh a thank-you nod, and Amber and I entered the small green-walled interrogation room.

"What's up, Gunnar? Waiting for that special sentencing day when you get to move to the big house?"

"Go to hell."

"Sure thing, but I have some questions first." Amber and I took seats facing Gunnar on the other side of the steel table.

"Why should I talk to you pigs? My trial is already over with except for the sentencing phase."

I nodded. "That's right, and you could get anywhere from three to five years behind those big boy bars, but we might have some say in that. We could recommend the max to the judge or ask him to be a little more lenient because you were helpful in a case we're working on."

He huffed. "Fine. What do you want to know?"

I smiled. "Glad you asked."

Amber pulled out the list of questions we had prepared

and dove in. I'd be the one taking notes.

"You were the heroin kingpin of the county for some time. There has to be competition in the area that was pretty happy when you got busted for the second time. Care to share names?"

"Hell no. I don't intend to be locked up forever."

"Right. So have you ever laced heroin with fentanyl?"

He stared at the table and kept silent.

"Okay, I guess we're done here. Enjoy your five years in Waupun, and I promise you won't be the same guy when you get out."

We pushed back our chairs and turned toward the door.

"Wait a minute. I had to think before I answered."

Amber looked over her shoulder. "Yeah, let's hear it. We don't have all day, and you'll miss dinner if you don't start talking soon."

"Fine, I'll admit it. I've laced heroin with fentanyl. It gives you a crazy high."

We took our seats again.

"That's nice," Amber said, "and where did you get it?"

"You can order the shit right online. I thought you cops did your homework."

"Limit your concerns to yourself. Who did you sell the laced heroin to?"

"Street guys who resold it. I never dealt with the final user. That's what the minions are for. It limits my visibility."

I laughed. "Not that well or you wouldn't be sitting here talking to us. Give us names. Do you know Cory Norman?"

He stared at the ceiling as he let out a groan. "Yeah, but

he's a lightweight. Only deals Oxy. I did business with three guys in town. If there's any more than that, you'll have to find them on your own."

I flicked his hand with my fingers. "Let's get to the names."

"John Cinq, Tony Wesley, and Marques Gates. What they did with the stuff is on them. They're the only people I dealt with."

"And do they all live in the county?"

"Yeah."

We stood and walked to the door.

"We have a deal, right?"

Amber smiled. "Depends if your information helps our investigation or not. We can find two-bit drug dealers on our off days without your input. We'll let you know."

We returned to the bull pen, and I made a call to Jack. "Are you at Cory's apartment?"

"Yeah, we're just heading in. Why?"

"You need to ask if he has any connections to John Cinq, Tony Wesley, and Marques Gates. Gunnar gave up their names as the guys he used to sell the fentanyl-laced heroin to."

"Got it. Nice work."

"Thanks, Boss." I hung up the phone and made a new pot of coffee. "Now we wait to hear what Cory has to say."

An hour had passed, and I was fidgety—we needed answers. What we had given the press did little to ease the anxiety of students, their parents, and the university. Luckily the press wasn't aware of Daphne's initial toxicology results.

They'd have a field day with that information.

We had already updated Horbeck and Jamison with what we knew so far when Jack and the guys finally returned at five forty-five.

I spun my chair toward them. "Well, what did you find out?"

Jack plopped down in my guest chair. "I had Silver transport Cory to lockup, and a warrant is being issued for his home. The mom had a choice to leave the house and stay somewhere else until the search is complete or join her son in lockup, for harboring a drug dealer. She surrendered the house keys."

I looked at Amber and smirked. "I guess the noose is tightening around the necks of all the local players. What about the guys Gunnar gave up?"

"Cory knew their names but said they don't run in the same pack. I'll have Patrol shadow them for a few days and see what they're up to. It'll be much easier to make an arrest stick if we catch them in the act of selling the drugs."

"What about a possible connection between Vince and Gunnar's guys? Gunnar said Cory only dealt Oxy, but maybe Vince had a connection with them," Amber said.

Jack fisted his eyes. "We'll figure this out, but for now, go home and get some rest. Horbeck and Jamison are on the clock, so let them do their share of the work. I'm heading upstairs to drill Cory about Vince and to see if he has any knowledge of Daphne's death."

Chapter 36

Naomi couldn't wiggle out of the agreement she'd made with him earlier that day. He'd promised her a failing grade if she didn't show up at his house by six thirty, and that time, he'd accept no excuses. She was the last to go, and he had to come up with a good place to dump her body. With the hot days and early summer rains, the heat, humidity, and bugs would take care of her rotting corpse in no time.

Where to dump her is the question. I don't want her found or connected to me in any way. I'll have to get rid of her car too.

Mike remembered seeing her drive an old van. He would put his bicycle in the back of it, drive the vehicle to Riverview Park after closing hours, and leave it there. The parking lot wasn't noticeable from the road, and all he'd have to do was drive to the farthest end of the lot, park the van, and ride his bike home. Since it was a city park and often patrolled, he'd have to act quickly and ride out from a different exit. Nobody would notice anything until the next day, when the park opened. The van would be ticketed and eventually taken to the impound lot if nobody claimed it. He'd keep Naomi's phone handy and assume her identity in text messages to buy him enough time until her body was eaten away by the elements.

He heard a car door open and close just beyond the house. He pushed the kitchen curtain to the side and peered out. From where he stood, he could see the back end of the van.

Good, at least she brought the right vehicle.

He had given it more thought as he prepared dinner. Once she was dead—and it wouldn't take long—he'd dump her deep in the Jackson City marsh. At that time of year, the place was rarely visited since there were too many mosquitos and the ground was still soggy. He wouldn't have to drag her far off the trail, maybe fifty feet in. The underbrush was dense enough to engulf her, and she'd never be found. He'd strip her clothes off to speed the decomp and to allow the forest animals easy access to her body. He'd burn the clothing in his firepit, and he'd check her messages only when he was in the center of town and around dozens of other people.

The doorbell rang, and he dried his hands on the kitchen towel, tossed it on the counter, and walked to the foyer. He pulled the door open to see Naomi dressed as he'd insisted—in a tight-fitting low-cut red dress that came well above her knees.

"Now aren't you a sight? And you dressed to please me, yes?"

She muttered a quiet yes.

"I must admit, Naomi, you really stank up your final exam. You're lucky I'm willing to give you a passing grade, but no promises yet. We'll have to see how the evening goes before I make my final decision." He led her to the master bedroom and pointed at the bed. "First things first, you seem tense, and I have the perfect way to relax you. Take off that dress," he said as he unbuttoned his shirt and closed the door behind them.

They emerged from the bedroom forty-five minutes later. Mike stretched and walked to the kitchen.

"Have a seat on the couch, and I'll get you a glass of wine."

She did as she was told.

"I hope you like spaghetti and meatballs with mushrooms. I made salad and garlic bread too. Dinner should be ready soon. I just have to warm everything up."

"I don't feel well, and I'm not really hungry."

He peered around the corner and stared at her. She wasn't about to ruin his plans, and if she didn't eat the poisonous mushrooms in the spaghetti sauce, or the belladonna berries in the salad, he'd have to administer the old standby— fentanyl in her wine. He'd insist she have dinner with him. Her grade depended on it.

"I'm sorry, Naomi, but the night is going to go my way. You understand the consequences, don't you?"

"I'm just not that hungry. Maybe it's nerves."

He handed her the glass and sat down next to her. "Then drink this wine and loosen up. I didn't make a special dinner for nothing. We have to celebrate you passing your botany exam, right?"

"I suppose so."

"Good, otherwise I'll fail you." He stood and walked to the kitchen. "We'll eat, drink, and be merry, and then we'll retire to the bedroom again." He glanced at the mantel clock. "You can leave at midnight. How's that?"

She remained silent.

In the kitchen, Mike dished up two plates of spaghetti. Hers was tossed with slices of Destroying Angels mushrooms. His wasn't. He carried both steaming plates to the table and set them down then returned to the kitchen to get the salads. He made sure to place the one with belladonna berries next to her.

"This salad is to die for. Baby greens, feta cheese, walnuts, and blueberries drizzled with my homemade balsamic dressing. Please, dig in. I'll get the garlic bread and the wine."

Mike took a seat across from Naomi. He wanted the perfect view of her facial expressions. He watched as she swirled the pasta around her fork and lifted it to her mouth.

She nodded. "It's very good."

"Great. I aim to please." Mike filled his fork with baby greens and took a bite. "These blueberries are fresh from the Farmer's Market downtown."

Naomi speared a mushroom and popped it into her mouth. "I had no idea you liked to cook."

He smiled as he watched her dig into the salad. "I enjoy it on special occasions."

It took only fifteen minutes for him to see the confusion begin. Mike attributed that to the berries. The mushroom symptoms would take longer to kick in—five hours or so. She'd have waves of violent nausea and vomiting before her liver was destroyed and she died. Waiting that long wasn't necessary since the berries were already taking effect. Naomi's speech had begun to slur, and her fork fell to the table. Mike watched with interest. He hadn't witnessed the effects of the berries before.

"You're a living test subject, Naomi, and it's amazing how fast the poison is working."

A string of drool ran from her lower lip to her plate.

"Let me help you." He took a seat next to her, stabbed more mushrooms, and forced them into her mouth. "Chew them."

She tried to speak, but she couldn't form words.

"Here, have more berries." He filled her mouth with the deadly fruit.

Her eyes rolled back in her head, and she slumped in her chair. Seconds later, she slid to the floor.

"Damn, that was quick. I barely had time to enjoy watching you suffer." He knew she wasn't dead, only unconscious, but he'd address that after he finished dinner. Food that good wasn't about to go to waste. Mike ate in silence, rose from his chair, then grabbed a pillow from the couch. No need to prolong the inevitable. He dragged her out from under the table and pressed the pillow over her face. He held it in place for a good three minutes before checking her pulse. She was dead.

He pushed off his knee and stood. "How about some dessert, Naomi? What, not hungry? Okay, well, I'm going to enjoy a dish of spumoni, and then you and I are going for a drive."

Chapter 37

With his Explorer backed into the garage, Mike raised the liftgate then returned to the house. He carried out Naomi's wrapped nude body and placed her in the back of the SUV, tossed a tarp over her as a precaution, then pushed up his sleeve and checked the time. Most people—other than cops and criminals—were fast asleep after midnight. Tomorrow was a workday, and the streets of North Bend were nearly empty as he headed east on Washington Street. He turned right at the highway entrance, merged onto the four-lane road, and drove south for five miles. He didn't use his blinker when he turned east again on Pleasant Valley Road—nobody was behind him, anyway. At Division Road, he turned south and continued on until he reached the marsh.

I hate this shit—dark, eerie, and dead quiet except for the crickets and frogs.

He flicked the cigarette out the window as he shifted into Reverse and backed the SUV down the dirt and gravel trail. He passed the grassy parking lot on his right and continued as far as he could until the path narrowed to the point that branches were scraping the sides of his vehicle. From that point on, the trail was meant for pedestrian traffic only.

I guess that's as far as I'm going.

Mike killed the engine and climbed out. He clicked on his headlamp and maneuvered through the branches and twigs as he made his way to the back of the SUV. He raised the liftgate, tossed the tarp to the side, and pulled Naomi's body out by her legs. He panned the light left and right as he looked for the best place to enter the woods. The forest was thick with brush and groundcover. Carrying her farther than fifty feet would be difficult. He was thankful she was tiny. He dipped down and, with a groan, heaved her over his shoulder and headed into the darkness.

It took a good half hour, but the deed was done, and he'd covered Naomi with sticks and rotting leaves left behind from last winter's snow melt. He bundled the plastic sheeting under his arm and headed to his vehicle.

After climbing in, he pushed the plastic under the seat and fired up the engine. A cold beer, a hot shower, and a good night's sleep were on his agenda once he got home.

That should do it. There's nobody left that I had an arrangement with and nobody that knew about it. The timing couldn't be better. The exams will be done in two days, and the semester will be over. UWWC will be nothing but a ghost town for the summer. I'll move on to another city if I have to, but that depends on how smart North Bend's cops are. From what I've seen so far, none of them can outsmart me.

Chapter 38

I stumbled up the stairs to the kitchen as my nose followed the scent of fresh coffee wafting through the air.

"Good morning, Kate. How'd you sleep last night?" Jade sat at the breakfast bar while sipping a cup of coffee and eating a toaster pastry.

I looked around as I poured coffee for myself. "I slept okay. Where's Amber?"

"She woke up late, hence the quick breakfast. No time for real food." Jade tipped her head toward the hallway. "She's showering."

I took a seat next to Jade. "Have you ever had a case where the serial killer poisoned his victims?"

She looked surprised. "You still think that was the cause of death for the two UWWC girls?"

"I think so but convincing everyone else has been a challenge. It doesn't help that the tox results for poisoning haven't come back yet."

"So it's a wait-and-see case?"

"Not really." I blew on my coffee. "We're working it hard, and the initial drug and alcohol results for Daphne came back with fentanyl found in her system. That still doesn't prove she was poisoned, though. It could have been a suicide for all we know."

"Damn. Waiting isn't my strong suit. I'd go bonkers."

"You? Really?" I smiled.

"To answer your question, no, I've never been on a case where the serial killer used poison as their means of murder. It's too slow, and it isn't messy enough. They're looking for instant gratification using something as gruesome as possible."

I shook my head in disgust, but I had an idea. I would research poisons fatal to humans and see what results I found. If the deaths were homicides, there was a reason the killer chose poison instead of a physical weapon. It could be a weapon of convenience, or possibly he was just that smart. Poison could mimic any number of medical problems or something instant, like heart attacks, strokes, choking to death, and seizures.

"And cause someone to have a fatal car accident."

Jade glanced at me. "Were you just thinking out loud?"

"Yeah, guilty." I grabbed the pad of paper and a pen from the countertop and wrote a note to myself. Even though we'd know the tox results soon enough, I still wanted to educate myself on the types of poison that could kill a human in less than twenty-four hours.

Amber emerged from the hallway, dressed and refreshed. "You better get a move on," she said as she poured cereal into a bowl.

"Yeah, yeah, I'll be ready in twenty minutes."

We pulled into the parking lot of the sheriff's office at 7:47. I was anxious to find out how the conversation had gone between Cory Norman and Jack after we left last night. If there was a connection between the three young men Gunnar dealt with and Cory himself, there could be a chance that the fentanyl found in Daphne's blood test was a direct result of a suggestion from Vince. There was still no account of where Daphne went after leaving Vince's apartment on the night she was last seen alive, and a lie detector test might be in order to prove or disprove Vince's statement.

Clayton and Billings waited in the bull pen with Jack for our arrival. Jack stood when we entered.

"Let's go. Conference room." His straight-to-the-point comment made me think something new had come up overnight.

I dropped my purse into the desk drawer, grabbed my notepad and pen, and followed my colleagues down the hallway.

Once in the conference room and seated, Jack took a gulp of coffee from his favorite chipped cup and began. "I interviewed Cory last night. I let him know in no uncertain terms that I wasn't there to tiptoe around the subject of drug dealing in my county. Of course he denied having anything to do with drugs and said he only knew Vince in passing. His story changed dramatically when I told him a warrant had been issued for the apartment and his mom had turned over the keys to me. He admitted to dealing Oxy on a small scale, and we'll see how small it actually is if we find some in the home. Then he suddenly remembered being friends with Vince after all."

I took notes as Jack continued.

"I asked if he ever sold fentanyl or knew if Vince contacted Gunnar's boys about buying some. Maybe Vince had suspicions of Daphne cheating and only wanted to teach her a lesson but accidentally overdosed her. He may have mixed it with something else since heroin wasn't present in her body. Cory swears he's never sold fentanyl personally but said it's widely available online, and that puts us back to square one. Without proof, blaming Vince for Daphne's death would be a circumstantial case at best."

I caught Jack's attention. "How about suggesting a polygraph test? If Vince didn't do anything wrong, it would get us off his back."

Jack grinned. "I can suggest it, but I don't know if he'll fall for those tactics. We can't harass him without something that leads us to him as the guilty party. Let's wait for the full tox report on both girls before barking up that tree, but"— he looked at Clayton and Billings—"I want you two to pay Vince another visit. Tell him that Cory is sitting upstairs and he told us everything. Check his temperature. Go ahead and have Billy tag along."

Clayton nodded. "Got it."

"What about us, Boss?" I asked.

"Go see if Lena got the final tox reports back yet."

"I'll let Amber take care of that."

Jack nodded. "Right. Okay, you can empty everyone's desks of the paperwork that needs to be filed in the records room."

I frowned. "Awesome."

Back in the bull pen, I made short work of the filing. I wanted to get online and start my research of poisons that were capable of killing a human in a short period of time.

Amber burst into the bull pen ten minutes later. "Jack, Lena has the reports. She's reading them first herself, then she'll come up here and go over them with us."

"That's great news, and I'll have to call the tox lab and give them a personal thank-you for getting that done so quickly. Did Lena say when to expect her?"

"She said it would be a half hour or so."

"Okay, Detectives, you better clear your plates and be ready to go. There may be more people to speak to, parents to update, and possible arrests to make. I just got word that the warrant is on its way from the courthouse. We're tearing apart Cory Norman's apartment today, and depending on what Clayton and Billings find out, Vince's might be next."

Before Lena announced the findings, I had a small window of opportunity to research poisons that were capable of killing people quickly. I wanted to know what I was talking about in case she and I got into another debate.

Chapter 39

Clayton turned the key in the lock and pushed the door inward. Billy Bachaus led the way into the cluttered, unkempt apartment.

"What's with the people who live in this complex?" He wrinkled his nose as he hit the light switch. "Let's air out this place. It smells like cat piss in here."

Clayton pushed open the drapes and slid the windows to the side. A fresh breeze wafted in, and the family cat scurried out the door.

Billings pointed as it ran past. "What the hell are we supposed to do about that?"

Billy shrugged. "It's a cat, and they have nine lives. Either chase it down and lock it in the laundry room or don't worry about it. Cats like being outside better than indoors, anyway." He looked around the living room and shook his head. "What a shit hole. Everyone gloved up with plenty of evidence bags?"

Clayton and Billings nodded then dug in. They methodically went from room to room as they opened drawers and cabinets, overturned cushions, and looked under furniture. Clayton pulled out the clothes in every drawer and checked pockets, and Billings did the same with the clothes that were hanging. Billy opened freezer and refrigerator containers to make sure no Oxy was hidden inside.

"I found a bag of pot and some papers," Billings said after lifting Cory's mattress.

Billy walked in. "Enough to get him on intent to sell?"

Billings held up the sandwich bag. "Looks like it's meant for personal use."

"Okay, let's keep searching. Don't overlook anything in the mom's room either. That might be the perfect place to hide drugs."

Clayton pulled pictures off the walls and checked the back sides. He stuck his head in each kitchen cabinet and checked to see if bags were taped to the inside walls. "I'm not finding anything." He and Billings gathered in the living room and looked it over carefully to see if they'd missed anything. "Did you check inside the washer and dryer?"

"Not yet." Billings tipped his head in that direction. "There could even be something in the dryer vent."

"Yeah, we should check that too."

They entered the laundry room and went through the washer and dryer—neither had drugs hidden inside.

Clayton glanced at the cat's litter box and raised a brow. "Are you thinking what I'm thinking?"

"I hate to admit it, but yeah. At least there's a scoop."

They sifted through the cat litter and found two sandwich-sized zipper bags containing hundreds of Oxy pills.

"Impressive," Clayton said. "I'll admit, that's a great

hiding spot, and the street value of this stuff is pretty damn high. Looks like Cory has some explaining to do."

Billy walked out of the mother's bedroom with a sandwich bag of Oxy pinched between his thumb and index finger. He laughed when he saw Clayton and Billings sitting in front of the litter box. "Cory must have a thing for places to relieve oneself. I found this baggie in the toilet tank of the mother's master bathroom."

Billings rolled the gloves off his hands in obvious disgust. "She may be looking at charges too."

"Let's lock up this place. We have plenty to charge Cory with, and we need to make a stop at Vince's apartment before we leave."

Clayton made the update call as they rounded the corner to Vince's apartment, and Jack said he'd get another warrant issued.

Billings knuckled the door when they reached it. They saw a flash to their right as the blinds opened then closed.

Vince pulled the door toward him and rolled his eyes. "This is harassment."

Billy pushed past him. "Sit down and shut up. We don't need your opinion."

Clayton took over. "We have Cory Norman and Gunnar Tobias in custody. Seems like you're all pals."

"I don't know either of them."

"That's the story you're going with, Vince? You know damn well that Cory lives four apartments from here. We just went through his apartment and found enough Oxy to put him behind bars for some time, and your apartment is next.

There's a warrant heading this way any minute now."

"You don't have any grounds to search my apartment."

Billings chuckled. "Sure we do. Cory is sitting in our county lockup, and he suddenly became very chatty. He told us about your connection to Gunnar's lackeys. You know, John Cinq, Tony Wesley, and Marques Gates, the guys you got the fentanyl from."

Vince buried his face in his hands. "You're handing me a line of shit, and I don't know what the hell you're talking about. I've never used or sold fentanyl in my life. I don't know those three guys or Gunnar Tobias, other than by reputation. I smoke pot, okay? That's all I can afford, anyway."

Clayton sat next to Vince on the couch. "Did you kill Daphne? Maybe you found out she was seeing someone else and you wanted to teach her a lesson. Fentanyl killed her, Vince, so how did that happen?"

"I swear to you, I don't know. I really cared about Daphne."

Clayton's phone rang seconds later—it was Jack. He stepped outside and answered. "Hey, Boss, what have you got?"

"Silver is heading your way with the warrant. I'll have him escort Vince back here, and we can legally detain him for twenty-four hours."

"Sounds good."

"Lena has the final tox results for both girls, and I'd like you and Billings to sit in on the meeting. Show Vince the warrant, lock up his apartment, and head back. You can search it later, and Billy doesn't have to join in unless the chief wants him to. That warrant is our golden ticket."

"Sure thing. We'll be watching for Silver."

Chapter 40

My notes were compiled and sitting in front of me in case something in the toxicology report seemed off. Lena was due to walk in any minute.

The security door beeped, and Clayton and Billings entered the bull pen.

Jack addressed Clayton. "Has Vince been secured upstairs?"

"Yep, Josh is processing him right now, and each detainee is in a separate cell. They can't even see each other."

"Good, I don't want to give them the ability to concoct stories to support one another." Jack filled his coffee cup then answered his ringing phone. "Yep, we're all here, and we'll meet you in the conference room." He turned toward the hallway. "Grab whatever you need and let's go."

We each took our usual seat at the table. Amber had her laptop, I had a folder of notes about poisons, and Billings and Clayton had the pages of their notepads turned to clean sheets. Jack had his coffee in front of him and the blank whiteboard at his back.

The clock ticked over to eleven just as Lena walked in. "Morning, everyone."

We returned her greeting with our own.

"Okay, I'm sure you're all interested in hearing the tox report results for both Daphne and Becca."

I was more curious about how Becca had died, but I kept that to myself. We already knew fentanyl was in Daphne's system, and the confirmation of the amount would tell us beyond a shadow of a doubt that it was what killed her. Becca's cause of death was still an unknown. I fidgeted.

"Daphne had a lethal dose of pure fentanyl in her bloodstream, meaning it wasn't cut with anything else. A few granules are enough to kill a full-grown adult."

I glanced at my sheet and crossed that off my list. The tox report substantiated what I had read. "So somebody deliberately killed Daphne?"

Lena shrugged. "We have no way of knowing that, only that the fentanyl killed her."

Jack ran his fingers through his hair then pushed back his chair and stood. He wrote that information on the whiteboard and remained standing, as if he was ready to record another round of bad news.

Lena sucked in a deep breath. "I had the lab double-check their work on Becca. They did and confirmed that she died from the bacteria clostridium botulinum. She had toxic levels of the poison in her body. Botulism is deadly if not treated immediately and it also causes paralysis of the nerves, hence the reason many people have Botox injections. Of course, those treatments are done by experienced professionals who only use the recommended amounts of the product." Lena checked our expressions. "That could explain why Becca never pressed the brake pedal. I've never heard of anyone who was subjected to a lethal dose, but I imagine it's possible that she couldn't move her foot from the gas to the brake."

Clostridium botulinum wasn't even on my poisons list, and I didn't know anything about it. I had to ask the question. "Can that poison cause severe stomach pain, and if ingested, would it show esophagus and stomach irritation?"

Lena nodded. "It would indeed, Kate, and I apologize for questioning your theory. Each of us has a field of expertise, and I didn't trust yours. What I would suggest is to go through Becca's home, look through her food—especially canned goods—to see if anything was beyond its expiration date. There might be a can in the garbage from the night before. Who knows? Like I said a few days back, her stomach contents only revealed her breakfast food, and that was cereal."

"Could spoiled milk contain the poison?" Clayton asked.

Lena shook her head. "No, it's primarily found in low-acid foods such as canned goods and vacuum-sealed meats, vegetables, and fish. Check everything in her cupboards and look at leftovers in the refrigerator."

Jack wrote that on the whiteboard. "So at this point, we can say with certainty that Daphne met with foul play and Becca is still an unknown."

Lena tapped her fingers on the table. "Not necessarily, Jack, and I may have to write the manner of death as undetermined. There's still the chance that Daphne committed suicide."

Jack sighed. "True enough. Thank you, Lena. We'll check all the food in Becca's home and go from there. It would be nice to have a lead that pointed us in a definitive direction since we're still at murder, accidental death, or suicide for both cases."

Lena stood and said, "If you don't find expired canned goods in Becca's cupboards or questionable food in her refrigerator, I'd lean more toward it being a deliberate act. Keep in mind, though, it would take a very knowledgeable person, likely with a degree in chemistry, to make that toxin." After stating her final opinion, she headed out of the room.

Jack waited for Lena to leave then checked the time. "First things first, I have a call to make. Start thinking of ideas we can brainstorm while I'm gone." Jack walked out to the hallway and closed the door behind him but returned in a matter of minutes. "Okay, Becca's folks are on their way to North Bend with her spare apartment key. I told them I had an update to share, and I'm going to conduct another interview with them too. There has to be more they can tell us. Is there anything you guys came up with that might steer us in the right direction?" He stared at me.

"You want my honest opinion, sir?"

He took his seat. "I'd appreciate it."

"I think the girls were murdered. What are the chances that two young women from the same college would both die of accidental poisoning and only one day apart? Especially with two poisons that aren't commonly found in a home."

Amber added her two cents. "That's true. It isn't like clostridium botulinum and fentanyl are found in everyone's medicine cabinet like aspirin is, or in the garage like antifreeze and rat poison."

I doodled on my notepad as I spoke. "The thing is, we don't have to go back to square one. I'm still curious to know who that Mike was that found Becca so interesting. If we find him and he knew Daphne too, we might be onto something. It's like you said a few days ago—find the connection and we'll find the killer."

"Okay, let's go over the list of people we interviewed again. Talk to that friend from Becca's hometown one more time, the one who told you about Mike. See if there's more she can add." Jack looked at Clayton. "You sure Michael Taylor is a dead end?"

Clayton scratched his chin, as if in thought. "Ninety-nine percent sure, Boss. The kid is a straight arrow, and he did give us Cory's name. He didn't have to do that."

"Finals end Friday, and then tracking down the students and professors will be a nightmare. People will be leaving North Bend by the weekend. The students will go home for the summer or get jobs, they'll take vacations, and reaching out to them will be tough. Dig in, people. We don't have much time. Go ahead and take your lunches now." Jack turned to Amber and me. "Once the Morbecks arrive, you'll go to Becca's apartment and inspect the food, and Clayton and Billings, you'll check every square inch of Vince's place."

Chapter 41

I jotted down notes as I ate my grilled chicken wrap.

Amber scooted closer to me. "What are you doing?"

"Making sure I don't forget anything. My mind is usually too full to store everything I'm thinking of." I took another bite and glanced at her. "It really helps."

"I'll try it. So what did you write?"

I ran down the list with my index finger. "To check everything in Becca's apartment, not just her food. There could be a clue to that Mike's identity somewhere in plain sight."

Amber nodded. "Good idea. What else?"

"To call Jodi Prentice again and ask more questions about Mike. Also, I want to review the list of people Clayton and Billings talked to at UWWC and have a look at all the classes both girls took. We need to have another conversation with Jennifer Tenley too."

"Why?"

"Because she wasn't asked if she knew anyone named Mike. If Daphne knew other Mikes, then we have to track them down and have a chat with them. This case is going to get a lot harder to solve after Friday when classes end and everyone goes about their summer activities. In other words, we have to give everything we've done one more look to make sure nothing was missed."

We were back in the bull pen by twelve fifteen. Jack exited his office and told Clayton and Billings to head out. We still had to wait for the Morbecks to show up with Becca's extra apartment key.

Amber straightened her desk while we waited. "Why didn't we just track down the apartment manager for the key? We could have been going through it already."

"Jack said something about him being out of town."

"Then the owner?"

I shrugged. "Don't know. I guess Jack thought this was the fastest way to get inside, plus he said he wanted to tell the Morbecks of Lena's findings."

My ears perked when I heard Jack's phone ring on the other side of his closed door. Seconds later, he walked out.

"The Morbecks are here. I'll get the key right away, and you two can leave. Here's the address." He gave us a concerned look as he handed the slip of paper to Amber. "Be thorough."

I tipped my head. "We will, Boss."

With the key safely tucked in my pocket, I left with Amber and reached the eight-unit brick apartment complex in Kewaskum fifteen minutes later. It had one central parking lot and no garages. I imagined it being a real pain in the winter.

"Which unit is hers?" Amber pulled into the parking lot and stopped.

I pointed to the far right. "Park over there by the side driveway. It's number four, so I guess it's an end unit."

Once parked, we exited the cruiser and walked to the door. I jiggled the knob.

Amber gave me an eyebrow raise. "Why did you do that?"

"If anyone is inside, that jiggle was their only warning." I slid the key into the slot and turned it, then I pushed the door inward.

We entered the living room of what appeared to be an efficiency apartment. It looked smaller than the one I'd had above the hardware store on Main Street, and it took only a second to view the entire unit. The living room opened to the closet-sized kitchen on the right, and the only bedroom was straight ahead. The single bath and a storage closet were at the end of a five-foot-long hallway.

Amber took in the apartment. "Damn, this place is tiny. We'll be done in a half hour."

I looked around. "Remember, we're searching for anything that could be a clue, not just tainted food."

Amber took a seat on the couch as she slipped on her gloves. "How do you want to do this?"

"Let's work together, that way the chances of missing something will be far less. We'll start in the bedroom and work our way out. Check everything, top to bottom and left to right." I stretched the gloves over my hands. "Okay, let's dig in."

We stripped the bed, shook the sheets, and removed the pillows from the cases. We pulled the mattress and box springs off the bed, looked under it, then put those items back in place.

I walked to the dresser. "Help me scoot this out."

Amber took one side, and I took the other. We lifted it and moved the dresser three feet forward. The only thing below it were the impressions of the feet in the carpet. We pushed it back and began going through each drawer.

"Hey, this seems off." Amber held up a lacy purple bra with matching panties.

"Off how?"

"This entire drawer is full of lingerie. I thought Becca didn't have a love interest other than sports. Where are the sports bras?"

I grinned. "Maybe she just liked girly stuff or she had a boyfriend some time back. Nobody throws out their lingerie just because the boyfriend is out of the picture. Check a different drawer."

"I guess you're right." Amber pulled open the next drawer. "Here it is—all sports bras and panties."

We continued on and found nothing in her bedroom that raised any red flags. We moved to the bathroom. I lowered the lid and took a seat on the toilet as I rummaged through the three-drawer vanity. Amber opened the medicine cabinet above the sink. "Humph, I thought Becca didn't take any medicine."

I stood. "What did you find?"

She turned the pill tray toward us. "What the—"

I cut her off when I saw the individual pills encased in the plastic-and-foil tray. "Birth control pills? Now that is interesting. When was it filled?"

Amber checked the date and the number of refills left. "It

was just filled last month by Dr. Manthei."

"That's my doctor." I reached in my pants pocket and took out my phone and list. I snapped a picture of the prescription information then retrieved a pen from my purse that sat on the coffee table. I added to my list a note to call Dr. Manthei as soon as we left the apartment.

We finished in the bathroom and found nothing else of importance.

"I'll get started on the kitchen. Why don't you clear that storage closet since there isn't enough room for both of us to work in the hallway?"

"Sure thing." Amber hit the wall switch and brightened the area before she began clearing each shelf.

I entered the galley kitchen and counted the cabinets— only four along with a pantry behind a folding door.

This won't take long, then I'll have that chat with the doctor and Jodi Prentice. There's a chance Jodi knew Becca was on the pill, but why, if Becca didn't have a love interest?

Minutes later, Amber appeared from the hallway. "There's nothing important in the closet, just towels and clean sheets." She looked around. "I'll take the pantry. That's usually where canned goods are, anyway."

We went through every drawer, cabinet, and pantry shelf. Nothing that was labeled had an expired date.

"Okay, so that's clear. Let's check the fridge and garbage can." I pulled open the refrigerator door and was surprised to see how empty it was. "Damn, she must have starved herself to save money."

Lined up side by side in the refrigerator door rack were a

jar of kalamata olives, a plastic bottle of brown mustard, two ketchup packets from a fast-food restaurant, and a pint of sour cream. The shelf in front of me held a bag of apples and a container with leftover macaroni and cheese inside. The shelf below that held three cans of soda and two cheese sticks. I pulled open the freezer and found an eight-pack of burritos, three of them missing, and a tray of ice cubes. I took a seat at the corner table and gave Lena's original assessment some thought. She had said Becca's stomach contents were from breakfast—a bowl of cereal.

I turned to Amber. "Is there an open box of cereal in the pantry?"

"Yep, some type of almond cranberry stuff, and it looks good. Why?"

"Because there isn't any milk in the fridge, and Lena said Becca had cereal for breakfast the morning she died."

"Maybe she ate it like granola."

"Humph—maybe. I'm going to start on the garbage can." I pulled out the trash can from beneath the sink and carried it to my chair. I hated that part of my job and had gone through people's trash more times than I cared to remember. "Something is wrong."

Amber took a seat in the only other chair and stared at the contents I was digging through. "It looks like trash to me."

"Exactly, but there isn't an empty milk jug in here."

"Okay, what do you have?"

"There's a couple of coffee filters with grounds inside, two tissues, a few crumpled pieces of paper, and a bag from Pizza

Pie." I saw a receipt stapled to the outside of the bag, tore it off, and handed it to Amber. "Check the date on this."

"It's from Monday evening, and she ordered a carryout calzone."

"And she died Tuesday morning. Check those balled-up pieces of paper. See what they are."

Amber opened each piece of paper and flattened them on the table. "One is a grocery store receipt for milk, cereal, ramen noodles, facial tissue, a jug of water, and a pint of three-bean salad."

"What's the date?"

Amber looked at the bottom of the receipt. "Last Saturday."

"And that was five days ago, yet there aren't any empty containers for those items in the trash can. They sure as hell aren't in the refrigerator either—that thing is almost empty." I grabbed the apartment keys and stood. "Come on. Let's bang on a few doors. There are three vehicles in the lot, so somebody must be home. We need to find out when the garbage is picked up here."

We took the sidewalk to the other end of the building, where two of the three cars were parked. Amber rapped on the door of apartment one, and we waited, but nobody answered. We moved on to apartment number two. I knocked and heard footsteps getting closer.

"Good, somebody is home." I made sure my badge attached to the lanyard around my neck was clearly visible. Amber did the same just as the door opened.

An elderly woman stood in front of us. "May I help you?"

175

"Yes, ma'am. We're detectives from the sheriff's office." I wiggled my badge so she would take note of it. "We're wondering if you know when the garbage is picked up here."

"Well, sure. That big truck comes early in the morning and makes all kinds of racket. It wakes me up every time. I mean it isn't even daylight—"

I had to interrupt or we'd be standing there all day. "Ma'am, we only need to know what day of the week that is."

"Oh. It gets picked up on Fridays."

"And there's only one pick up a week?" Amber asked.

"Yes, thank God. I swear, if—"

I tipped my head and smiled. "Thank you, ma'am."

Amber and I headed back to Becca's apartment. Inside, sitting in the kitchen and looking at the contents of the garbage can, we knew that items were missing.

"The groceries were purchased on Saturday, the day after the trash pickup, yet there isn't an empty water jug, a milk jug, or a deli salad container in the trash. What the hell, Amber?"

"We need to tell Jack about this discovery, but we can't do it while the Morbecks are there. Those people are under enough stress already."

"Let's lock up this place. Forensics may have to go through it even more closely than we did. I have a bad feeling that the poison that killed Becca didn't come from expired food. Let's head to Dr. Manthei's office and see what she's willing to tell us. I'll make the call to Jodi while you drive."

Chapter 42

My call to Jodi Prentice went unanswered, so I left a message saying I needed her to call me as soon as possible. Amber turned in to the doctor's office parking lot just as I hung up.

Inside, the receptionist saw me and flipped through the pages of the appointment book. "Kate, I don't believe you're scheduled to see the doctor today."

With the waiting room empty, I didn't feel the need to whisper. "Linda, I have to speak with Dr. Manthei. It's official business."

"Okay, give me a second. She's with a patient now, but I'll find out how much longer it'll be."

"Appreciate it."

Amber and I sat in the waiting room—and waited. I pulled my phone from my purse and texted Jack. "Are the Morbecks still with you?" I didn't get a response, which in essence was the answer I needed. He was still with them. I grabbed a magazine and mindlessly flipped the pages. What we had, or hadn't, found in Becca's apartment weighed heavily on my mind.

"Kate? Can I help you with something?"

I looked up to see Dr. Manthei at the door to the hallway. I placed the magazine on the coffee table and stood. "May we?"

She motioned for us to follow her, I presumed to her office. Inside, she closed the door and offered us seats. "What is this about, Kate?"

"We're here on sheriff's office business, and I was hoping you could help us."

"Sure, if I can."

I opened my picture gallery and showed her Becca's birth control pill prescription. "You've heard about her death, haven't you?"

"I have, and it's so sad, but why do you have a picture of her prescription? I assume you know about doctor-patient confidentiality, right?"

I slipped my phone back in my purse. "Dr. Manthei, there isn't confidentiality anymore—she's dead. Becca didn't have a boyfriend, yet this prescription was just filled last month. We need to know how long she has been on the pill and if it was medically necessary or strictly for birth control reasons."

She let out a sigh of what I took as apprehension and logged on to her computer. "Becca was very healthy and didn't have problems with her monthly cycle or any reproductive issues." She tapped the computer keys. "I'm pulling up her chart now." She scrolled through a few pages. "Here it is. Becca started using birth control pills two months ago."

I glanced at Amber. "And before that?"

Dr. Manthei shrugged. "No idea. That was the first time she asked for a prescription. Becca had only been my patient since last fall."

"How was that bill paid? Did it go through her parents' insurance?"

"No. She asked for a three-month prescription and paid with her own credit card."

"Had she mentioned being in a relationship?" Amber asked. "You know, anything to the effect of 'My boyfriend Mike and I have become intimate and I need birth control.' Something like that?"

"No, but now that I think back, she almost seemed embarrassed to ask for it, and she didn't mention a boyfriend at all."

We stood, shook the doctor's hand, and walked to the door. "Thank you for the information. It's been very helpful. We'll show ourselves out."

My phone rang as we crossed the parking lot. Jodi was returning my call. "Hello, Jodi, I'm so glad you got back to me." Amber clicked the fob, and I climbed into the passenger seat and fastened my belt. "I'm putting you on Speakerphone, and my partner, Detective Amber Monroe, is with me. We need more information about Becca."

"What can I tell you that I haven't already, Detective?"

"I need to know more about Mike, the guy who had a thing for Becca."

"Becca said two sentences about him. That's it. He was a creep, and she couldn't wait until school was over so she wouldn't have to see him again until fall."

"Meaning he was a freshman too?" Amber wrote while I talked.

"I didn't read anything into it. I'm just telling you what she said."

"Did she mention his last name? Please, think hard about it."

"No, she didn't."

I thought she answered too quickly, but I let it go since I wanted to keep her talking. "Did Becca mention being intimate with him?"

"God no!"

"How about anyone else?"

"Becca didn't have a boyfriend, and she would have told me if she did."

I let out an audible breath. "You're sure?"

"One hundred percent sure. We talked on the phone almost every night."

A thought popped into my mind. "Did you talk on Monday night?"

"Yes, I'm pretty sure we did."

"And did she say what she was up to?"

"Only that she was studying. She ordered carryout and was cramming for her chemistry exam."

"And her disposition was how?"

"Normal I guess, other than the studying part. We joked around, talked smack, and then she said she had to go. That was the last time I spoke to her."

"Did she seem sick, like she was in pain?"

"No, not at all. Just busy."

"Okay, thank you, Jodi. I really appreciate your help." I clicked off the call and rolled my eyes at Amber. "The more we work this case, the more confused I become."

Chapter 43

It was midafternoon by the time we entered the bull pen. I saw Jack sitting in his office alone, and Clayton and Billings busied themselves at their desks. The scene appeared calm.

"By the looks of it, I assume you didn't find anything at Vince's apartment."

Billings cracked his neck then gave it a rub. "And you assumed right. Jack already cut him loose."

"Damn it," Amber said. "Good thing we have tons of information. We just don't know where to go with it."

Jack walked out of his office and leaned against the doorframe. "Yeah, let's hear it."

"The Morbecks are gone, right? They aren't in the lunchroom or anything?"

"They're downstairs getting a crash course in botulism from Lena. They aren't coming back up, if that's what you're asking. What did you two find out?"

I took my seat, and Jack perched himself on the edge of my desk. "To put it simply, somebody has been in Becca's apartment."

"Hold that thought." Jack walked into his office, and I

saw him pick up his phone. He talked for several minutes, hung up, then returned to the bull pen, this time choosing to take a seat on my guest chair. "Just checking to make sure the Morbecks haven't been in the apartment since Becca's death. They said they haven't stepped foot in there. It's too soon and too painful. So, what's going on, and why do you think somebody has been in her apartment?"

Amber took the lead. "There are several things that didn't sit well with us, but mainly it was the lack of food in the refrigerator and the receipts we found in the trash that proved alarming."

"How so?"

"The receipt from the grocery store contained items that weren't in the apartment or the trash can. We asked the neighbor when the trash pickup was, and she said Friday, but Becca bought the groceries on Saturday. The milk, a jug of water, the creamer, and a three-bean salad were all missing from the refrigerator, and none of the containers were in the garbage can. There weren't expired canned goods in the pantry or empty cans in the trash either. A receipt from Pizza Pie was in the garbage from the night before Becca died. She ordered a carryout calzone, and according to what Jodi Prentice told us, she spoke with Becca that night. She said Becca was studying for her chemistry final and didn't mention anything about feeling sick."

Jack wrinkled his forehead until his brows nearly touched. "That's very odd. Check with the pizza joint, anyway, and see if they've ever had food poisoning complaints or fines from the health department for spoiled food."

I wrote that down on my to-do list.

"Anything else?"

I set the pen on my desk. "There's definitely more. We found lingerie in Becca's drawers and birth control pills in her medicine cabinet, yet Jodi swears Becca didn't have a love interest. She said Becca would have confided in her if she had."

Amber added her two cents. "And if Becca cared enough about a man to be intimate with him, she would have been over the moon. I know I would have told my closest friend everything about the guy if I were in her shoes."

Adam nodded. "I concur. I've heard the gushing that goes on between Mia and her friends every time one of them has a crush on a boy."

Jack scratched his chin. "So Jodi was adamant about Becca not having a boyfriend?"

"She was, Boss, and that leads me back to the mysterious Mike that Becca couldn't stand. Jodi didn't know his last name, but she said Becca hoped she wouldn't have to see him again until the fall semester starts."

"So he's a student and likely going into his sophomore year like Becca would have been?"

I looked at Amber. "We assumed so."

Jack turned to Clayton. "Becca wanted to go into the biochemistry field according to what her mother said, and both girls took chemistry lab."

"Yep, they sure did."

Jack headed to his office. "Take a ten-minute break. I need to look through my notes to see if the Coles mentioned what Daphne was planning as a future career."

Amber started a fresh pot of coffee while everyone else scoured their notes for anything that could be a clue.

Jack returned to the bull pen ten minutes later. I poured coffee for everyone and took my seat.

"Okay, the Coles said Daphne wanted to be a horticulturist once she graduated college. See if Becca took horticulture classes."

Billings logged on to his laptop and pulled up the school's curriculum. "They don't offer horticulture classes, but they do teach botany."

"And that takes us back to Mike," Clayton said. "Daphne and Mike were in the same botany class."

I grimaced. "And I still bet he's the same Mike who had the hots for Becca."

Adam shook his head. "I'm not so sure. The professor said he never noticed any interaction between Mike Taylor and Daphne other than as classmates."

"Maybe Mike was only interested in Becca, and Daphne wasn't on his radar," Amber said.

"Nah, Mike Taylor was a straight arrow. We didn't sense anything off about him, and Becca didn't take botany classes, anyway."

Jack sighed. "Okay, talk to the chemistry professor again since that was the only course Becca and Daphne had in common."

Clayton rubbed his forehead. "But we already talked to him for the second time yesterday. He's—"

"Shit," Adam said. "He's the botany *and* chemistry

professor. There has to be a different Mike in one of Becca's classes, and apparently it isn't the Mike Taylor that Daphne knew."

"It is a common name," Jack said. "And without a last name, finding the right Mike is going to be a lot harder."

"Maybe not. The admissions department would know every Mike who had just finished his freshman year. Becca told Jodi she wouldn't see him again until fall, meaning he was a freshman too."

"All right, let's switch this up. Adam, you and Chad go interview the pizza joint. Pull the health department records on them and make sure everything looks kosher. No fines, no dirty dining complaints, etcetera, etcetera. Kate and Amber, head to the university. See what you can get from the admissions office as far as anyone named Mike on their freshman roster from last fall." He gave us a scowl. "Be nice too. We don't want them to force us to get a warrant. Oh yeah, I need the apartment key back."

I dug it out of my pocket and dropped it into his open hand.

"I'm sending Forensics over there to do a thorough search for prints and DNA. Hopefully something will pop."

Chapter 44

It was late in the day when Amber and I headed west on Washington Street. We didn't know if anyone would still be at the admissions office, but if not, we'd walk the hallways and interview anyone and everyone we came across.

My gut feeling was that the girls were murdered and Mike was the culprit. I was sure the mystery would unravel as soon as we learned who he was. The connection, I felt, was him, but we needed the why. I checked the time on my cell phone—4:57. We turned right, into UWWC's entrance, and passed the faculty parking area as we headed to the small visitors' lot. I noticed how empty it looked. Amber parked the cruiser, and we walked to the main entrance. Once inside, I took note of the dimmed lights, and I sensed that only a handful of staff and students remained in the building. Many doors had already been closed as we made our way down the hallways toward the admissions office.

"I'm not feeling good about this. There really isn't a reason for anyone to be here other than a few professors and students taking exams."

"Can't you just twitch your nose or chant something for good luck?"

"I'm not a witch, Amber."

She laughed. "Jack said to be nice, so I guess that means to you too."

I rolled my eyes. "Hey, look, the admissions office door is open."

"So you did twitch your nose?"

"I'll deal with you later." I stepped over the threshold with Amber at my heels. I cupped my mouth and whispered to her. "Remember, we have to play nice and put on the charm. That means I'll do the talking."

Amber frowned as I stepped up my pace and reached the counter first. A middle-aged woman seated at a computer glanced up. Her name tag read Constance B.

"May I help you ladies?"

I stuck out my hand and shook hers as I made the introductions. "Hello, Constance, I'm Detective Pierce with the sheriff's office, and this is my partner, Detective Monroe."

Amber nodded and held out her badge.

Constance perched her glasses on her nose and took a closer look. Apparently satisfied, she placed the glasses back on the desk. "What can I do for you, Detectives?"

"We're kind of in a time crunch, and we'd hate to make you ladies stick around longer than necessary." I caught a glimpse of two other women glancing at the clock. "We'd really appreciate your help."

"I'll do what I can."

I smiled. "And that's all we can ask of you. What we need is a copy of the registered students who started as freshmen last fall, particularly male students."

"There's no way to separate male from female."

"I understand. Then I guess we'll need a list of all of them."

Constance looked at her colleagues and then at the clock. "Um, I don't know if that's allowed. Something about student privacy, I think."

"Sure, go ahead and pull out the college bylaws. I guess we'll have to wait while you go through them. I'm sure they're lengthy."

Another woman wearing a name tag that read Beverly approached the counter and took over for Constance. "I believe you'll need a warrant for that information."

"Possibly, but you'll have to wait here for it to arrive since each of you will have to verify its authenticity. It could take a few hours—you know how courthouse red tape goes. I hope none of you have plans."

"Give us a minute." Beverly pulled Constance aside. We heard whispering between the women from behind the cubicle wall. I smiled at Amber. The women returned to the counter minutes later, and Beverly once again took the lead. "We'll need something in writing that says we'll be held harmless for handing over that information."

"Sure thing. Go ahead and write it up. We'll look it over and sign it. Our lips are sealed, and I'm sure you aren't about to tell your supervisor, am I right?"

"Of course we won't tell anyone. The paper is just for our peace of mind."

189

Minutes later, with the list of students' names in hand, Amber and I followed the hallway back to the main entrance. I pushed open the double doors, and we headed to the cruiser. As we walked, I glanced at the faculty parking lot again, remembering the morning Daphne was discovered dead in her car. We had to solve this case for both her and Becca. Justice needed to be served.

I stopped dead in my tracks when I saw a man walking toward a white SUV. "Amber, isn't that Mr. Morton?"

She looked over her shoulder. "Where?"

"Over there in the faculty lot." I pointed at the vehicle, but he had already climbed in and was pulling away. I yelled and began chasing the SUV, but it was too late. He had turned onto the street and was gone.

"What the hell were you doing?" Amber asked as I returned to the cruiser.

"I swear that was Mr. Morton."

"Leaving the faculty parking lot? He said he was a real estate investor, not somebody who works at the university."

"I know one thing for sure. I'm looking over those witness statements again to see what he drives. That looked like an Explorer to me."

Amber got in behind the wheel and started the car. She tipped her head toward the dash-mounted computer. "Just pull his name from the DMV database. It's faster."

"Yeah, smart thinking. I'll do that right now." I woke up the computer and logged in. Seconds later, I was on the DMV site for Wisconsin and typed in his name. I turned to Amber, and my jaw dropped as if its hinges had snapped.

"Amber, his name is Mike. Mike Morton, remember?"

"Yeah, but he isn't a freshman or a student. Don't get stuck on the name Mike. There are plenty of them. We need to find the right guy, and that man you saw in the parking lot probably wasn't even Mr. Morton."

I ignored Amber's comment and glanced at the screen as the computer was doing its search. "Shit, there are two hundred and seventeen men named Michael Morton with vehicles registered in the state. What town did he say he lived in?"

"He didn't."

"Fine, then I'll pull up each driver's license photo." I set the page to show fifty thumbnails at a time. I gave each one on the first page a glance then moved on to page two. "There he is, the fourth person on line three." I clicked on the thumbnail, and his driver's license photo filled the screen. "It shows that he lives on the outskirts of North Bend."

Amber stopped at the red light. "Is the address beyond the city limits and in the county's jurisdiction?"

"Give me a second to check the map. Yep, off of Highway Z. Now let's see what vehicles are registered to him." I tapped the options on the sidebar, and the next page showed his registered vehicles. "Sure as shit, a white Explorer, and it looks like that's his only car."

"Okay, so because he was at the university, that makes him a killer? I doubt if Jack would go along with that."

I huffed. "No, but why was he parked in the faculty lot?"

When the light changed to green, Amber pressed the gas. We were two miles from the sheriff's office. "Maybe he saw a nearly empty lot and parked. Remember that picture in Becca's phone gallery? He was probably at the college to sign something as a parent."

"Doubt it. I'm digging deeper. The guy was a tool, anyway, talking down to us like he did. Plus, I got a raging headache when he showed up. Maybe he's a misogynist who likes killing college girls."

Amber frowned. "I think you need some coffee. You're going off the rails. Let's review the list of students, separate all the Mikes from the rest, and see if they had any classes in common with Becca before we start accusing random people of murder when they happen to walk out of the university's door."

"Whatever. I'm still running it by Jack." After Amber parked in the empty space meant for the cruisers, I climbed out of the car and crossed to our building. We entered the bull pen to see two people sitting with Jack in his office. I raised my brows at Billings, who was on the phone. He shook his head, so I turned to Clayton and whispered. "What's going on, and who are those people?"

"We're in the middle of a new shit storm."

"Something with the pizza place or Becca's apartment?" I asked.

"Neither. Pizza Pie was clean, no complaints or issues with the health department, and Kyle and Dan are still working the apartment."

Amber nodded toward Jack's door. "Then what?"

Billings hung up the phone and shook his head. "Damn it. The van that was towed in this morning and sitting in the impound lot *does* belong to their daughter."

I took a seat at my desk. "Keep your voice down, Adam. Who is the daughter, and why are they here?"

"They're Mr. and Mrs. Hahn, and their daughter, Naomi, went missing. Nobody has seen her since Tuesday, when she left the campus."

Amber cupped her hand and whispered. "Another student?"

Chad gave her a nod. "The parents weren't that concerned until yesterday, when they couldn't get through to her on the phone. They texted her but said the return texts seemed suspicious. They weren't written the way Naomi speaks. They contacted every friend they could think of, but without Naomi's phone, they were sure they missed some. Anyway, nobody has actually seen her or heard her voice. Patrol noticed a van at Riverview Park yesterday and ticketed it last night when it was still there after the park closed. This morning, it was towed to Impound, where it's still sitting. Now the parents showed up to file a missing persons report."

I glanced through the wall of glass. "The shit keeps piling up."

Clayton agreed. "That's putting it lightly."

"Kate is rubbing off on you, Chad. I think you need some coffee too. We know nothing about this Naomi other than she hasn't been in contact with her parents for two days. She's considered missing, not dead. Maybe she went on a quick out-of-town trip with one of her friends to celebrate the end of the school year. You know how teenagers are."

I gave Adam a quick look and noticed his furrowed brow.

I was sure his concerns went to Mia and her safety while she was away at college. Amber crossed to the coffee station, came back with the carafe, and filled our cups.

"Here, calm your nerves. It doesn't mean this case is related to the others."

Minutes later, Jack stepped out of his office and escorted Mr. and Mrs. Hahn to the door. "I think I have everything I need for now. One quick question, though. Did Naomi go to Riverview Park often?"

The couple looked at each other and shook their heads. "Not to our knowledge, Lieutenant Steele."

Jack put his hand on Mr. Hahn's shoulder. "Keep in touch with Naomi's friends and let us know if you hear anything. Meanwhile, the missing persons alert with all Naomi's identifiable features will hit every police department in the state. She'll show up, and hopefully she just went on an impromptu trip with a friend."

Mrs. Hahn wiped her eyes. She didn't look as optimistic as Jack tried to sound.

"I'll have my patrol units scour the county, and I'll contact the city boys. Is there any place in particular Naomi hung out?"

Mr. Hahn held the door open for his wife then looked back at Jack. "She liked to jog along the bike trail through town."

Jack nodded. "I'll let Chief Sanders know that, and we'll be in touch. Since her van is in the impound lot, anyway, we'll take a good look at its contents and let you know what we've found. Riverview Park will be searched thoroughly too."

"Thank you, Lieutenant."

Jack closed the door behind the couple and let out an exhausted-sounding sigh. "Can this week get any worse?"

Billings spoke up. "That was a rhetorical question, right?"

Jack pressed his temples. "Go home, it's after six o'clock. I'll let Horbeck and Jamison know about Naomi Hahn."

Chapter 45

A chilled bottle of beer sat on the table and formed a ring of condensation around its base. He wiped the water away with his forearm and placed the bottle on the classified section of the newspaper. His eyes searched the front page for the latest news on the deaths of the two university students.

"Aah, here we go. That's it—three paragraphs?" He chuckled at the lack of evidence from the buffoons who considered themselves law enforcement. "North Bend is the perfect place to commit crimes. The cops here are a joke." The article was the same as yesterday's, with a slightly different spin on the reporter's theory. He'd suggested the girls took their own lives, and he was convinced foul play wasn't the cause. Since no tampering was discovered with Becca's car, he was sure the pressures of college exams were to blame. "Not a bad theory to run with. Obviously, the cops are keeping tight-lipped about the real cause of death. I'm sure the toxicology reports have come in by now."

Mike had his doubts that Naomi would ever be discovered. Becca and Daphne's deaths could very well be blamed on food poisoning and an accidental drug overdose.

Neither could be proven as murder. And Naomi? She had disappeared without a trace. The cops had nothing.

I'll get away with this just like I got away with Isabelle's death. Not a trace of evidence led back to me. I outsmarted the cops then, and I will again. Anyone can be a cop, but it takes real intelligence to be a chemist and a killer.

Chapter 46

"You may not realize this, but I can read your mind."

I gave Amber my best eye-roll. "Really? So what am I thinking right now?"

"You're thinking about Mike Morton and how the second we get in the house, you're going to power up your laptop and do an internet search on him."

"Humph." I looked out the window so she wouldn't see my smile.

"Nothing to say?"

I shrugged. "I just want to eliminate him from our suspect pool."

"We don't have a suspect pool." Amber turned in to the driveway and pressed the remote. The overhead lifted, and she pulled in next to Jade's bright orange Mustang.

"Whatever, let's just say I'm being proactive." Inside the house, Spaz was immediately under my feet. I gave him a quick petting, ran down to my basement bedroom, and grabbed my laptop. Back upstairs, I settled in at the kitchen table with a notepad and pen at my side.

Jade opened the slider and came in from the deck. "I

thought I heard you guys in here." She glanced at the clock. "Another long day and now you're on the computer? You're like a dog with a bone, Kate." She took a seat next to me. "What are you looking up?"

Amber piped in. "She's trying to turn a real estate investor—who just happened to be a witness when Becca crashed her car—into the university student killer."

"Is that what you guys gave him as a moniker?"

"No, it's just what I called him in the moment. To be honest, we don't know anything for sure."

I reminded Amber of the unusual lack of groceries and empty containers in Becca's apartment. "Somebody removed those items, Amber. There's no denying that."

"True but let me play devil's advocate for a second. What if Becca bought those groceries for somebody who was less fortunate? Maybe they weren't for her at all."

Jade looked at me. "Amber does have a point, you know."

"Whatever. I'm still going to do an internet search on Mike Morton." I typed his name into the search bar and got thousands of results. I groaned. "I think I better narrow this down to Wisconsin only." I changed my search parameters and checked again. "Now there's twice as many names as there were in the DMV database."

Amber poured three glasses of iced tea and set two of them in front of Jade and me. "That's because not everyone in Wisconsin named Mike Morton has a car."

I let out an irritated sigh and typed "Mike Morton real estate investor" into the search bar. Nothing came up. I deleted that search and typed in his name with his address—

the results showed only the last time that property was sold. My frustration grew quickly. "Why doesn't anything come up other than his driver's license information?"

"Who knows? What do you guys want for dinner?" Amber walked into the kitchen and pulled open the freezer door. "How about a pizza? It's getting too late to make something from scratch."

I nodded. "Yeah, sure."

"So why are you checking out this guy in particular?" Jade asked.

"Because I saw him walk out of the university earlier."

"So?"

"So, it's odd for a real estate investor—as he claims to be—to walk out of the university and climb into an SUV that was parked in the faculty lot."

"Then search his name and add UWWC next to it."

"Yeah, good idea." I tapped away at the keys and hit Enter. "Holy shit! His name came up as a professor at the university."

"No way!" Amber jammed her face in front of the screen and blocked my view. "What courses?"

"I don't know. I can't see the screen." I pushed her away and clicked the link to the "Rate my professor" website. Dozens of student reviews for both botany and chemistry classes popped up. I grabbed my phone. "Oh my God, it has to be him."

"What are you doing?" Amber asked.

"Calling Clayton. Why didn't he or Billings mention the professor's name? Both Daphne and Becca took chemistry classes."

"Wait a sec. Let's think this through before we jump the gun."

I reluctantly hung up my phone.

"Mike Morton's name never came up when we were all together. Donnelly interviewed him at the scene as a witness to Becca's accident, you and I interviewed him later at the restaurant along with those other witnesses, and Clayton and Billings interviewed him as a professor at the university. All of our notes are in different files."

My mind went back to Lena's comment after the tox report showed Becca had died of botulism poisoning. I looked at Amber. "Do you remember what Lena said to us when we were going to check out Becca's apartment?"

"Something to the effect that if we didn't find any expired foods, she would lean more toward Becca's death being a deliberate act."

"Yeah, and she also said it would take a very knowledgeable person, likely with a degree in chemistry, to make that toxin, and I bet Mike Morton has that knowledge."

"You're absolutely right, but what about the fentanyl?" Amber asked.

"Who knows what his credentials are? Maybe he's able to order it online."

Jade added her opinion. "So you have a chemistry professor named Mike and two dead college students. I still don't see the connection, and neither will the district attorney. In America, you can't arrest somebody based on mere suspicion. Without probable cause or substantial evidence, the DA will never let this go to court."

I objected. "But he's capable of making the botulism toxin."

"How do you know that, Kate? He's a chemistry professor, not a mad scientist. You need proof."

I ground my fists into my eyes. "And how do we get that?"

"Was there DNA or prints at either scene?"

"Nothing that was in the system," I said.

"Did Lena print both girls?"

Amber pulled the pizza out of the oven and sliced it. She brought it to the table along with plates and a stack of napkins. "She said she did."

"Most cunning criminals wear gloves. It's the rage killers who don't plan ahead. If Daphne and Becca were really murdered—"

I began to interrupt, but Jade held up her hand. "Just hear me out. It's likely that the killer's prints won't be found anywhere if those deaths were planned. If you really feel this professor is your guy, you're going to have to come up with a valid reason why he'd do such an act."

"He did seem like a jerk when we interviewed him."

Jade smiled. "Being a jerk doesn't make somebody a killer. You need to dig into his background. Maybe he has a criminal record. Interview his neighbors, his associates at the college, that type of thing. Get into his head. You won't have a case unless you do. Just keep in mind to tread lightly. Without a shred of evidence, the county could be looking at a lawsuit for ruining a man's career."

I backed off for the moment. Jade was right, and we'd discuss it with Jack tomorrow. God knew he needed a night without drama. We had to play it smart since we were dealing with an educated man, not a two-bit street thug. I didn't know how we'd prove Mike Morton was our man, but my gut told me my instincts were right, and so far, it had never steered me wrong.

I powered down my computer but not my brain. I knew I had a restless night of sleep ahead of me. We dug into the pizza without saying much, and I was sure our minds were full of questions, but at that point, we had no answers.

Chapter 47

I shook three ibuprofen tablets into my hand and gulped them down with a glass of water. I wasn't about to let that throbbing headache ruin my day. I couldn't get to work soon enough, and my to-do list was growing exponentially. A quick cup of coffee and an English muffin would hold me over until lunch. I yelled down the hallway toward Amber's bedroom as I popped a muffin in the toaster for her. "Are you ready to go?"

"Jeez, where's the fire? I need something to eat first."

"There's an English muffin in the toaster for you, and I've already poured your coffee."

Amber sat at the breakfast bar and waited for the muffin to pop up. "You really are like a dog with a bone."

A plate sat on the counter, and I grasped the knife that already has a slab of butter balanced on the tip. I stared at the toaster, waiting for the muffin to pop up. "It's him, Amber. I can feel it."

"Did you dream about him?"

"Maybe, and whatever I dreamt gave me a pounding headache. I just don't remember the details."

"You had a headache when we interviewed him at the restaurant too."

I remembered. "It could be that transference thing again."

"But why a headache?"

I shrugged. "I don't know yet, but it will come together. It has to." I slid the plate across the breakfast bar. "Hurry and eat so we can go."

It was my turn to drive, and I was sure I exceeded the speed limit by ten miles an hour. I couldn't help myself, and I saw Amber's side-eyed glance.

"Looking for a speeding ticket?"

"No." I let off the gas. "Sorry, but this case needs to be solved before another student dies."

Amber patted my shoulder. "Tomorrow is the last day of finals before the summer break. We'll get the perp, whether he's a professor, a student, or neither. I'm confident in our ability to solve cases and we've proved ourselves time after time. This is a really tough one since we don't know without a doubt that the cause of death was murder. Lena still hasn't filled in that box on the death reports."

I knew we had our work cut out for us. "Should I tell Jack my theory first, or should we go through the list of students' names?"

"Jack definitely needs to know that Mike Morton, the witness, and Mike Morton, the professor, are one and the same."

"Damn it, I just thought of something else." I jerked my head toward the back seat floor. "Grab my purse and pull out my list. I want you to add something before it slips my mind."

Amber opened my purse and flattened the list out on the dash. "Okay, go ahead."

"Write down the fact that Mr. Morton was behind Becca on her way to school that morning. The question is why? He doesn't live anywhere near Kewaskum. Was he following her? Was he waiting to see if she'd crash? And if he was, he had to know she was going to. Donnelly's account of Morton's witness statement said he acted detached and indifferent about the whole thing when he was interviewed."

"That's right, it did. Way to go, girl. That's what I call thinking like a top-notch detective."

I felt a sense of relief. We might get the evidence we needed after all. "Also, we have to check out whether there are any video cameras near Becca's apartment. If he was lying in wait, we might catch his vehicle in the area."

"You're absolutely right, and Pizza Pie was only a block from her apartment. They might have cameras. I'll write that down too, and if he came from North Bend, he'd have to pass the pizza parlor on his way to her apartment."

I inhaled deeply and let it out gradually. "But it's all circumstantial. We're trying to make a case out of something that might be nothing more than a crazy coincidence. Just like Jade said, we still need proof."

"And as soon as we rally our team together and narrow down the students named Mike who had classes with Becca and eliminate them, we can focus on Morton. We'll get the proof we need, one way or another."

We arrived at work at seven fifty. I needed to catch Jack right away before our day began to fill with unplanned events. We entered the bull pen, and my eyes shot toward his office immediately. I was thankful Jack was inside and sitting alone at his desk.

I headed toward his door. "I'm going to suggest we go into the conference room for this powwow."

Amber stashed her purse in the bottom desk drawer and headed toward the coffeemaker.

I rapped on Jack's half-closed door.

"Yeah?"

I pushed the door open wider and peeked in. "I need to speak with you, Boss. Is this a good time?"

Jack minimized the screen on his laptop and gave me his attention. "Better now than later. There's always the chance of a shit storm heading our way, you know."

"I know that all too well. I have a theory on the UWWC case that I'd like to share with everyone. I think it holds merit."

Jack looked surprised. "Really? Then I say let's get to it." He tipped his wrist. "Give me five minutes, then we'll meet in the conference room. I just need to close out a few things."

"Sure thing, thanks." I closed Jack's door and gave Amber a nod.

Clayton grinned. "Got a covert operation in the works?"

"Nope, you're both expected to sit in. Conference room in five."

Clayton and Billings grabbed their notepads, pens, and coffee cups then took off. I carried Amber's cup and my own, and she took the carafe and the tray containing creamer, stirring sticks, napkins, and the sugar packets. With each of us seated at the long oval table, we waited for Jack to arrive.

Chapter 48

Jack coughed into his fist then took a sip of water from the plastic cup in front of him. "First off, Amber, thanks for making a decent pot of coffee." He glanced at Adam. "Sorry, Billings, but your coffee could put hair on a woman's chest." We laughed, and Jack turned to me. "Okay, all joking aside, Kate has something important to share with us about the UWWC case, so let's give her our full attention."

Clayton rearranged himself in his chair to face me and opened his notepad. He was ready to go.

I began with everyone's eyes focused on me. "What I saw yesterday when Amber and I left the university is what started the ball rolling. I guess you'd say the timing couldn't have been better. I walked out of the building with the list of freshmen's names when I glanced over to the faculty parking lot with thoughts of Daphne on my mind. Seconds later, I saw Mr. Morton climb into a white Explorer, which absolutely threw me for a loop."

Billings frowned. "You mean Professor Morton?"

"Yes, but we didn't know he was a professor. It's the same Mr. Morton that Donnelly interviewed from the crash site and the same man Amber and I interviewed at the restaurant. He told us he was a real estate investor."

Jack spoke up. "Why does that surprise you? He could be both."

I looked at Chad. "Go ahead, Clayton. Tell Jack what kind of professor he is—and by the way, his first name is Mike."

Chad looked at Billings and shook his head. "He's a chemistry and botany professor, but we didn't know he was a witness at the crash site since nobody mentioned the witnesses' names to us. Kate, you and Amber took over that side of the investigation while we focused on the school. That seems really coincidental."

"Too coincidental for my liking," I said. "Remember Lena telling us it would take somebody with a chemistry degree to make clostridium botulinum?"

"Damn it." Jack rubbed his brow. "She did say that, didn't she?"

"Oh my God, I just thought of something else, and it explains the next thing I was about to say."

Jack locked eyes with me and took a sip of coffee. "Go on."

"While we were driving to work this morning, it occurred to me that Mr. Morton doesn't live anywhere near Kewaskum."

Jack raised a curious brow. "And you know that how?"

"Like I said, this began yesterday. I pulled up his driver's license last night, and then Jade suggested—"

Jack rolled his eyes. "Kate, how many times have I told you two that Jade doesn't work with us anymore."

"I know, but we live together, and she's super smart. She gave us good advice."

"Which was?" Adam asked.

"To do a search for his name with UWWC after it. That's when it came up that he was a professor at the college. Anyway, back to my original story, I wondered why he was at the accident scene when he lives in North Bend. The fact that he stuck around tells me he wanted to witness the devastation and see if Becca was dead."

"Good point," Chad said.

Amber added her two cents. "We asked him what he was doing that morning and where he was going. His response was that he was just driving around."

"Right—an insomniac who likes to hang out at fatal car accidents," Clayton said.

I smirked in agreement. "My theory is he wanted to see if she would crash her car. Meaning, he's the one who took those items out of her apartment because he didn't want them found. He tainted the milk, the creamer, the water, and the three-bean salad. He knew she didn't have long to live, and maybe he was even surprised that she made it through the night. That's why he followed her down the highway."

Jack set down his pen and scratched his cheek. "So he was sitting on the sidelines and watching from his car to see if she would leave for school or not."

"Exactly! He has the capability and intelligence to make the botulism toxin. He put it in her food when she was at school then took the containers away later. There's no other explanation."

"But there weren't any signs of forced entry."

I let out a sigh. "Well, he got in somehow. I think we should check the area for video cameras. Maybe we'll catch his vehicle near her apartment."

Amber turned to Jack. "The question is, since he's our only person of interest so far, should we focus on Morton or the students named Mike?"

"We don't have evidence against him yet," Jack said. "And until we do, we can't let on that we suspect him. There's a fine line we have to walk until we get proof that he's the killer. Forget the creepy-boy theory and focus all of your attention on Morton. Why Becca and Daphne? Did he have a thing for both of them that wasn't reciprocated?"

"Wait! I just thought of something else. Becca was on the pill, yet she didn't have a boyfriend. Do you think Morton was forcing her to have sex with him? She did tell Jodi that she couldn't stand him, yet she didn't give her best friend any details. If that's what was happening, I'm sure Becca was humiliated and embarrassed but wanted to confide in her friend."

Jack nodded. "That makes sense, but how could he compel her to have sex unless he was blackmailing her about something? Dig in, people. Find out more about Becca and Daphne and look into their grades, see if they were failing any classes. Maybe he held their final grade over their heads. Check Morton's background, look for criminal activity, see if he has ever been arrested, hit every bullet point."

"Boss?"

"Yep." Jack lowered his cup and looked at me.

"I couldn't find any personal information on him last night. The only thing I could track was his driver's license and the UWWC site."

"Was there a professor biography on him?"

"I haven't looked into it yet, but that should give us something."

Jack jerked his chin toward Chad. "Clayton, get on that. Billings, start looking for bank records, previous addresses, etcetera. Enlist the help of Tech if you need to. Amber and Kate, head to Kewaskum and find a camera near Becca's apartment. We need irrefutable proof that Mike Morton followed her from her apartment that morning. He's going to be surveilled from this point forward as we gather every shred of evidence we need to make an arrest."

Chapter 49

Amber and I headed out. I drove as she used her phone's map to search the retail spaces near Becca's apartment. Even though Kewaskum was a small town, we wanted to see which stores or gas stations Mike Morton would have had to pass to get to Becca's apartment.

"Okay, there's that Quick-Mart on the left at the intersection of Highway 45 and H, a used-car dealership on the right at the edge of town, Pizza Pie a block south of the apartment, and everything else is farther north."

"Of those three places, somebody should have a camera, and I'm thinking the gas station is our best bet. If I remember correctly, it isn't very old, and everyone who drives north on Highway 45 would have to pass it to get to Kewaskum. Let's stop there first."

I turned in ten minutes later and parked alongside the gas station. I noticed a few corner-mounted cameras as we walked toward the building—a good sign. We entered, introduced ourselves to the very young-looking clerk, and asked about their surveillance system. We got a deer-in-the-headlights stare from him, meaning he didn't have a clue what we were talking about. He glanced at the clock. "The manager doesn't come in until ten. He'd know what you want, and the office is locked, anyway."

"How about giving the manager a call?" Amber said. "We can really use some help here, and we don't have a lot of time to waste."

"I guess I can do that."

"Great, thanks."

We walked outside to take a better look at the cameras. They both appeared to be facing the pumps, a position commonly used to catch the plate number and description of anyone who attempted a pump-and-run tactic.

I shielded my eyes as I looked up and then out. "I wonder if those cameras actually catch the highway at all since the gas station is set back off the road."

"I guess we won't know until we check the footage." Amber turned toward the building. "Let's see if the kid got ahold of the manager."

Back inside, we approached the counter, where the young man had just hung up the phone.

"What's the verdict?" I asked.

"The manager is heading out soon, but he lives in Fond du Lac. It's going to take an hour or so since he was just getting up."

I frowned. "Okay, thanks." I handed him my card. "Call the bottom number on this card when he gets here. Meanwhile, we're going to check out a few other places in town."

Amber climbed into the passenger seat and buckled her

belt. "Let's try Pizza Pie. The chances of catching Becca on tape from Monday night are pretty good if they actually have cameras. I'm sure that living only a block away, she would have walked there to pick up her calzone."

We bypassed the used-car dealership for the time being, but we'd stop there later if necessary.

I pointed to the left as I slowed down to the posted speed limit. "There it is. Tiny place and an even tinier parking lot." I pulled in and parked in one of the four spots. Everything else in that area was street parking only. I glanced farther down the road as we exited the cruiser. "I can see the apartment building from here."

"That's all fine and good but check out the storefront. I don't see any cameras."

"Crap." I walked to each side of the building and looked down the entire length of the wall—no cameras. I groaned my disappointment. "Let's have a quick talk with them, anyway."

Inside, we asked to see the manager. While we waited, I scanned the room and caught sight of a camera mounted above each side of the counter. I elbowed Amber. "There and there." I pointed at them. "They must catch the cash registers and the customers standing at the counter."

Seconds later, a thirtysomething gentleman walked out from a back room and approached us. "I'm the manager, John McKay. Is there something I can help you with?"

We introduced ourselves and asked to speak privately with him. He escorted us to his office behind the kitchen and offered us two folding chairs. "Sorry about the cramped quarters, but we want to keep as much floorspace as possible for the dining area."

"Not a problem, Mr. McKay."

"Please, call me John."

Amber nodded and pulled out her notepad. She flipped the pages until she found what she needed. "We'd like to see your counter camera footage from Monday evening."

"Sure thing. Do you have a time in mind?"

Amber checked her notes. "Yes, according to a receipt we have, a take-out calzone was purchased at six fifty-two."

"Take-out?"

"That's correct," I said.

"I'm sorry, but the carryout counter is across the hall. The people pick up their food at an outside window similar to a drive-through. We just don't have the space at the counter for people to wait around for their food."

"So, you're saying what?"

"We don't have cameras at the take-out window."

"Shoot. Sounds like that's a dead end."

We thanked him for his time and left. Outside, we walked to the apartment complex and checked every building along the route. Most were small houses that had been turned into commercial properties. A laundromat, a law office, and a real estate office were squeezed between Pizza Pie and Becca's apartment building. We glanced at the corners of each structure but didn't see cameras mounted anywhere.

Amber turned around. "Damn it, let's head to the cruiser and check the used-car dealership."

We had turned to go back when an idea popped into my

216

head. "Let's make a stop at the real estate agency. Maybe they know Mike Morton or the person who owns Becca's apartment building. It's a small town, and many people use local agents to buy properties."

"Sounds logical."

A bell rang out when I pushed open the door. Since the office had only two desks less than ten feet away and facing the front windows, I thought the presence of a bell was odd unless the agent happened to be in a back room when a potential client walked in. One desk was occupied by a middle-aged woman, and the other was empty. A name plate with Marla Cannon written across it in gold text sat at the front of her desk.

"Good morning, ladies. How can Midwest Properties help you find the home of your dreams?"

I chuckled to myself as I pulled out my badge and noticed how quickly her cheerful expression faded.

"Oh my word, are we in trouble for something?"

"Not at all," Amber said, "unless there's something you need to disclose."

"No, of course not, so please, have a seat. I take it you aren't here to ask about properties for sale."

"That's correct, but thanks, anyway," I said. "We need to know if you're familiar with a local real estate investor named Michael Morton."

She rubbed her chin. "No, that name doesn't ring a bell. Should it?"

"Not necessarily. Would you happen to know who owns that eight-unit apartment building to your north?"

"Oh, sure. We worked with a Martin Glover on that purchase. He signed off on everything and mentioned possible future purchases on behalf of a C Corp. He was an odd one, though."

I furrowed my brows. "Odd how?"

"He just preferred to do everything via email and phone calls. He contracted with our agency on that building without ever meeting us in person. I've never had a client do that before. He purchased the property sixteen months ago."

Amber pulled out her notepad. "Is Martin the owner of the property or just the person who handled the sale?"

"Sorry, we aren't privy to the actual mortgage documents, so I couldn't say either way."

Amber wrote that down. "And you said it was sixteen months ago?"

"Yes, that's correct. A year ago February."

We stood and shook her hand. "Okay, thanks. You've been very helpful."

When we left, the bell rang at our backs.

"I don't know if that information does anything for us or not," Amber said.

"True, but it doesn't hurt to have as many names as possible. The owner will know soon enough that Becca's unit will be available for rent again. Maybe we should contact this Martin Glover, anyway, and he can pass the message on unless he actually is the owner." I glanced at my watch. "Let's go back to the gas station. The manager must be there by now."

Amber checked in with Jack as I drove. The call was short,

and she hung up just before I turned in to Quick-Mart's driveway.

"What did he say?"

"Silver has eyes on Morton's Explorer. Guess he's at the college doing whatever he does there."

"Probably mixing up poisons."

Amber groaned. "That's a scary thought. Billings is trying to access his accounts and phone records, but he's hitting a brick wall."

"And Clayton?"

"According to his biography, Mike Morton has been at UWWC for a year and a half, is originally from Madison, and taught chemistry at UWM for nine years prior to moving here."

"He'd go from there to a two-year university in North Bend? That doesn't make sense to me. Married, unmarried, kids?"

"The bio said unmarried."

"Everything should be easy enough to confirm with a phone call."

We entered the gas station and approached the same clerk as before. "Has your manager arrived yet?"

"Yep, he just walked in. I'll get him." The young man returned seconds later. "He wants you to come to his office. That's where the security system is, anyway."

I shrugged. "Yeah, sure. Lead the way."

We followed the attendant down the hallway to a closed door bearing a plaque with Office written across it. He knocked twice, and a voice from the other side said to enter.

The young man opened the door, allowed us through, then walked away. Inside sat an attractive man looking very casual in shorts and a T-shirt. The space, about the size of a normal bedroom, was filled with football memorabilia, particularly that of our favorite green and gold team. I liked him already. He stood, introduced himself as Anthony Calderone, and offered us the comfortable-looking guest chairs that faced his desk. "Tommy said you're detectives from the sheriff's office?"

Amber spoke up. "We are, and we can really use your help. We're looking for a white late-model Explorer that may have passed by here anytime between Monday afternoon and Tuesday morning."

"So not *getting* gas, just passing by on the highway?"

I felt a letdown coming. "That's what we're looking for, yes."

He scratched his head. "To be honest, I don't think you'll catch anything because of the overhead awnings. Our cameras are meant as deterrents for pump-and-runs. Being right off the highway made it too easy for passersby to fill their gas tank and make a run for it. Our problems have gone down significantly since we installed those cameras."

"Can we take a quick look, anyway?"

"Sure, be my guest."

He tapped a few computer keys and asked us to come around to his side of the desk. "This is what the cameras catch from both angles." He pointed. "See how the rooftop blocks the entire highway? You only see the six bays and the vehicles at each pumping station. You can't even see the driveway."

"Yeah, so unless he stopped here and filled up, we've got nothing."

"That's right. You're welcome to sit here and watch the in-and-out footage if you like, but from Monday afternoon to Tuesday morning at normal speed will take a long time."

"How about from six thirty until seven thirty Tuesday morning?" I asked.

"Probably about twenty minutes if I speed it up a bit."

Amber nodded. "Let's give it a try. You never know when something helpful might fall in your lap."

"Okay. I'll set those parameters and leave you to it. I'll be out front if you need anything. Just toggle these buttons to go back and forth."

"Thanks, Mr. Calderone."

He walked out and closed the door.

I looked at Amber as she began playing the footage. "Do you think Mike would have actually stopped here for gas on his way to watch Becca's apartment Tuesday morning?"

"No clue, but what's twenty minutes of our time?"

"I guess you're right."

Chapter 50

We scored a big fat zero at Quick-Mart—Mike Morton never pulled into the station.

"I guess the car dealership is our last hope to see him drive by. He had to unless he sat on a side road off the highway and just watched for Becca to pass him."

I shook my head. "I don't know. He strikes me more as the type who would like to savor every minute of that morning, from the second Becca walked out of her apartment until she died in the crash." I pulled into the lot and parked then rolled the kinks out of my neck. "I hope this isn't going to be strike three."

Inside, we made our introductions and were led back to the room with the surveillance system. The general manager told us that they'd had a rash of vandalism and just recently installed wide-angle cameras to catch the entire lot. I hoped it would show us what we were desperate to see. We gave him the same parameters as we did at the gas station—late Monday afternoon to Tuesday morning around seven thirty. He called in the technician to assist us then excused himself.

With my fist under my chin and my elbow on the desk, I

stared at the screen, afraid to blink. Amber sat like a matching bookend on the other side of the technician. Every so often, I glanced at the time stamp at the lower right of the screen. We had only twenty minutes left. My chair squeaked under my weight as I squirmed anxiously while trying to think of how Morton followed Becca without being seen on any surveillance system.

He's an intelligent man and planned her death. He had to know that cameras faced the main road coming into Kewaskum.

"Keep your eyes on the monitor, Amber. I have to check something on my phone."

"Sure thing."

I pulled up a map of Highway 45, knowing Morton wouldn't come across any camera until he reached the Quick-Mart station. I backtracked to see where intersecting roads turned off the highway and ran parallel all the way to Kewaskum. There were a few. I glanced back at the screen. "Anything?"

"Nope," Amber said.

I powered down my phone and watched the monitor until we had reached seven thirty-five—the reported time of the crash. Again, we had nothing. We thanked the technician and left. It was after eleven o'clock, and we hadn't made any headway.

"Here's what I think," I said as we climbed in the cruiser. "He had to have taken a parallel road into town. The guy isn't stupid."

Amber huffed. "He's on our radar, so he can't be that smart. He just thinks he is."

"I agree, but we need to go to the apartment, follow the street that exits out the side driveway, and see if it connects with a road farther back that runs parallel to the highway. There's a chance a business north of the apartment could have captured the Explorer on video beyond or behind the apartment. He had to be lying in wait, just not in a place where Becca could see him."

Amber nodded. "Yeah, that sounds good, but I want to give Jack the name Martin Glover first. Maybe he or one of the guys can track him down and pick his brain. Who knows, if the guy is local, it's possible he's seen the Explorer in Becca's neighborhood."

"Right, and Jack should follow up with the onsite manager too and see if he's back in town. He ought to know Becca's habits and what kind of company she kept."

I inspected my neglected manicure and listened to Amber's side of the conversation as she spoke with Jack.

"That's interesting. This case definitely has its twists and turns. Sure, we'll go back and bang on the door, and then we're going to see if there's a parallel road to the highway, one that Morton might have taken to avoid passing cameras. Yep, see you later." Amber clicked off the call.

"What's interesting?"

"The fact that Martin Glover *is* the on-site manager."

"What the hell? So he's the operations man and the property manager?"

"Sounds like it. Jack said his voicemail message said he'd be back in town as of last night. Let's shake his tree and see what he knows."

We returned to the apartment building and rapped on the first door. A shirtless man wearing pajama bottoms pulled the door open. It was nearing noon. I imagined we looked as startled as he did.

"Martin Glover?" Amber asked.

"Nope, Danny Greenly. Who are you?"

I jiggled my badge at the end of the lanyard. "Is this Martin Glover's residence?"

He looked upward as if he had to think of the correct response. "Technically, yeah, but he subleases it to me, and I forward maintenance issues to him. Guess you'd call me the middleman. Why?"

I ignored his question—we were conducting the interview, not him. "Do you know where Martin lives?"

"Nope, never asked."

"Does he ever shine around?"

Danny stared at Amber. "Not really. There's no reason to. He has me, but if you have concerns about the building, why don't you talk to him?"

"That's why we're here, but we need to speak to him in person."

He scratched his head. Sorry, like I said—"

I interrupted. "We're cops. We'll track him down. Did you know Becca Morbeck?"

"No, she never had any complaints. I did hear about her death, though—a real shame."

I cocked my head. "Do you have a key to her apartment, Danny?"

"Sure, I have a key to all the apartments, not that I've ever used them."

Amber wrote that down. "And Mr. Glover does too?"

He shrugged. "I assume so."

I gave Amber a glance. "Okay, one more question before we leave. Why do the manager calls go to Mr. Glover instead of you?"

"I guess he handles the C Corp business too, but like I said, I'm the middleman for the tenants here—a face, if you will. They don't have his number, only I do. Guess he doesn't want to be bothered unless it's absolutely necessary. You know how tenants can be. They tell me the problems, if there are any, and if it's warranted, I pass the information along to Mr. Glover."

Amber frowned. "Yeah, that seems like more work than necessary. Why not just have a real manager on site?"

He shrugged. "My rent is cheap, so I don't ask questions, and doing this doesn't interfere with my life. I do have a real job—a late-night gig stocking grocery shelves."

"Got it." I handed him my card. "You'll let us know if anything else comes to mind?"

"Yeah, no sweat."

Amber and I left and exited out the side driveway next to Becca's apartment onto Clinton Street. I checked my map again and handed the phone to Amber. I showed her the route I wanted to follow. "We need to get to Edgewood and then go south. That'll take us to H, we'll head to Kettle View, and that runs parallel to the highway."

"Yep, I see it."

We were back at the sheriff's office by twelve fifteen. I was curious to learn more about this Mr. Glover—a man who seemed to have a reason to stay in the shadows.

Chapter 51

With the ham-and-cheese sub unwrapped and a diet soda at my side, I settled in at my desk. I powered up my computer and typed Martin Glover's name into the search bar.

Jack leaned against the doorframe of his office and dug into a bag of kettle chips. "Why don't you turn off your brain for a half hour and take a real lunch break with the rest of the gang?"

I smiled. "Isn't that like the pot calling the kettle black?"

"Touché." He crossed the room and took a seat next to me. "What are you working on?"

"This Martin Glover is an enigma, and I want to know why. There isn't a logical reason that he'd stay in the shadows if he's the manager of Becca's apartment building, but even the real estate woman said he was odd. In essence, he handled the purchase, yet the real estate agency never met him face-to-face."

"Yeah, that is odd. Go ahead and research the guy."

"So Billings didn't have any luck with Morton?" I asked.

"Nope. There aren't any credit cards or bank accounts that come up for him."

"So how does he pay his mortgage?"

"Good question unless he just rents the property and pays with money orders or cash. Billings is going to walk over to the courthouse after lunch and check with the Register of Deeds office for Morton's address. We'll need a copy of it, anyway. We should know who the actual owner is soon enough."

"Did Clayton check with UWM about Morton's claim of working there for nine years?" I asked.

"He left a message, but nobody has called back yet."

"Hurry up and wait, right?"

Jack crunched a chip and held the bag open for me. I reached in and pulled out a handful.

"Yep, it seems like we do that a lot around here." Seconds later, his desk phone rang. He stood and excused himself. "Go ahead and finish the chips. I need to start eating healthier, anyway."

I stared at the bag then placed it on Clayton's desk. A round of cursing and the sound of Jack's fist connecting with his desk got my immediate attention. Something was definitely wrong.

He stormed out of his office. "Gather the team and head to Jackson City marsh. Donnelly was just flagged down by the DNR as he was making his rounds south of town. Sounds like they found a female body in the marsh while they were grooming the trails. I'll be right behind you after I round up Lena and Forensics."

"Damn it!" I leapt from my chair, grabbed my gear, and headed for the lunchroom. "Guys, we have a dead female at the Jackson City marsh. Jack wants us to leave now."

Clayton jammed his sandwich in his mouth and headed for the bull pen, with Amber and Billings on his heels.

I called out to Amber. "I'll start the car."

Twenty minutes later, our group of four arrived at the state wildlife area.

"Looks like Karen is here too." I killed the engine along the four-foot-wide gravel shoulder and climbed out of the car just as Clayton snugged his cruiser at our rear bumper. We headed down the trail toward Tim and Karen, who were standing alongside the DNR truck with the two rangers.

Clayton asked a few questions while we waited for Jack, Lena, and the forensic team to arrive. "How'd you guys happen to find the body?"

Tom Rollins spoke up. "It wasn't hard. We just followed our noses. We assumed it was a coyote kill—a deer, most likely—and were going to remove it from the park. That's when we saw her nude body partially exposed under a pile of leaves. We backed out of the scene immediately."

"Good thinking," Clayton said. "The forensic team and the medical examiner should be here any minute. Did you guys notice tire tracks leading back?"

Bill Franklin pointed at the ground. "With the heavy tree cover, it's pretty dark back here. To be honest, I wasn't looking for anything unusual as I backed in. I focused on avoiding tree limbs."

"Understood. We'll probably need you to pull out to the road, but let's wait for our team to show up first. They may want to take pictures of how things look right now."

Moments later, Jack, Lena, Jason, Kyle, and Dan arrived. They followed Tom Rollins to the body then asked him to wait back at the truck. Minutes later, Kyle and Jason stepped out of the brush and said Bill should park the truck along the road so they could back in the vans. With that done, Kyle grabbed the forensic bag, and Dan secured his camera's strap around his neck. They spent the next twenty minutes at the body while the rest of us waited on the trail.

Dan emerged from the woods first. "I've taken the initial photos of the body before and after we cleared away the leaves. Go ahead, Lena. We're good for the time being."

Jack and Lena disappeared into the brush.

"The only noticeable injuries on the body are from the wildlife. It's strange that we didn't see a wound substantial enough to kill her," Kyle said, "but Lena may find something definitive after the body has been cleaned."

I looked at Tom. "If you guys hadn't come out here to groom the trails, she could have gone undiscovered. Over time, there would have been no evidence of her being out here at all."

"That's especially true with the dense underbrush," Bill said. "This place is a haven for all kinds of animals, and at this time of year, the bug population is off the charts." He swatted a mosquito on his neck.

I jotted comments in my notepad as we waited.

Minutes later, Jack stepped out of the woods. "I think that's Naomi Hahn. The deceased has a four-leaf clover tattoo on her right ankle, and Naomi's mom described the same tattoo."

I dropped my notepad to the ground.

Jack looked startled. "You okay?"

My response was garbled as I knelt over to pick up my pad. I teetered for a second, and Jack grabbed my arm. "Amber, get her out of these woods and into the cruiser. Keep your eye on her and call me in five. If her head doesn't clear by then, take her to Emergency."

"You got it, Boss. Put your arm around my shoulder, Kate, and let me help you to the car."

Through my ringing ears, I heard Jack's voice in the distance. "How far back do you think the body is?"

Amber had a tight grip on me as I stumbled to the cruiser. "It's fifty feet."

She pulled open the door. "What are you talking about?"

"The body—it's fifty feet from the path."

"How would you know that? Never mind. Just lie back and close your eyes."

Chapter 52

Kyle nodded. "I was going to check the distance, anyway. Give me one second." He reached into his forensic bag and pulled out the laser tape measure then knelt to the ground and found a clear spot where he could see Lena through the brush. He aimed the tool at her back, clicked it on, and took a reading. "From here to the body is fifty-one feet."

Clayton wrote that in his notepad as Jack flicked a gnat off his arm. "How soon can my detectives begin searching the area?"

Dan scanned the surroundings. "We have no problem with you searching the trail and out by the road, but as soon as Lena finishes her field exam, we're going back in to take more pictures. We don't want to disturb the scene until we've photographed everything."

Jack tipped his chin at Clayton, Billings, Donnelly, and Karen. "Go ahead and look around on the trail then work your way to the road." He glanced at the patches of sky between the tree canopy. "It's dark back here, so use your flashlights if you need to. Anything that isn't native to the marsh needs to be bagged and tagged."

Clayton and Donnelly walked to the cruisers to grab the flashlights. Clayton peered in through our passenger window. "How are you doing, Kate?"

I sighed. "I'm better now, but I really got loopy back there after Jack said the deceased could be Naomi Hahn."

Clayton frowned at Amber then me. "Think it's that transference thing again?"

"I don't know, Chad. Naomi was a student at the university, just like Becca and Daphne were. If Morton is the culprit and these weird feelings I get are actually transference, then I'd put my money on him being Naomi's killer too. I felt like I had been drugged, like I was in some kind of stupor."

"I'll pass that information on to Jack and Lena. She'll do the usual exam and a tox screen for sure."

I reached for the door handle.

"What the hell are you doing?" Amber asked.

"I'm okay now. I just need to keep my distance from the body."

Chad jerked his chin toward the trail. "We're grabbing some flashlights to take back in. Why don't you two stay out here and search along the shoulders? Jack said if it isn't native to the marsh, then pick it up."

I stepped out of the cruiser. "That sounds good."

"I'm still going to keep my eye on you. One misstep and you're going back in the car," Amber said. After popping the trunk, she grabbed evidence bags and gloves, and we began searching the roadside. Amber searched the side our vehicles were parked on, and I took the east side of the road.

I combed through the ditches and gravel shoulders for anything that didn't belong there. Fifteen minutes into my search, I caught a glimpse of a shiny object when the sun hit it just right. I knelt to take a look.

Amber yelled across the road. "What have you got?"

"A pull tab from a soda can."

"Go ahead and bag it."

I did and continued on. Minutes later, the black van pulled out. Lena, Jason, and the body were on their way to the coroner's office. I waited until they passed, then began backtracking. I nearly missed it as I was about to cross the road. Lying where the gravel met the weeds was a cigarette butt. I picked it up and carried it to Amber's side of the road. "A memory just came to mind."

She glanced at the cigarette in my hand. "What do you remember?"

"Mike Morton's odor when he took his seat at the restaurant. He smelled like cigarettes."

"Let me have a look." Amber pinched the butt between her thumb and index finger. "Marlboro. Good memory, Kate. Now we just have to find out what kind of cigarettes he smokes."

We began our walk back to the trail. "Did you find anything?"

Amber shrugged. "A screw in the gravel and a glass shard. Nothing else."

We reached the guys halfway down the trail. "Anything?" Billings asked.

"I found a cigarette butt and a pull tab." I held up the

evidence bag. "How about you?"

"Karen found a few threads tangled in the brush. Whoever carried the victim there left a little bit of their shirt behind."

"That's something we can work with."

Jack put his hand on my shoulder. "Kate, how are you doing?"

"I'm okay now, Boss." I jiggled the bag. "This cigarette butt reminded me of the day when Amber and I met Mike Morton in the restaurant. I remember him smelling like cigarettes. The butt I found is Marlboro."

"I'll let Silver know to keep a close eye on Morton to see if he lights up. If he's lucky, he might be able to snag the butt when Morton puts it out."

Donnelly joined in on our conversation. "He was smoking when I interviewed him at the crash site. I saw him with my own eyes as he stomped the cigarette into the gravel. What are the odds that it's still out there?"

"I don't know, but you're about to find out. Do you think you remember where he was pulled over?" Jack asked.

"Sure, within a hundred feet or so."

"That's close enough for me. I'll give the evidence bags to Kyle, and you five head out. Karen, take over for Silver while he grabs a bite to eat, and then get back to your patrol duties. I'm going to stop at the station and touch base with Lena. I have to read over Naomi Hahn's description one more time, and if she is the victim, I'll have to make that difficult call to her parents."

We left in our cruisers and followed Donnelly to the

southbound lanes of the crash site. If luck was on our side, we'd find that one cigarette butt that would prove Mike Morton was the killer. Having matching DNA on both cigarettes would give us the evidence we needed to issue a search warrant on his property and end his killing spree once and for all.

Chapter 53

Jack returned to the sheriff's office, poured a cup of stale coffee, and took a seat behind his desk. He opened Naomi Hahn's folder and began reading through it.

Clayton's phone rang in the bull pen. Through the glass, Jack gave Chad's phone a glance.

It could be the university getting back to Chad.

He rose from his desk, crossed the bull pen, and answered it. "Lieutenant Jack Steele speaking. How may I help you?"

A female voice spoke up on the other end of the line. "Hello, this is Mary Johannsson from the administration office at UWM calling for Detective Chad Clayton. Is he available?"

"He isn't at the moment but go ahead and tell me about Michael Morton. I'm Detective Clayton's supervisor, and we've been waiting to hear back from you."

"I'm sorry for the delay, Lieutenant. Our entire system was recently updated, and some files have been archived. I had to do a little digging."

"Not a problem. What did you find out?"

"Many of the professors here are tenured, so the faculty

doesn't change often. The only professors who left our university on their own in the last few years were Isabelle and Martin Glover but at separate times. When Isabelle disappeared, gossip spread throughout the university about infidelity and possible foul play, but nothing ever became of it. Mr. Glover made his exit several months later, citing something about wanting to live in the US Virgin Islands. I think he really left because of the rumors. But as far as a Michael Morton goes, we've never had any professor here by that name."

Jack ground his fists into his eyes. "Do you still have the files for the Glovers at the university?"

Silence filled the other end of the phone line.

"Mrs. Johannsson, this is a very serious criminal matter. The Glovers aren't employed there any longer, so you don't have a confidentiality agreement with them, correct?"

"I suppose that's true."

"Then please don't make me go through the red tape of issuing a warrant."

"What exactly do you need, Lieutenant?"

"Both of their entire files emailed to me in PDF format right away. It's imperative that their photographs are included."

Jack heard a sigh on Mary's end. He was hopeful.

"Fine, I need your email address."

"Thank you." Jack gave her his email address and clicked off the call. He grabbed Naomi's folder and headed downstairs as he waited for the Glover files to land in his in-box. He rapped on the door then pushed it forward.

Jason sat at his desk in the coroner's office.

"Is Lena in the back?"

"Yep, she's washing the body before the initial exam. Give me a minute to let her know you're here."

Jack sat on a guest chair and reviewed Naomi's file. A minute later, the door to the autopsy room swung open. "You can go on back."

"Thanks, buddy."

Jack entered the cold room outfitted with stainless steel equipment. The victim lay on a washing table, and Lena had temporarily draped a white sheet over her body. Jack noticed her wet hair. "Sorry to interrupt, but what have you got so far?"

"Poor thing. She was such a tiny girl, just over one hundred pounds. Upon a visual exam, I haven't seen a COD yet. I haven't felt any head wounds under her hair, and she doesn't have anything jammed down her throat. I'll have to finish cleaning her thoroughly to see if I can locate any puncture wounds, but all of these insect and animal bites are going to make it difficult."

"No visible signs of a wound could mean poison like the others."

"It certainly can, and I'll send the blood samples to the lab immediately. This is obviously a homicide, Jack. I'd like to check her stomach contents as soon as I can."

Jack tipped his head toward a table near the wall. "I want to show you the description of Naomi Hahn given to me by her mother." They walked to the back of the room, where he opened the folder and handed his notes to Lena.

"Identifying features—black shoulder-length straight hair, green eyes, a scar on her left elbow from a bicycle injury when she was a kid, a tattoo of a green four-leaf clover on her right ankle, and fillings in two of her top left molars." Lena walked to the body. "Luckily rigor is subsiding." She lifted the arm of the deceased and checked the elbow with a magnifying glass. "I see a scar that looks like it had been stitched, and we already know she has a clover on her ankle." Lena used a mouth mirror to check for fillings. She turned to Jack. "Two on the top left."

"Okay, I'll give the parents a call and hopefully get their permission for an autopsy. I'll let you know as soon as they tell me, one way or another."

Jack took the two flights of stairs back to the bull pen and dropped into his office chair. The email had arrived. He bypassed the employment files for the moment and clicked on the photos. On the screen in front of him was the same photo Mike Morton had used on his UWWC biography.

"Arrogant son of a bitch." Jack grabbed a pen and paper.

I have to connect the dots. So Mike Morton and Martin Glover are one and the same. His UWWC bio said he wasn't married, but clearly, he was. So what happened to the wife?

He squeezed his head between his palms. "There's too much here for one person to figure out." Jack tapped his contact list, scrolled to Donnelly's cell number, then pressed the green call symbol.

Donnelly picked up immediately. "Hello, sir."

"Are you guys at the location?"

"We just exited our cars and began walking the shoulder."

"Okay, good." Jack jotted down more thoughts as he talked. "How much help do you really need out there?"

"One or two people should be fine."

"Okay, then tell Amber and Kate to head back. I need them here."

"You got it, Boss."

"And, Donnelly."

"Yes, sir?"

"Find that cigarette butt. It's crucial to this case."

Chapter 54

Jack made the difficult call to Mr. and Mrs. Hahn and asked them to come to the sheriff's office right away. He glanced through the glass wall when Amber and Kate entered the bull pen.

"What's up, Boss?" Amber asked.

"We need answers now. I have no doubt that the female from the woods is Naomi Hahn, and her folks are on their way. While they're here, I want both of you to work in the conference room and establish time lines, causes of death, and the evidence we have, beginning with Becca and through Naomi. Find everything you can about the girls, bullet point your notes, and put something together. There's a common factor between all of them that gave Morton a reason to kill them, so work on that too. The families want to bury their loved ones, the press is demanding answers, and the community wants to feel safe. Write down what we've done that has moved this case forward and what we still need to do. It turns out that Mike Morton and Martin Glover are the same person. I don't know what that's telling us other than he's changed his identity yet still uses his real name for certain things. A woman from UWM called back and said they've never had a chemistry professor named Mike Morton. She did say that they had a tenured couple named Martin and Isabelle Glover, but the wife just up and disappeared one day on a camping trip. Gossip about foul play surfaced due to rumors of infidelity on Isabelle's part, and several months later, Martin quit. She thought the rumors tarnished his sterling career, but he said he only wanted to fulfill their dreams of moving to the Virgin Islands."

"Well, that didn't happen, and his bio said he was unmarried."

"That's right, Kate, so find out what you can on Isabelle Glover. See if you can track down her location while I talk with Naomi's parents."

I rubbed my chin. "Two tenured professors giving up those kind of jobs? That already raises a red flag with me."

"Exactly. Why would anyone leave that kind of job to come to North Bend and start over? I want to know what he's hiding."

"Which one is his real name?" Amber asked.

"Not sure, but I'm leaning toward it being Martin Glover. He must have fake credentials for his alias. Gather every note you've taken so far, your laptop, a couple of legal pads, and head to the conference room. I'll join you as soon as I've finished talking to Mr. and Mrs. Hahn." Jack answered his ringing phone, said he'd be right out, and hung up. "Okay, they're here. Jan is going to forward all incoming calls to the conference room while I'm with Naomi's parents. I'm counting on you two. Dig deep."

Jack rolled his neck then headed to the reception area, where the couple was waiting. He reached out with a handshake. "Mr. and Mrs. Hahn, let's talk in my office."

"Do you have news of Naomi's whereabouts?"

"I do, Mrs. Hahn." Jack opened his office door and pointed at the guest chairs. "Have a seat."

Chapter 55

Amber and I sat at the table. She took notes while I entered information into my laptop. I had several tabs open that showed newspaper articles dated two years back about interviews with Martin Glover. His wife, a fellow professor at UWM, had vanished. The cops were suspicious, but his story never wavered. They were home by four thirty that Thursday before spring break and, with a week off, had plans to hike, camp, and fish at Devil's Lake State Park in Baraboo. In his statement to police, he said his wife, Isabelle, often hiked alone. As a botany professor, she liked to observe the plant life everywhere they went, and on that last day, she never returned to the campsite. In his account, he insisted they were deeply in love, had no marital problems, and planned on retiring to the US Virgin Islands one day. The search for Isabelle went on for weeks, but she was never found, and no proof of foul play was ever discovered.

I rubbed my forehead. Just reading the newspaper articles about him gave me a headache. "What he said to the police is a total contradiction to the rumors at the college, according to what Jack was told. The gossip mill said Isabelle was cheating, so he had to know about it, and stories like that spread like wildfire. Do you think he killed her? Maybe she was what sent him to crazy town."

"It's possible," Amber said, "but if the cops in Madison never arrested him, they obviously couldn't find enough evidence."

"And that's probably why he kills the women in such unusual ways. He uses his expertise to his advantage, and there aren't any physical signs of how they were murdered." I stood at the whiteboard and began jotting down my thoughts. "First, he has a God complex and is seemingly very narcissistic. I'm sure he thinks he's smarter than everyone else. Isabelle was a professor who could have been fooling around with other professors right under his nose. That's the worst kind of humiliation." I noticed Amber's eyes widen.

"What if she was fooling around with male students?"

"Whoa, that didn't occur to me. Maybe that's why he set his revenge on students." I began rifling through our notes. "I remember somebody saying Becca and Daphne were tutored in chemistry. If they failed their finals, it could push back their education. What if Morton was that tutor, or even worse, what if he promised them a passing grade for personal favors?"

"You may be onto something, Kate."

The phone centered on the table rang, and I grabbed it. "Kate Pierce here. Yep, hang on." I pressed Speakerphone. "Go ahead, Donnelly. Amber is with me."

"Why are you answering Jack's phone?"

"He's with Naomi's parents so the calls were transferred

to the conference room where Amber and I are working. Did you find the cigarette butt?"

"Yep, and it has to be his. It was the only one we found, and the location was right."

I sighed with relief. "And it's a Marlboro?" Tim's pause was too long and I felt my shoulders sink.

"No, it's a Salem. Was the one at the marsh a Marlboro?"

Amber let out a groan. "Yeah, maybe you hadn't stepped in on the conversation yet when we said that. So we *think* he smokes Salem, but we have to prove it without a shadow of a doubt. Somebody needs to go to his house and search the yard for cigarette butts, but we'll have to clear that with Jack first. Have the guys drop that cigarette butt off downstairs so the lab can extract DNA from it. We really need their help here getting our ducks in a row." I clicked off the call and glanced at the clock. We had to speak to Jack, but the only thing we could do at the moment was continue bullet pointing our theory until he walked through the door. Still, we needed questions answered before Mr. and Mrs. Hahn left. I fired off a text to Jack, saying we needed to know if Naomi took botany or chemistry classes and if she was failing either one. We'd get the physical proof soon enough, and Mike Morton or Martin Glover—whatever his name was—would spend the rest of his life in prison.

My phone vibrated as a return text came in seconds later. I checked the message, and the answer was yes to botany and yes to failing.

"Add Naomi's name to the failing-in-botany and tutored list. So we have two girls who were failing chemistry, one who was failing botany, and all three were in Morton's classes. At least we're establishing a connection between them."

We heard footsteps heading our way. "Finally," Amber said when Jack rounded the corner.

"Sorry it took so long. I escorted Mr. and Mrs. Hahn down to the coroner's office, and Lena pulled me aside and said she had checked for signs of sexual activity simply because Naomi was discovered nude."

"And?" Amber grabbed her pen.

"And she found evidence. Of course, I didn't share that information with the parents since they told me Naomi wasn't dating anyone. Both Becca and Daphne were fully dressed, so that exam wasn't deemed necessary, but now, in hindsight, I told Lena to go back and examine both girls, anyway."

"That's smart."

Jack took his seat at the head of the table. "They've agreed to an autopsy too. So what have I missed during the last hour?"

I gave Amber a side-eyed glance before speaking.

Jack noticed. "That didn't look promising."

"The guys are headed back with the cigarette butt they found."

Jack slapped the table. "Perfect! So what's the problem?"

"It doesn't match the one from the marsh."

Jack squeezed his temples. "Why can't we catch a break?"

"Boss, I have an idea."

"Yeah, what?"

"You have Silver sitting on Morton at the university, so

how about I run out to his house and check the yard for Salem cigarette butts."

"Not on your life." Jack stood and paced around the table.

"Come on, Boss. Karen can meet me there. We'll be in and out in a few minutes. Everyone else is needed here, and Amber is killing it—excuse the pun—with note taking. We'll knock on the door as if we expect him to answer. When he doesn't, we'll just walk the yard for a bit before we leave. We might even find a cigarette butt on the ground somewhere."

"Trespassing and snooping are the same thing, Kate."

"But he'll never know we were there. Silver will make sure of that. And in my opinion, killers don't get special breaks."

Jack pushed up his sleeve. "Call Silver and make sure Morton is still at the university. I want you back in that chair"—he pointed at the seat I was in—"in forty-five minutes. Do we have an understanding?"

"Absolutely." I leapt from my chair and headed down the hallway.

Jack yelled out the door. "You better have your phone and your sidearm with you."

"I will, I promise."

Chapter 56

He turned the wand on the blinds and looked out for the tenth time. The cop was still parked on the corner.

What a moron. Does that imbecile think his patrol car is invisible? I know he's watching my Explorer since there's nobody here other than me that's guilty of anything. This school is nearly a ghost town since tomorrow is the last day of finals.

Mike grinned. "I have to commend the sheriff's department for actually doing their job. I'm flattered that they're so curious about me. Maybe I need to rethink my exit strategy—my coups de grâce, if you will."

He made the call, was picked up on the other side of the building by an independent driver who advertised in the free newspaper, and was home ten minutes later. Inside, he began to pack the items he'd need to lay low in one of his apartment units until he had his final plan figured out. He'd hide behind the Martin Glover identity since law enforcement wouldn't connect him to that name. No matter what, he was still smarter than the cops and could outwit them without breaking a sweat.

The sound of gravel crunching beneath tires perked his

ears. Mike moved the curtain aside and peered out. He watched the driveway until the vehicles came into view.

"A cruiser and a patrol car?" He chuckled. "I guess somebody needed to back up somebody else." He was interested to know who was in the cruiser. It had to be a detective, but which one? He had likely met them all. He grabbed a handful of aspirin and chomped them like peanuts while he watched the action unfold in front of him. A woman stepped out of each car. The patrol officer rounded the front of her squad car and had a brief conversation with the detective.

Mike grabbed his binoculars and focused on the woman in the blazer. "Just as I thought. It's the bitch from the restaurant—Kate something." He rubbed his chin with curiosity and walked to the dining room window to watch—a good fifteen feet from the front door. Mike wondered why they were there, especially when one of their own was watching his car. He was sure they thought the house was empty—his vehicle wasn't there. The women walked to the door together, gave an obligatory knock, then waited. He could hear their conversation from his position. "So they're going to snoop around for cigarette butts? Looking for DNA, are ya? But how did you know I smoke?" He thought about the number of times he'd flicked butts into the yard—it wasn't often and none recently that he could remember. He'd raked the yard several weekends ago to clean up the remaining winter debris.

He watched as they parted at the porch, each going in a different direction. The pounding in his head was increasing, and so was his anger. The aspirin did little lately to relieve his pain. From room to room, he followed the patrol officer, watching out each window until she disappeared around the garage.

I'll strike now while she's hidden from view of the detective.

He turned the knob and slinked out to the patio then crossed the backyard to the detached garage. He didn't like the thought of them snooping around his botanical gardens either. He had his doubts that inexperienced people knew what poisonous plants looked like, but the belladonna berries could easily be identified during an autopsy.

No worries—Naomi will never be found.

He heard that cop rummaging through the trash scattered behind the garage. He peeked around the corner then sneaked up behind her while she was preoccupied. "Psst." She turned, and with a coiled fist, he coldcocked her in the face. She hit the ground like a ton of bricks, then he stomped her in the ribs. He gave her one more punch for good measure, ripped out her shoulder mic, and tossed it in the trash heap. Mike flattened himself against the walls of the garage until he got a bead on the detective. He saw her near the firepit.

Shit—that's where I burned Naomi's clothes.

He watched as the detective picked a piece of cloth out of the ashes. His moves took only a second. Mike charged her at a full run and knocked her feet out from under her. Kate hit the ground but got her bearings before he had time to deliver another blow.

She jumped up, ready to strike back, but immediately grabbed her head. She was stunned as she cried out and fell to her knees. He kicked her to the ground, where she moaned in pain. Kate couldn't move.

"What's wrong, Detective? Giving up that easily? I have a right to protect my home, and I don't see a warrant in your hand. I'll sue the county for trespassing on private property. Now get the hell off my land."

She lay in the dirt, her head grasped between her hands, and rocked back and forth.

"You call yourself an officer of the law? You're pathetic and can't even defend yourself." He reached inside her blazer, released the holster's thumb break, slipped the weapon into his waistband, then tossed her phone into the brush. Mike delivered a final blow to her gut and walked away.

Chapter 57

Worry took over Jack's thoughts. His leg bounced involuntarily as he watched the clock.

Over the last hour, the team had concluded that all three girls must have been tutored by Morton since they were failing his classes.

"If his wife really was cheating on him with somebody at the university, especially young hunky students, I could see how that would set him off. From what I noticed during our interview, he appeared to be a narcissistic, overbearing man who thinks women are the weaker sex—likely because of his wife's actions. He may truly hate women and used that hate to kill those female students he was tutoring."

Billings spoke up. "I've overheard Mia talking to her friends about some creepy professors. Many have God complexes and hit on the female students. Maybe Morton blackmailed them and they were going to turn the tables on him."

"Blackmail about what, though?" Clayton asked.

"It *is* finals week, Chad. Maybe he promised them a passing grade in exchange for personal favors. They got sick of it and threatened to rat him out," Amber said. "Don't forget, Becca had birth control pills in her apartment, yet she didn't have a boyfriend."

Jack ground his fingers into his scalp. "And during the table exam, Lena confirmed the fact that Naomi recently had sex." He glanced at the clock again. "Where the hell is Kate? She promised to be back ten minutes ago."

Clayton lifted his hip and pulled his cell phone from his pocket. "I'll give her a call." He dialed Kate's number, but the call went directly to voicemail. "That's odd. She doesn't answer."

Amber tried to alleviate Jack's concern. "She probably left her phone in the car's cup holder, where she always puts it, and lost track of the time."

"Maybe, but I'll have Jan radio Lawrence," Jack said. He dialed the reception counter and had Jan in Dispatch contact Karen's squad car radio. Jan called the conference room several minutes later. "Jack, Lawrence doesn't answer."

"Son of a bitch. Call Silver and see if he still has eyes on Morton's car." He set the phone back on the base. "I have a bad feeling about this." The phone rang a second time. "Jan, what did Silver say? He does? Okay, thanks." Jack shook his head. "Silver says the Explorer is still in the university's lot." He took one more look at the clock. "If Kate isn't back here in ten minutes, we're heading out, and she better have a damn good excuse for worrying us." He looked at each face. "Let's tighten up what we have against Morton so I can make the call to Judge Pemberley. I'd say with the information we've put together, there's probable cause to search Morton's house, and at sunup, we'll take him by surprise with that warrant in hand. He won't have time to hide the evidence that's likely stashed there. I want to see Mike Morton behind bars by this time tomorrow."

"And there's one more bit of evidence we can use to put a nail in his coffin," Amber said.

Jack raised his brows. "I like the sound of that."

"The fact that he and Martin Glover are the same person tells us he had a key to Becca's apartment. A break-in wasn't necessary when all he had to do was wait for her to leave, turn the key in the lock, then add the clostridium botulinum to her food. Who knows? The owner behind that C Corp could very well be Martin Glover too."

"You're probably right, Amber." Jack waved his hand back and forth over the table. "Gather up this paperwork and take everything back to the bull pen while I try to reach the judge. Have Jan transfer the calls to my office. Clayton, run downstairs and see how Kyle is doing with extracting DNA from that cigarette butt and then find out if Lena has started Naomi's autopsy. We need the swabbed DNA from Naomi to match the DNA on the cigarette. Still, if we can prove that Morton smokes Salem cigarettes, and the same brand is found on his property, we can tie all the evidence together. We'll have him dead to rights if they're a match. The rest of you keep trying Kate's phone and Karen's radio." Jack left the conference room and returned to his office.

"This is getting real," Amber said as she returned to her desk. Another call to Kate's phone went to voicemail. Amber stared at Jack's office door. "Be ready to go the second he walks out."

Billings hung up his phone. "Jan just tried Karen's radio again—no answer."

"I don't like this waiting." Amber grabbed her phone and called the reception desk. "Jan, please check with Silver one more time."

Clayton stormed into the bull pen. "Lena checked Naomi's stomach contents already. It was full of whole berries and unchewed sliced mushrooms."

"That sounds like she was force-fed, and what are the chances that those items were store-bought?"

Billings holstered his weapon. "I'd say slim to none."

Jack's door flew open. "The warrant is being processed for Mike Morton aka Martin Glover. Anything from Kate or Karen?"

"Can't reach them, Boss," Amber said.

"Then grab your gear. We're heading out."

Chapter 58

After trudging through the woods for twenty minutes with the backpack slung over his shoulder, Mike came out on the other side and into a country subdivision. He pulled the folded piece of paper and his phone from his cargo pants front pocket and made the call. The driver said he was on his way. He arrived minutes later at a house Mike had chosen randomly. He liked the way it looked. Climbing into the back seat, Mike tossed the backpack on the floor and let out a groan.

The driver looked over his shoulder. "Hard day, man?"

"You can say that."

"Where you heading?"

"Allenton, just off Maple Street. I'll guide you in once we're closer."

"You bet. It should only take ten minutes or so."

Mike thought about the detectives and how they'd ruined his plans of driving away, never to be seen again. He wouldn't be able to get his Explorer and leave town before he became the most likely suspect. They were already onto him. His hopes of humiliating the police and sheriff's departments, just as he had in Isabelle's unsolved case, were gone. They'd dashed his plans of making sure they had two unexplained deaths on their hands and a missing girl who would never be found. He wanted them to face scrutiny from John Q. Public and have to explain why they couldn't give the families closure or justice for their loved ones. The crimes would tarnish the county's reputation, and law enforcement would be deemed incompetent. Mike would hear all about it on the news and read the latest articles in the online newspapers and he'd enjoy proving once again how much smarter he was than the cops.

"But no, you had to screw up everything for me!"

The driver frowned at him through the rearview mirror. "Are you talking to me?"

Mike rubbed his brow. "Sorry, kid, I'm just thinking out loud. Tough day, remember?"

The driver nodded. "Yeah, I hear ya. No sweat."

The car slowed at the curb after turning off Main Street onto Maple.

Mike pointed through the windshield. "It's the yellow house on the right."

The driver pulled forward. "Is this okay?"

"Yeah, good enough." Mike handed the driver a twenty, grabbed his bag, and stepped out. He waited until the car turned the corner then made a call to another independent company. He looked up at the house address. "I need a driver at 684 Maple Street in Allenton as soon as possible. Fifteen minutes? Yeah, that'll work."

Chapter 59

Karen opened her eyes and saw nothing but blue sky. "What the hell?" Instinctively, she reached for her shoulder mic, but it was gone. A searing pain shot through her ribs when she tried to sit, so she repositioned to her hands and knees. Blood ran from her nose to the dirt below. Short breaths helped as she braced herself against a rusty fifty-pound barrel and stood. She held her side and tried to regain her composure.

A broken nose and ribs? That bastard got me good.

Karen had to get around the garage and find Kate but breathing deeply enough to yell was too painful. She looked at her watch—forty minutes had passed since she began rummaging in the trash. With her hand above her eyes, she looked for movement but saw none in her immediate field of vision.

I didn't even hear him come up behind me. Where's Kate? She would have found me if she was okay.

With short steps forward, Karen used the wall of the garage to steady herself. When she reached the corner, she carefully peeked around it. Nobody was there.

"Kate, where are you?" She gingerly drew her gun—every

movement hurt—then she continued on. She had to get to her squad car to call for help. It was a hundred feet ahead, and she was thankful that he hadn't taken either vehicle. Kate's location was still an unknown, and Karen called out again, but her voice wasn't strong enough to go the distance. A noise sounded from the east side of the house, and her startled turn caused her to grab her side. With slow breaths, she got through the pain, but she needed to know who was there. It could be Kate, or it could be Morton, but with her gun ready to fire, she had a decision to make—turn in that direction or continue to the car. She turned.

Chapter 60

Jack's phone chirped as he drove. With his right hand, he dug it out of his left chest pocket and handed it to Amber. "See who that is."

"Lieutenant Steele's phone, Detective Monroe speaking. Hang on, Lena, Jack's driving. I'll put you on Speakerphone so you can talk." Amber tapped the icon and set the phone on the console.

"What do you have, Lena?"

"I've identified the type of berries and mushrooms in Naomi's stomach—both poisonous, of course."

Jack slammed his fist against the steering wheel and let out a snarl. "That son of a bitch forced them down her throat too."

"It does appear that way. The berries would have acted first, causing severe dizziness, slurred speech, loss of motor functions, and unconsciousness."

"What kind of berries were they?"

"Belladonna or deadly nightshade, and extremely toxic. They resemble blueberries, and that's why children should never get their hands on them. The mushrooms would have taken Naomi out for good, but they act slower. Five hours or so before they would have kicked in. They're the Destroying Angels variety and very deadly. She'd have had severe vomiting, and eventually her kidneys would shut down and she'd die."

"Okay. Great job, Lena, thanks."

Amber grabbed the dash as Jack slammed on his brakes, backed up, and made a sharp right-hand turn. According to the numbers on the mailbox, they had arrived, and Mike Morton's house was directly to their right and well hidden by trees. Clayton's cruiser was on Jack's bumper. They reached the clearing at the front of the driveway, where the house was located. Both Kate's cruiser and Karen's squad car were parked there. Jack leapt from the driver's seat, his gun already drawn, and yelled out to move in.

"Amber, you and I will clear the house. Clayton and Billings, check the yard."

Jack called out to Kate as he pounded on the front door. With no response, he backed up, rushed the door with his shoulder, and broke it off the hinges. He turned left, and Amber went right. They cleared each room, one by one.

Clayton yelled out from the east side of the house. "I have them. They're both back here by the firepit."

Jack and Amber raced out the back door and turned left. Behind the garden and near the shed, a firepit surrounded by large stones was dug into the ground. Two plastic lawn chairs sat next to it. Billings and Clayton had already helped both women off the ground and onto the chairs.

"Are you okay?" Amber asked as she ran to their sides.

"Oh my God, you guys are a mess. What happened?"

Karen's weapon lay in the dirt next to her feet. She groaned as she tried to speak. "He sneaked up on me, punched me in the face, and stomped my ribs. Then he ripped my radio off my shoulder and tossed it in the garbage pile behind the garage. Thankfully, I still have my gun." She turned to Kate. "I imagine Kate's scenario is the same. His car wasn't here, Jack. Silver still had eyes on it, but somehow—"

"Don't worry about it. We'll find him," Jack said. "Right now, we need to get you medical attention."

Kate shook her head. "I'll be all right. He knocked the wind out of me and roughed me up, but nothing feels broken. The pain in my head is what took me out. It was so intense I couldn't move, but now that he's gone, it's not as bad. Jack, he has my gun."

"It's okay." He looked at Clayton. "Put an APB out on him right away—armed and dangerous." Jack examined Karen's face. "Your nose looks broken, and your eyes are almost swollen closed." He jerked his head at Billings. "Get an ambulance out here." Jack turned to Kate. "Are you sure he's gone?"

"He was wearing a large backpack and disappeared through there." She pointed toward the woods. "That was the last time I saw him."

Chapter 61

"Once the ibuprofen kicks in, I'll be okay. Now that Karen is in good hands at St. Joe's, we can focus on finding Morton and arresting his sick ass."

Jack sat on the edge of my desk and rubbed his chin. "I still wish you had been checked out."

"I'm fine. Sore, yes, but not seriously hurt. There's something going on with Morton, though."

Amber sneered. "Other than he's a sicko who likes to beat up female cops and kill female students."

"Don't forget his wife disappeared without a trace," Billings said.

"Yeah, that too."

"No, I mean there's actually something physically wrong with him."

Jack frowned. "As in an illness?"

"I'm not sure, but if this transference thing is real, my head starts pounding whenever I'm near him. Today was much worse than at the restaurant. It was debilitating."

"Yet he still gets around," Clayton said.

Jack turned to me. "Is the headache going away?"

I nodded. "It's getting better."

"Good. Do you remember anything that could be a clue to where he went? Did he say anything to you?"

"Only personal insults, nothing that was important to the case. Maybe there's something in the Explorer that will help."

Jack checked the time. "The flatbed should be back with it any minute. Kyle and Dan are standing by."

I squeezed my eyes closed. "Oh my God, I just remembered something. Seconds before he jumped me, I saw a piece of burnt cloth in the firepit. I picked it up, and that's when he tackled me. It was red and stretchy like Spandex. It could have been clothing."

"And Naomi was nude," Amber said.

Jack pointed at Billings. "Call the courthouse and see if that warrant is ready. Better yet, run over there, pick it up, and then hit the Register of Deeds office. Find out if that property is deeded to either Michael Morton or Martin Glover. While you're at it, get the address of every property in the entire state that is deeded to either name. It's time to start tearing places apart." Jack walked to the window and parted the blind's slats. "The sun is dropping in the sky. Before long there will be too many shadows outside to search the grounds. I suppose you didn't find any Salem cigarette butts before he jumped you?"

"No, but there will probably be plenty in the house, plus he attacked two law enforcement officers. That's grounds enough to put him away."

Jack cracked his neck. "I know, but we have one chance with the DA to get a conviction. I want all the evidence we can get our hands on." Seconds later, he answered his ringing office phone, and I heard excitement in his voice. He hung up and stepped into the bull pen. "Clayton, run down to the evidence garage. Kyle said he has something we need to see."

"On it." Clayton disappeared down the hallway toward the back staircase. He returned in less than five minutes. "This, my friends, just sealed Morton's fate."

Jack stood. "Thank God. What is it?"

"Would you believe he had a journal belonging to Becca in the glove box? There was also plastic sheeting jammed under the seat. Kyle is going to test it for prints and DNA. It could be what Naomi was transported to the marsh in."

I smirked. "And he thinks he's smart? No criminal with half a brain leaves evidence right in their own vehicle."

Jack slipped on a pair of gloves and pulled out the journal from the evidence bag. He turned the pages and read a few entries. "Just like we thought. That sick bastard told her he'd fail her in chemistry if she didn't have sex with him."

I rubbed my temples. "And she must have threatened to expose him. Instead of backing off, he killed her."

"And I'm sure that's the same reason Daphne and Naomi died too," Amber said.

"I'll read this entire journal later, but I doubt if this information is something I'll share with Becca's parents. They're dealing with enough sadness the way it is."

The door beeped, and Billings walked in waving the warrant above his head. "We're good to go."

"What about other properties?"

"The Register of Deeds had records for Becca's building

in Kewaskum, a four-plex in Horicon, and a duplex in Fond du Lac, registered to a Martin Glover. They said it would take longer to find others that may be owned by the C Corp."

"Okay, we'll check out his own house first and then see if we can find information on more properties in our county. I'll alert Fond du Lac and Dodge Counties about the other properties, and they'll have to conduct those searches on their own. Let's head out while we still have some daylight left. Horbeck and Jamison agreed to come in early and hold down the fort."

Chapter 62

"Shut up, old woman, and be happy I don't pour drain cleaner down your throat. You're going to stay in that bathroom until further notice." Mike heard sobbing coming from the other side of the door.

She cried out, "I don't understand. You seemed like a nice landlord. What happened? I pay my rent on time and—"

"I said to shut up! My head is throbbing, and you aren't helping things. You're a means to an end, so keep quiet and you live. Get on my nerves and you die."

She went silent.

"That's better."

Mike sat at the table and weighed his options while he stared at the vial in his hand. He gave it a swirl, thought about its contents, and returned it to his chest pocket.

I can take the old woman's car and hit the road now, or pack it up with food and supplies, eat a filling meal, get a good night's sleep, then reevaluate everything in the morning. I bet that old bag has plenty of money stashed too.

He went to her purse and dumped it over the table. Her cell phone, a checkbook, and that all-important wallet fell out along with a bottle containing nitroglycerin pills.

Heart problems, huh? I bet you could use one of these about now.

His phone rang just as he was heading to the bathroom with the bottle in hand. He fished the phone out of his pants pocket.

Danny Greenly? What the hell does he want?

"Danny, what's up?"

"Mr. Glover, I thought you ought to know."

"Know what?" Mike walked outside and sat on the porch. He didn't need the old woman to hear his side of the conversation through the bathroom door. He shook a cigarette out of the pack, held it between his lips, and flicked the wheel on the lighter. The end of the cigarette glowed orange as he took a deep pull.

"The cops called me and asked if I knew of other properties you managed for the C Corp."

"What'd you say?"

"I said no."

"That was the right answer, Danny. Expect to see a bonus in your mailbox soon, and don't tell them anything if they call again."

"You bet, sir, and thank you."

Mike powered down his phone. No need to give the cops any help tracking him down. He picked up the old woman's phone and stuffed it in his pocket.

So the sheriff's office knows for sure that Mike Morton and I are the same person. That means they're tracking down the properties under my real name. It'll take longer to get the information they want from the C Corp, though, especially since those records are being held at the title company in St. Thomas. Nothing happens quickly in the Caribbean. I'll be safe here for a while.

Mike walked back in and locked the door behind him. He pulled the curtains closed, jiggled the handle on the patio door, and peeked into the garage. The house was buttoned up tight. With everything secure, including Mrs. Kittleman, he went to the kitchen and opened the refrigerator. "Hmm... so what looks good?"

Chapter 63

Back at Morton's house, Amber and I picked apart the contents of the firepit until dark. We placed in the evidence bag a burnt heel of a shoe, several pieces of red fabric, and a lone bra strap with the plastic slide still intact but melted.

"Those bits of clothing definitely belonged to a woman," I said, "and likely Naomi."

The guys, already in the house, had gone through the botanical garden earlier, and with Lena's help, had determined through photographs that at least ten poisonous plants were being nurtured in that garden. Ashtrays filled with Salem cigarette butts sat on most flat surfaces.

I wrinkled my nose when we walked through the door. "That guy was quite the smoker. This house stinks to high heaven."

Jack tipped his chin at us. "What did you find in the firepit?"

"A little bit of everything—pieces of shoe leather and a heel, a bra strap, and more of that red stretchy material."

"Enough evidence to suggest an outfit, then?"

"I'd say so," Amber said. "How's the search in here going?"

"Billings and Clayton are rummaging through paperwork in Mike's office. They had to break the lock on the file cabinet. Guess he didn't have time to gather everything and no vehicle to put things in. He likely took what was most important to him in that backpack."

"Do you think he hitchhiked?"

Jack frowned. "Doubt it. That would be too undignified for someone with a superiority complex like he has."

"But there wouldn't be a paper trail. Independent drivers and taxis have to report their rides."

Amber cocked her head. "Independents who are self-employed don't have to if they work under the table and deal only in cash."

"Then we'll never find him." I opened a drawer and began rifling through it. It was apparently the kitchen junk drawer since I found nothing of interest inside. I moved on to the living room and opened the lower cabinets of the bookcase then took a seat on the floor, with Amber at my side. "There's a ton of paperwork in here, so we might as well dig in." We spent a tedious hour going through every sheet of paper. Some dated back to when Morton lived in Madison.

"I guess this is a good sign," Amber said. "If he keeps every slip of paper he's ever had, then we're bound to find something."

Jack moved his stack of papers to the side, stood, and rubbed the back of his neck. "Everything is kinking up on me." He called out to Clayton and Billings. "Find anything yet?"

Clayton walked out of the office. "Yeah, several mortgage

documents that were filed by the county and signed by Martin Glover."

"Any that we aren't aware of?"

Billings spoke up from the other room. "Not yet."

I shook my head. "I still don't understand why he has some properties purchased by a C Corp and others by Martin Glover."

"I imagine he's trying to hide income and have zero liability with the ones under the C Corp," Jack said.

"Hey, check this out." I handed four slips of paper to Amber. "He kept receipts from a trip to the Virgin Islands. Who does stupid things like that?"

Amber pointed at the stacks of paper in front of us. "Apparently he does."

Jack knelt at our side. "What kind of receipts?"

"Here, take a look." Amber passed them to Jack. A wire transfer to a title company, a bank deposit, a drugstore receipt for a five-hundred-count bottle of aspirin, and a bar tab had been folded together and secured with a paper clip.

Jack looked at each one. "They're all dated during the same week eighteen months ago. Didn't he tell UWM he wanted to retire to the US Virgin Islands?"

Billings walked out of the office. "Yep, he sure did."

"The receipts were signed by Martin Glover, and it shows the last four digits of his credit card number. Start looking for credit card bills under that name." Jack looked around. "Damn it. He must have stashed his computer in that backpack. I don't see one anywhere."

"What about all the other mail? Is it being delivered to

Michael Morton or Martin Glover?"

We searched the house and didn't find a single envelope with a name on it.

I pointed at the full-size shredder near the office door. "That's probably where all the envelopes went."

Jack pointed at Clayton. "Chad, run down to the mailbox and check for new mail. I doubt if he thought about getting it today."

Clayton did and was back minutes later. "Looks like everything comes to Martin Glover, and get this, one envelope is from the bank. That could be a gold mine of information."

"Open it."

My head nearly spun off my shoulders. "That's a federal crime, Jack."

"Not when we have a warrant in hand. Now go ahead, Clayton."

Chad ripped open the envelope and smoothed out the three sheets of paper that showed deposits and withdrawals.

Jack looked over his shoulder. "More wire transfers, and they're all going to a bank in St. Thomas. So maybe some renters give him personal checks, he deposits them here, and then the funds are wired to an account in the Caribbean. That account is probably attached to the C Corp, which buys more properties back in the states."

"That seems like a lot of work for no obvious reason."

"True but following these bread crumbs might tell us where he's holed up. That bank in the Virgin Islands is only a phone call away." Jack pushed up his sleeve and checked the time. "Unfortunately, that will have to wait until tomorrow. Banking hours are over for the day, so for now, let's keep digging through these papers."

We'd spent hours going through useless paperwork and realized our best bet was still to contact that bank the next morning. With our evidence bags full, we buttoned up the house and called it a night.

Chapter 64

The knocking wouldn't stop that Friday morning. Mike peered out the window and saw an elderly lady standing on the porch. She continued to pound and called out Mrs. Kittleman's name. "Mildred, open the door. Did you forget about breakfast and bingo? Are you home?"

Mildred's ringing phone would give him away. He quickly silenced it and hoped the nosy woman outside hadn't heard it ring. He watched as she dropped her phone back into her purse and walked to the garage.

Did I make sure that side door was locked last night?

He couldn't remember. He ran to the door between the kitchen and garage and secured it. Seconds later, the woman banged on that door.

I can't believe that damn old hag came into the garage. Now she saw the car and knows for sure that Mildred is home.

Mike crouched under the picture window that faced the driveway and peeked out. He watched the woman try the phone one more time before climbing into her car and pulling away.

Good, maybe she gave up—or maybe she's going to report this to the police. I better see what Mildred can tell me. It might be time to go.

Mike knocked on the bathroom door. "Mildred, I'm coming in, so don't do anything you'll regret." He cracked open the door just enough to get a glimpse of the full-sized vanity mirror. In its reflection, he saw Mildred slumped over the tub. "Son of a bitch." He rushed in and went to her side. It was too late—she was cold and stiff. "Damn it, it's just my luck the old woman had a heart attack. Now I've really got to make myself scarce."

Mike grabbed everything he could use for the foreseeable future, including her wallet, and ripped the keys off the hook by the garage door. He raised the overhead, got in the car, and squealed the tires as he shifted into reverse. He had to get out of the county, the state, and then the country. He patted his chest pocket to check—the vial was still there.

Chapter 65

I noticed Jack leaning against his doorframe. He blew on his steaming coffee and began the morning update.

"Okay, listen up, people. The lab confirmed that the DNA on the cigarette butts matched each other as well as the swab sample from Naomi's body. The proof is irrefutable that Glover is our guy, and the DA has agreed to go forward with murder charges against Martin Glover, aka Mike Morton. Now, all we have to do is find him. I've checked the website for the bank Glover uses in the Virgin Islands, and it opens in forty-five minutes. Our warrant for his information will hold up at the bank and at the title company he wired money to. Even though the accounts may be under the control of the C Corp, Martin Glover is the person who made the transactions. The US Virgin Islands is a territory of the United States, and they have to abide by our laws."

"Have all of his buildings that we know of been checked?" I asked.

"Both Fond du Lac and Dodge Counties sent deputies to search the buildings. He wasn't at any of them." Jack's sigh was discouraging. "We don't know his next of kin since he isn't local to our area. I've reached out to Dane County and asked for their help. For now, we wait, at least until I talk to the right people in the Virgin Islands."

When his desk phone rang, Jack pushed off the door. He took a seat and answered it. "Yes, this is Lieutenant Steele. On the outskirts of Addison? That isn't the Allenton police station's jurisdiction. Okay, I'll send a deputy out there." Jack dialed Dispatch and gave Peggy the address. "Who's out that way? Yep, that's fine. Have him update me when he knows something." Jack returned to the bull pen and took a seat in Amber's guest chair.

"What was that about?" Billings asked.

"An old lady called in for a wellness check on her friend. She said the woman doesn't answer the door or the phone, but her car is in the garage. They're missing breakfast and bingo."

I smiled. "What a life to look forward to."

Clayton chuckled. "Yeah, you young pups have a long wait." He turned to Jack. "Who are you sending?"

"Ebert can be there in less than ten minutes." Jack rolled his neck and glanced at the clock.

"The time isn't going to go any faster by staring at the clock, Boss," I said.

"Yeah, I know. I finished reading Becca's journal last night. She wrote that she was going to tell the counselors what Morton was up to. It sounded like she was scared to death of him."

Amber groaned. "Yeah, literally."

Jack's phone rang again. "Sure, patch him through.

What's wrong, Ebert? Uh-huh, that's what the old lady told Allenton's police department. Yeah, go on in, and I'll stay on the line." Jack covered the mouthpiece with his hand. "Ebert said the overhead is wide open, and the door from the garage to the house is unlocked. A complete contradiction to what the caller told the police."

"That's odd," Billings said. "Maybe dementia is setting in."

Jack shook his head. "Yeah, I'm still here. That's troubling. Okay, watch your moves, Ebert, and call out to her." Jack turned toward us. "The contents of her purse were dumped out on the table."

My interest was piqued, and the four of us sat on the edges of our seats as we listened to Jack's side of the conversation.

"Shit! Clear the house and get Silver out there. Amber and Kate are on their way."

Jack hung up. "Ebert said the old lady is dead in the bathroom, and it looks like the house has been gone through."

I stood, secured my shoulder holster, and grabbed my purse. "And that probably explains why the car is gone and the overhead was left open. The burglar was actually in the house when the friend stopped by. He made a quick exit after she drove away."

Amber turned back to Jack as we headed to the door. "Do you think this has anything to do with Glover?"

"At this point, I have no idea, but anything is possible. I'll let Lena and the guys know what's going on. They shouldn't be far behind you."

Amber and I took off, the siren engaged and the lights flashing red and blue. Twenty minutes later, we reached the small house set back off the road. Two patrol cars sat in the driveway, and Ebert approached us as I pulled in.

"What have you got, Tim?" I killed the engine and climbed out. Amber and I walked with him to the house.

He pointed at the garage and explained his every move. "The overhead was open when I arrived, and the door between the garage and house was unlocked. Once in the kitchen, I noticed the purse's contents scattered on the table. I checked the living room for the homeowner, called out her name, then continued down the hallway. That's when I saw her body slumped over the tub—she was ice cold and stiff."

I jerked back my head. "That wouldn't make sense if the perp just committed a burglary and killed the woman in the process. The call came in less than an hour ago, and apparently he was still in the home."

Silver walked in. "I agree with you, Kate. Let's see what Lena gives the woman as a TOD."

"Got a name for her?" Amber asked as we entered the bathroom and took a look at the deceased.

"Mildred Kittleman, aged eighty."

I rubbed my head. It was beginning to pound. "First things first. Pull up her name in the DMV database and put a BOLO out for her car. The perp couldn't have gotten far. We also need to know if she owns this house or rents it. We can't conduct a thorough search without a warrant unless we're absolutely sure the home belonged to her. We need to interview that caller too. Have the PD pick her up."

Amber and I walked each room. She noticed me squinting. "Something wrong?"

"My eyes are blurring, and my head is pounding."

"Again? Maybe this problem has been a sinus infection all along."

"I don't think so."

We continued on and saw that the house had definitely been gone through. We returned to the kitchen and stared at the contents of Mildred's purse.

"The wallet is missing." Amber looked around. "I don't see a house phone or a cell phone anywhere. Ebert, the friend said she tried calling Mildred, right?"

"That's correct."

"Okay, tell the Allenton PD we'll interview the friend at their station. Meanwhile, talk to the closest neighbors and find out everything you can about Mildred."

When I heard cars approaching, I peered out the window. Lena and the forensic team had arrived, and we needed an estimated time of death before anything.

"I have to get some ibuprofen from the car. I'll be right back." I returned to the house minutes later with Lena, Jason, and our forensic team.

"Hey, guys." Amber tipped her head toward the hallway. "The deceased is in the bathroom."

Kyle nodded and headed in that direction.

"We'll need your best guess at a time and cause of death as soon as possible, Lena. That'll tell us something about the perp and how long he was here."

"You got it." Lena turned to Dan. "Go ahead and snap your pics so I can get in there and examine the body. That room is too small for all of us."

Chapter 66

I pulled into the Allenton Police Department's lot, and Amber and I headed for the front door. Lena had given us a rough estimate of how long Mrs. Kittleman had been dead—it was seven hours, give or take. Our forensic team photographed the residence while we waited for information on the property owner on record. The BOLO was in place for the car and covered the entire state.

An officer led us back to the interview room Mrs. Yahr sat in.

"Mrs. Yahr?" I extended my hand and Amber did too. "We're detectives from the sheriff's office and need to ask you some questions about Mildred."

"Is she okay? It isn't like her to forget our plans."

"Mrs. Yahr, we need Mildred's phone number, and does she own that house?"

"No, she rents it from a Martin somebody, but he said his wife is the actual owner." She leaned across the table and whispered. "I've never met a wife, and Mildred hasn't either. Mildred pays him with a money order every month for reduced rent. She *is* on a limited budget, so she jumped at the chance. I'm just afraid that isn't legal."

"I assure you it is, but it is an odd arrangement." I gave Amber a side-eyed glance, and she excused herself from the room. "Can you give me one minute here? I have to send off a quick text to one of our deputies."

"Sure, dear, take your time."

With that done, I continued the questioning. "Now, go ahead and tell me exactly what happened when you pulled up to Mildred's house earlier today."

Worry covered her face. "I got out of my car and knocked on the door, but she didn't answer. I tried her cell phone, and I swear I heard it ring in the house, but that went unanswered too. I walked to the garage and was surprised to find the side door unlocked. I was thankful because it would have taken a lot to see in that window with the blinds drawn. My vision isn't that great anymore."

I smiled and asked her to continue.

"Anyway, I couldn't believe my eyes. Her car was there, so I went to the door that enters the kitchen and turned the knob—it was locked. I pounded on it, called out her name, and when she didn't respond, I decided to ask the police to do a welfare check. I called her phone once more before I left, and it still went to voicemail. Please tell me she's okay."

I reached across the table and covered Mrs. Yahr's hand with my own. "I'm sorry to tell you that Mildred has passed away."

"Oh no, she's my dearest friend! Did she have a heart attack?"

"We don't know, ma'am. It's early in our investigation."

Mrs. Yahr dabbed her eyes with a tissue. "She took nitro, you know. Triple bypass two years ago, but she seemed to be doing fine."

My mind was going a hundred miles a minute as I tried to process the information I was hearing. I handed Mrs. Yahr my card and told her it was okay to call anytime if she thought of something else. I asked the officer to show her out, then I met up with Amber at the car.

"Did you call Jack?"

She nodded and pocketed her phone. "Yep, and they're on their way with the warrant. Good thing it covers any property owned by Mike Morton or Martin Glover."

"Did Jack get ahold of the bank and title company in the Virgin Islands?"

"He said he did. They're just waiting for the police department to review the warrant. Jack had to email them a copy of it. As long as Martin Glover's name is on record as the signatory for the C Corp, we should be good to go."

We returned to Mrs. Kittleman's house to wait for Jack, Clayton, and Billings. It didn't take long for them to arrive.

When Jack hit the brakes, his car skidded in the gravel. He jumped out of the cruiser and stormed inside. Clayton and Billings were right behind him.

"Start taking this place apart," he said. "Where's Lena?"

I pointed down the hallway. "In the bathroom with the deceased. Second door on the right."

Lena walked out at the sound of Jack's voice. "Jason is getting the gurney so we can take her to the morgue. Let's sit, and I'll tell you what I think."

"Hang on. Everyone gather around." Jack held up the warrant. "Look for anything with Martin or Isabelle Glover's name on it. There may be plenty of properties in her name that we aren't aware of. Find those rent receipts too. Now get started."

Everything was fair game, and at least Mrs. Kittleman kept only things that were important. Her files were in order, and we quickly found the money order stubs with Martin Glover's name on them, proving this was another Glover property. Jack had Clayton call the courthouse Register of Deeds again and check for properties belonging to Isabelle Glover. There were four.

"Work on those property locations while Lena updates me." Jack took a seat in the kitchen with Lena. "Okay, tell me about Mrs. Kittleman."

"There were no visible signs of a struggle. She's an elderly woman, and if my theory is right, she likely died of a heart attack. If Glover stormed in here and took over the house, who knows how much stress that may have put on her heart, and the scar on her chest confirms she's had open-heart surgery in the past. You'll probably find nitro somewhere in the house. She's been dead for hours, Jack, so I'm assuming Glover came here sometime yesterday."

Jack let out a hard breath. "Yeah, looking for a place to hide after the confrontation with Karen and Kate at his house. I'm sure that old lady banging on the door this morning was a sign for him to move on, and fast." Jack knuckled the table. "Thanks, Lena. Go ahead and remove the body." He called us over. "Any word on the BOLO?"

Clayton responded. "Nothing yet, Boss."

"Okay, he's originally from Madison, so maybe he's working his way back there. Do you have any homes in that general direction that were owned by Isabelle Glover?"

"There were two. One in Pierceville and one in Cottage Grove."

Jack nodded. "Get Dane County deputies out to those houses and remind them of the BOLO for Mrs. Kittleman's 2014 green Ford Escape. Make sure they know that Martin Glover is armed and dangerous."

The radios squawked in the patrol cars. Ebert's vehicle was the closest. He stepped off the porch and went to the car. Seconds later, he returned to our group. "Jan said the BOLO alerted in Jefferson County as the car passed a license plate reader in the westbound lanes of Interstate 94. The state patrol hasn't been able to locate the car, though."

Jack mumbled a few choice curse words. "He probably got off the interstate as soon as he saw the cameras." He looked at Clayton and Billings. "You two wrap up everything here with Dan and Kyle and then go back to the station. See what's going on with the authorities in the Virgin Islands. Silver, seal the house when they leave, then you and Ebert can go back to your patrol duties." He tipped his head at Amber and me. "You two follow me. We're heading to Dane County."

Chapter 67

"Did your headache go away?"

"Yeah, I'm okay, but I'm telling you, it's related to Glover. He was at Mrs. Kittleman's house just before we arrived, and it can't be a coincidence that my head started hurting then."

Amber pulled up a map on her phone and spread it with her fingers. "There's an exit by Lake Mills for Highway B. It runs parallel to the interstate then turns into BB and goes directly into Cottage Grove. There really isn't a convenient way to get to Pierceville from that area."

I glanced at her. "So you're thinking Cottage Grove?"

"Yeah, I'll call Jack and suggest having the sheriff's office put somebody on that house."

The drive to Cottage Grove normally took an hour and a half. With our lights and sirens engaged, we'd cut twenty minutes off that time. Amber made the call to Jack, explained her Cottage Grove theory, then hung up. Five minutes later, her phone rang. It was Jack saying he alerted the sheriff's office that Glover might be traveling on Highway BB toward the residence in Cottage Grove. Deputies were being dispatched to that area and would also watch the house. He reminded us to set our radio to the Dane County Sheriff's Office channel.

Amber set the channel then placed her phone in her lap. "I'm glad Dane County is all over this. Now we've got to get Glover before another person dies."

I exited the interstate behind Jack onto Highway B at Lake Mills. The radios had been silent, and no calls had come in—something seemed off. Cottage Grove was only twenty minutes away.

Amber called Jack again and tapped Speakerphone. "Any updates from Dane County?"

"Not a peep. If Glover exited onto B at Lake Mills, they should have had him in custody by now. Damn it, we'll be at the house in ten minutes."

I frowned at Amber. "What just happened?"

"He's got to be pissed. He abruptly hung up."

We made several turns off BB as we went deeper into farm country. We followed Jack down two-lane roads with thick woods on either side of the cruiser. Seconds later, his brake lights flashed red, and he stopped. Jack's door opened, and he climbed out and crossed the road.

"What is he doing?" I inched forward and then saw it. A patrol car sat in a hidden driveway ahead and to our left. Jack leaned in at the driver's-side window and talked to the deputy while we waited. I lowered the window when he turned our way. "What's the word, Boss?"

"The house is a half mile up on the right. Patrol cars are stationed there"—he pointed—"and on the west side of the property. The sheriff's office contacted the tenants, and they left the premises for the time being. None of the deputies have had eyes on the green Escape, though." Jack jerked his chin toward the deputy's car. "According to him, the entire patrol unit for the sheriff's office, as well as the city police, are on the lookout for Glover."

Amber busied herself with the map on her phone then leaned over the console so she could make eye contact with Jack. "We should split up. Kate and I could head toward the Pierceville property and watch for him on that side of the interstate. It's only a five-mile drive."

Jack scratched his cheek. "Not the worst idea. I'll let the sheriff's office know to send a few units that way too." He slapped the cruiser's doorframe. "Keep me posted and be careful."

I smiled as I waited for Amber to give me directions. "Yes, dad." I raised my window and turned toward Amber. "You ready?"

"Yep, go straight ahead until we reach Main Street. You'll turn right and go about two miles until we pass under the interstate. That's where the road turns into Highway N."

"Okay, let's get to that point, and then you can guide me from there." I rounded Jack's cruiser and continued west until we reached Main Street. I turned right with two miles to go before we'd see the interstate.

Amber tapped her phone. "I'm going to give Clayton a call and ask if the warrant for the C Corp went through without issues from the authorities. Oh yeah, just keep going straight on N when you get to the interstate. I'll be off the phone by then."

"No problem." The radio squawked a few times with unrelated issues. I turned it down and listened to Amber's side of the conversation as she talked to Clayton. The traffic going east and west zoomed by as the interstate came into view directly ahead. I'd pass under it and continue on. According to my calculations, the house was less than two miles away.

Amber hung up. "Everything is set, and they've emailed Chad the list of homes under the cloak of the C Corp."

"That should help us track him down." I passed under the freeway. "So I go straight for a mile or so?"

"Yeah, hold on, I'll check. Okay, Highway N veers left a little ways up. You'll continue straight on Lonely Road."

"Really? Why would somebody choose a sad name like that for a road?"

Amber shrugged. "Watch out!"

A car gunned it off a side road, nearly hitting the front right quarter panel of the cruiser. I slammed on my brakes and cranked the wheel left, ending up in a shallow ditch. The car sped off ahead of us.

"Son of a bitch, that was close."

"Amber, that car was green, and it looked like the same body style as an Escape. It has to be Glover." I threw the car into reverse, and the wheels spun on the wet grass. "Come on and grab, damn it!"

"Do it slower. Not so much gas."

I tried again with less gas, and the back wheels caught the edge of the asphalt. I was back on the road. I cursed as I shifted into Drive and floored the gas pedal. "Where did he go?"

"I don't know, but there aren't a lot of road choices out here. Just gun it!"

I had to slow at each intersection to look for movement. We weren't familiar with the area and didn't know the hiding places and shortcuts. Amber radioed that the suspect's vehicle was seen north of 94 on Highway N. It was all we had, and even though we were in pursuit, we had no idea where he went.

I pounded the steering wheel. "Son of a bitch, we've lost him."

"He won't get away, Kate. There are too many deputies searching the area. Keep your eyes peeled. He's surrounded, he just doesn't know it yet. Try Lonely Road."

I looked left and right and constantly checked my rearview mirror. Amber leaned forward and turned up the police radio. The flash of a vehicle came from the right. I yelled as the Escape appeared out of nowhere and slammed into Amber's side of the car. The jarring impact sent the cruiser into the brush on the opposite side of the road, and my head bounced off the window, stunning me. I turned to Amber—her side window had exploded from the hit, and she sat motionless against the dash. Glover stood at her door with my own gun aimed at my face.

Chapter 68

"And so we meet again, Detective Pierce. Why can't you just leave me alone? I'll die soon enough, anyway." His voice was getting louder and more urgent. "Damn women! None of you are worth a shit. This world would be a better place if none of you existed. I'm better and smarter than all of you put together. And you? You call yourself a cop? You and this bitch are a laughingstock, and we both know it."

I squeezed my head to keep it from exploding. I could barely speak because of the pain, but I forced out the words. "If that were true, then we never would have found Naomi, but we did. You weren't counting on that, were you? I'd say you were pretty stupid to leave your DNA all over her like you did." I forced a smile through my pain. "Cat got your tongue?"

He didn't respond.

"The deputies will be here any second, Glover. You aren't going to get away with this. Just give yourself up."

"Shut up." He waved the gun at me then pressed it against Amber's blood-soaked head. "I already have a plan, and you aren't going to ruin it."

"You'll be in custody any minute. Listen, I can hear sirens in the distance, and they're getting closer. They're coming for you, and you won't get away."

"That's where you're wrong—again. I'm the one deciding my fate, not you." With the gun still drawn on me, he used his left hand to reach into his right chest pocket and pulled out a vial.

I moaned in pain. "What the hell is that?"

"Don't worry about it. Like I said, I determine my future, not you or the clowns you call cops. I'm dying, anyway. Damn brain tumor is a real buzzkill, and the pain is nearly unbearable at times." He cocked his head to the right and smiled. "Must be similar to how you feel right now with that head injury."

I felt the large goose egg forming and wiped away the blood running down the side of my cheek. "What's in that vial?"

"Have your medical examiner figure it out during my autopsy. I'm giving you my permission to have her cut me up. Let's just say it's a fitting end to my suffering. Isabelle went out this way, so I figured I may as well too." He shook the liquid in the vial then snapped open the cap.

I yelled out for him to stop. "I want to know why you killed those girls? They did nothing wrong."

"I'm a highly educated man, Detective Pierce, and women should be flattered to spend time with me. Isabelle was the love of my life, yet she betrayed me. They all do sooner or later. Women who betray my trust should pay the price. I'm better than all of you, and I deserve respect!"

"The only thing you deserve is life in prison." I saw three patrol cars screech to a halt. The deputies leapt from their vehicles with guns drawn and ordered Glover to the ground.

He smiled, tipped back the vial, and drank the contents. Within seconds, the effects were taking place.

I unsnapped my seat belt and reached for Amber as I yelled to the deputies to call an ambulance. When Glover collapsed to the ground, they ran to his side.

The first officer kicked the gun out of his hand. "What's wrong with him?"

"I don't know, but he drank whatever was in that vial. Bag it as evidence. Try to get this passenger door open and call Lieutenant Steele. Detective Monroe needs help." I held Amber's head between my hands. "Amber, Amber, can you hear me?"

She moaned and opened her eyes. "What happened?"

"You have a good knot on your forehead and a few lacerations. You slammed into the dash when Glover hit us."

"Glover hit us? With what?"

"Never mind. The ambulance is on its way. I'll explain everything to you later."

Amber turned in the seat, and chunks of safety glass, metal, and plastic fell to the floor.

"Be careful. There's plenty of sharp objects next to you."

She looked out the mangled door as deputies pulled on it. Glover, surrounded by two officers, lay on the ground. "Did he get shot?"

"No, I think he drank poison, and well deserved, I might add. I don't know if he'll live or die."

An officer stepped over Glover just as the ambulance pulled up. "Detective Pierce?"

I rubbed my temples. "Yes, that's me."

"The suspect is dead."

I heard tires squeal to a stop, and behind the patrol cars, Jack was running our way.

EMTs rushed to the cruiser with a gurney and lifted Amber out. I crawled over the console, onto the passenger seat, then out to the ground. I leaned against the vehicle to stabilize myself and saw Jack at Amber's side.

"Is she going to be okay?" he asked.

"Looks like a good contusion and cuts about the head, sir. She doesn't appear to have any broken bones, though."

Jack let out a relieved sigh. "Where are you taking her?"

"She's being transported to University Hospital."

I shook my head as Jack approached me. "University Hospital? That's fitting, but to be honest, I'm tired of hearing the word *university*."

"That makes two of us. Your head is bleeding, Kate." Jack looked over his shoulder. "I need an EMT to check her out."

Another gurney was wheeled toward us.

I held up my hand. "That isn't necessary."

"Put her on that gurney and tie her down if you have to." Jack smiled. "I'll catch up with you two mavericks in a minute." He looked at Glover, still lying on the road. "Got a short version on him?"

"Poison, I think. Have the lab test that vial the deputy bagged."

"Okay, get these two out of here. I'll be along shortly after we clean up this mess."

Chapter 69

It was Wednesday, and five days had passed since the crash in Pierceville. I wondered if that was some kind of a sign. My last name was Pierce, and even though Glover tried to kill us that day, he was the one who met his demise on Lonely Road. It was ironic, and the demons that must have haunted him got the best of him in the end. A man who thought he was superior to the rest of the world died just like any ordinary person and alone in his own personal hell.

We sat in the conference room and waited for Jack. Our morning update was about to begin. Clayton and Billings sat across from Amber and me, chuckling like two grade-schoolers.

I gave them the best glare I could muster up. "Really, boys, what's your problem?"

"Us? We don't have a problem," Clayton said. He pulled his phone from his pocket and snapped a picture of Amber and me.

"You're so juvenile," Amber said.

"Here, take a look for yourself." Clayton turned his phone and showed us the picture. "I'm putting that on our social media site. It's priceless. Two detectives with butterfly stitches across their foreheads and one with black eyes. How are we supposed to take you seriously?"

I couldn't help laughing. We looked a mess.

Jack walked in minutes later and grinned at Amber and me. I rolled my eyes, and Amber shook her head.

"Okay, we have a lot to discuss this morning, and I promise to do it with a straight face. In all seriousness, I just spoke with Lena. The autopsy on Glover showed an enormous brain mass, likely cancerous. He did say he was dying, right, Kate?"

"That's what he said, sir, but that doesn't justify his actions."

"I totally agree. At least now that the investigation is over, the families can put their loved ones to rest." Jack flipped through the sheets of paper in front of him. "According to the lab, the residue in the vial was potassium cyanide mixed with water—a deadly cocktail for sure."

I spoke up. "He told me he was going to kill himself the same way he killed Isabelle."

"Yet her remains were never found, and now he took that secret to hell with him," Amber said.

"True enough." Jack summarized the first sheet of paper aloud. "So, when it was all said and done, Isabelle Glover was murdered by cyanide, Becca Morbeck was killed with clostridium botulinum, Daphne Cole died from a fentanyl overdose, and Naomi Hahn lost her life from being suffocated after eating poisonous berries and mushrooms."

"And poor Mrs. Kittleman had a heart attack because

Glover scared her to death," Billings said.

"I guess we'll never know why Glover had some properties set up in a C Corp in St. Thomas."

"Actually, I do know the reason," Jack said.

We all faced him and waited for the aha moment. I smirked. "Well, let's hear it, already."

"It's far from any reason we thought of. I called the bank yesterday before I left work to tell them of Glover's death. I thought I should make them aware of his passing and the legalities associated with his properties. Here, the ones under his name could possibly be sold, and the proceeds ought to go to the victims' families. At least, that's what I think should happen."

"But the ones under the umbrella of the C Corp can't be attached to him personally," I said.

"Exactly. It turns out the benefactor of everything owned by the C Corp will remain in the Virgin Islands. A clause in the paperwork states that the company will be dissolved, the properties owned by the C Corp will be sold, and the funds will be used as an endowment to remodel and enlarge the University of the Virgin Islands on St. Thomas and St. Croix."

We sat in silence, all likely shocked by the revelation. We couldn't make up something like that. An evil lunatic who was a true mad scientist actually had a generous and loving side toward a group of islands in the Caribbean that mattered to him deeply. I wondered why.

"Apparently, the banker knew Glover well. He told me that Martin met Isabelle on St. Thomas during a summer vacation. She had been living in Charlotte Amalie at the time and taught at the university. They got married at Bluebeard's Castle, high on the mountainside, and lived on St. Thomas for two years while they accumulated properties on the island. Their intention was to retire there and live out their lives in one of their ocean-view homes. That's all the banker knew other than that they moved to Madison, Glover's hometown. What likely happened was that Isabelle eventually grew tired of Martin's superiority complex and had extramarital relations with a few students at UWM. Martin went off the rails after that, and unfortunately, she was the first to die."

I sighed. "I wonder if the brain tumor affected his personality."

"Lena thinks so and said he had some pretty hardcore drugs in his system along with toxic levels of aspirin. His head must have been killing him—literally."

I nodded. "And I felt his pain, but it turned him into a narcissistic monster and a woman hater."

"It did, but now it's time to wrap up everything related to Michael Morton and Martin Glover." Jack glanced at the clock. "I could sure use a good cup of coffee. We have a full day of paperwork ahead of us."

Amber pushed back her chair and stood. "Although that was far from subtle, I can take a hint. How about a twelve-cupper of the best coffee in town?"

Jack grinned. "Now that's what I'm talking about. Thanks, kiddo, and thanks to all of you. I couldn't ask for a better team of detectives."

THE END

Thank you!

Thanks for reading *Imperious*, the second book in the Psychic Detective Kate Pierce Crime Thriller Series. I hope you enjoyed it!

Start at the very beginning of the Monroe sisters' world and meet each character as they're introduced. The **Detective Jade Monroe Crime Thriller Series** is where it all began, and *Maniacal*, the flagship book, is the first book in that series. Sergeant Jade Monroe, a detective in the sheriff's department of a fictitious Wisconsin town, is introduced. Jade has more crimes to solve and murderers to apprehend than most detectives, but she's a tough cop, determined to prove herself, and gets the job done. The books are listed in order below:

Maniacal
Captive
Fallacy
Premonition
Exposed

The Agent Jade Monroe FBI Thriller Series follows on the heels of *Exposed*, Book 5 in the Detective Jade Monroe Crime Thriller Series. Jade has advanced to the big leagues. She's now an FBI agent in the serial crimes unit. She has more ground to cover and more criminals to apprehend with her new partner, J. T. Harper. Currently available books are listed in order below:

Snapped

Justified

Donors

Leverage

Malice

The Amber Monroe Crime Thriller Series follows on the heels of *Malice*, Book 5 in the Agent Jade Monroe FBI Thriller Series. This series focuses on Jade's sister, Amber, a new recruit in the Washburn County Sheriff's Office. She has big shoes to fill, and all eyes are on her. Currently available books are listed in order below:

Greed

Avenged

Vendetta

Atrocity

Travesty

The Psychic Detective Kate Pierce Crime Thriller Series follows on the heels of *Travesty*, Book 5 in the Amber Monroe Crime Thriller Series. This series focuses on Kate Pierce, a psychic detective at the Washburn County Sheriff's Office. Kate has gotten her share of ridicule over the years for her work as a psychic, but it's that very gift that has landed her in the lead role in solving many cases that nobody else could figure out.

Stay abreast of my new releases by signing up for my VIP email list at: http://cmsutter.com/newsletter/

You'll be one of the first to get a glimpse of the cover reveals and release dates, and you'll have a chance at exciting raffles and freebies offered throughout the series.

Posting a review will help other readers find my books. I appreciate every review, whether positive or negative, and if you have a second to spare, a review is truly appreciated.

Again, thank you for reading!
Visit my author website at: http://cmsutter.com/
Find me on Facebook at
https://www.facebook.com/cmsutterauthor/

Printed in Great Britain
by Amazon